CELESTE

Book #3 of Glory

Dale Mayer

Book in this series:

Genesis

Tori

Celeste

Glory Trilogy

CELESTE
Beverly Dale Mayer
Valley Publishing Ltd.

Copyright © 2016, updated © 2022

This is a work of fiction. Names, characters, places, brands, media, and incidents are either the product of the author's imagination or are used fictitiously. Any resemblance to actual events, locales, or persons, living or dead, is entirely coincidental.

ISBN-13: 978-1-988315-83-6
Print Edition

About This Book

Celeste Chandler hates to be last, almost as much as she hates going home with her tail tucked between her legs. This time she's injured—her leg, not her pride. But none of that matters because she's being stalked, and going home may have been her worst idea yet. Whoever is after her also wants to destroy her sisters. The triplets are the last in the line of stargazers, and, once they're gone, there will be no one to care for their planet's most valuable resource—the energy reserve—and the key to all life on planet Glory.

Matt has waited anxiously for Celeste to not only return to town but also to him. Given her position as an energy worker, he had no hope of tracking her down after she left. Only if she wanted to be found could she have been located. He had never expected she would stay away for so long. He's even begun to wonder if she ever plans on coming back.

But their planet is becoming unstable, and the only ones who can save it are Celeste and her two sisters. United, they have the power to fight the cloaked enemy in their midst and to preserve all life on the planet. Apart from them, there will be no peace, no love, … and no life in any form on Glory.

Sign up to be notified of all Dale's releases here!
https://geni.us/DaleNews

CHAPTER 1

CELESTE CHANDLER COULDN'T go much farther. Her leg throbbed with pain. She should have returned before now, not waiting until the last minute. She closed her eyes and breathed through the discomfort. Then she took a deep breath and started again.

Finally Granny's cabin was just ahead of her. Celeste cautiously glanced around. Good, she was still alone. Her nerves tingling, her body tense with excitement, she stared at a wall of greenery, blocking her view. She was almost home, for the first time in over a year. And she had to admit that her heart ached with yearning to reconnect. She was the youngest of three triplets—by mere minutes—and she'd missed her sisters terribly.

So much had happened, and she didn't really understand all the changes. But she was home now, and, after she healed, then eventually she'd contact them all and catch up. Finally.

It was as if the bomb blast from Granny's death had destroyed the core of their lives and had blown the family apart. Genesis had stayed home to hold down the fort, which was always her thing, being a homebody and the responsible eldest sister. Tori, the middle child, had run as far and as fast as she could. Celeste? Well, she was like neither of them, but she'd gone into hiding close by to find herself. Close enough to keep track of the goings-on, but far enough away that no one could find her. Not that anyone was looking.

Except Genesis. And, damn, Celeste felt bad about that. Living several towns away, she'd been close enough to hear a lot of what had gone on but not enough to know all the details.

Her coworker, an avid gossip, who drove from town to town making deliveries, had shared that Genesis had been involved in a major kerfuffle, but she had a new partner, and they were living full-time in the Paranormal Center.

That had caused Celeste a ton of sleepless nights. It shouldn't matter, as she'd been the one to walk away from Matt, the new head of the Center. … However, no way would Celeste ever be okay with him being in a serious, committed relationship with her sister.

It had been weeks before she had found out that Genesis's partner was not Matt, Celeste's former fiancé.

After she could breathe again, she'd mentally beaten herself up for being such a fool.

Celeste leaned against a thick tree, catching her breath. Just a few more feet. Then she'd be safe. And home. Once she'd heard her other sister, Tori, had returned home recently, Celeste knew she was the last one to return to the fold. Granny had always said that she was the slowest of the bunch, and that was fine, as Celeste did things in her own time and rarely made mistakes.

Boy, had she been wrong. Devastated at the loss of the woman who'd raised them, destroyed by what she could only imagine as being a complete betrayal by her lover and the man she thought was hers forever, Celeste couldn't cope and had walked away. One year ago.

Leaving Genesis to mop up the mess behind Celeste.

She owed her sister a lot. Just the thought of seeing her

again made her arms ache for a hug. Genesis and Tori were special. They'd been the idols Celeste had looked up to. The models she'd always tried to copy.

And look at what she'd done.

Smurg, her owl spirit pet, flew down to land on a sweeping branch beside her. The look in his eye was one she'd seen many times before.

"I know. It's a big step. And, once again, I can't force myself to take it."

Smurg tilted his big feathered head and stared at her with those wonderful owlish eyes, silently encouraging her to take this step.

And she was rather desperate to do so. Her leg, injured only a week ago, hadn't improved. And now it was at the point that she was afraid she'd left it all too long. She needed Granny's healing pool. But it was on the other side of the energy barricade.

And, the minute she crossed it, she would trigger an alarm that would tell her sisters that Celeste was here.

Was she ready for that?

Did she really have a choice?

Her leg throbbed and pounded the longer she stood here. She looked back the way she'd come. That was the biggest issue. She wouldn't likely make the trip back with her leg like it was. And was she truly alone? The entire way in, she couldn't shake the sensation of being followed. Tracked. An abrupt flash of fear spurred her into motion.

"Okay," she whispered to Smurg. "I'm going."

A small paw slipped into hers. She looked down at Minkel, the spirit meerkat, who walked ever at her side. Her spirit pets were the only reason she'd survived being alone as long as she had. And technically the pets meant Celeste was never truly alone.

Granny had had many in her care. Some had left with Granny upon her death. Many others had left with Celeste, and some had found new homes. It had hurt to lose some of them. But she'd come to understand that these were needed changes. Granny would be proud of Celeste. Granny had often told Celeste how possessive she was and how she must learn to share.

Sharing was one thing, but what about when sharing didn't work, and you lost a special pet? How did one lose a special someone when you were bonded by love?

Silky the lemur whispered reassuringly in her ear. Celeste tilted her head into his warm belly. He stayed snugged up in the crook of her neck.

"I know. I know," she said. "You guys just don't understand how hard this is."

But that wasn't true. They did understand. They'd been here at the cabin before too. They had loved Granny as much as Celeste had. They'd been lost in the spirit world, as they'd never connected to their human soul mates or lost them before their time had come. Granny had been the one to rescue them.

But Celeste had an affinity for the spirit animals, and they'd bonded to her in a big way. But some were hers in ways she hadn't realized, until she lost a few and had seen the bond had only gone one way.

Silky murmured encouragement.

And Celeste knew she'd procrastinated enough.

Hopefully her sisters would give Celeste time to heal, to adapt to being here, before they crashed into the silence her world had become.

She bowed her head and raised her arms. In a gentle series

of flowing movements, she opened the energy barrier and stepped through the oversized foliage to the protected space around the small cottage.

It looked just the same, as though it had been frozen in time. As soon as her gaze landed on it, her tears started to flow. Would she ever adjust to Granny no longer being here? She'd been the stability, the rock, the driving force behind the three sisters. So much of their history had been mired in mystery, but Granny had forged a strong path for them. And, when she'd died, it was as if everything died with her.

How sad was that?

But first things first. Celeste shuddered as the pain in her leg deepened. As if it knew they were somewhere it could get help—but maybe didn't want that help.

She hated her wild imagination. How could her leg scream at her to leave this place? To go away before it was too late? Too late for what?

At the cottage door, it took another moment to open the locks. She frowned at the double-energy alarm system in place.

Trouble had been here.

And recent trouble.

She stepped over the threshold and carefully relocked the door. Dropping her bag on the table, she hunched over, her pain so severe that she could only focus on the healing pool. It called to her, yet her leg injury screamed at her forward progress. As if it didn't want her to move forward. She didn't bother looking around. She'd known that the cabin was empty of people as soon as she'd entered the protected space.

Good. She stripped, dropping one item at a time, as she crossed the room to the closed door on the far side. She pushed it open and cried out in joy.

Inside, in the deep recesses of her mind, she'd been afraid

that the healing pool wouldn't be here. That something really bad had happened to damage the pool.

Instead, the waves of glittering blue water surged toward her. Reaching for her. She kicked off her shoes and slowly, painfully removed her pants, crying out as her sore leg was free at last. Her socks and panties hit the ground afterward. It was all she could do to sit on the edge of the pool and swing her leg over the side, when the water surged up her calves and up to her thighs. By the time it hit her hips, she was lifted above the glistening waves for a tiny second, then slowly lowered into the bubbling pool below.

She cried out once, before her head was completely submerged, and then she sank to the bottom of the pool. Relief and joy washed through her.

Her last rational thought, as Silky detached from her ear to float at her side, and Minkel perched on the edge above, was, why had she taken so long to come?

MATT HANDED THE sheaf of papers to Connor. "Check out the disturbance at Grandfather's place. Take Devon with you. The investigation is going well over there, but something is still not as stable as it should be. And we need it to be."

As Connor reached out to grab the papers, Matt froze, his senses firing up inside. His hand still holding the papers, he slowly sank into his desk chair. "Jesus. Finally."

Connor frowned. "Matt? What's up?"

Matt released his pent-up breath and murmured, "Your soon-to-be sister-in-law just arrived."

The office door burst open, and Genesis raced in, Tori one step behind her.

"Matt," they both cried out.

He held up his hand. "I know. I can feel her too."

The two sisters hugged each other.

Genesis frowned. "She's hurt. She's triggered the healing pool."

"It's the first place any of us would go. Just think of the emotional trauma we all felt after Granny's death. Celeste is confronting that for the first time," Tori said softly, her hand gently stroking Genesis's back.

"True." Genesis stared out the window at the darkening sky for a moment, before she whispered, "Yet it seems that it could be more than that."

Another odd eruption of noise came on a different level, as their spirit animals conversed.

Matt stared as Darbo spoke with several other spirit animals crowding into the space. They could connect to Celeste's animals in a way that no one else could. And, in this case, since Darbo had been hers at one time, he had a deeper bond than most.

"She's hurt," Matt said, standing abruptly. "Darbo said her leg is bad. Can barely walk, Minkel says."

"Then it's a good thing she's in the pool," Connor said, wrapping an arm around Genesis. "Let's keep calm, everyone. We knew this time would come. We all want this. It's a good thing. I know she's hurt, but we can't go rushing up there and scaring her off. She's come back on her own …"

"What if she's only come back for the pool?" Genesis whispered, tears in her eyes. "Her leg must be bad, if that's why she returned."

"Hey, don't look at this as her being forced home for the pool," Tori said. "This all has to happen in its own time. You know that."

Genesis nodded, but her gaze was locked on Tori's face, as

if waiting for her to make a decision.

Matt knew the decision had to be made by the two sisters, not him. But, damn it, this one *should be* his decision. Celeste was *his*. She'd run from him and what they had, but she'd been in his heart. Part of his soul. And, damn it, she should have come home a long time ago.

His world had improved so much since adding Genesis and Tori to his life, but the one person who truly belonged here still refused to have anything to do with him. Maybe that would change now.

Darbo reached out a small paw and gently brushed it down his cheek. Matt stroked the super soft fur of the tiny lemur who lived attached to his heart, but hung most of the time from his ear. "I know. She's home, and she's hurting."

But the lemur's actions also said he knew that Matt was hurting too. So hard to deal with this when everyone was caught in their own cycle of pain and hope.

So much had happened since Celeste had left. Had she any idea of what had gone on? What was still going on? The world she'd walked away from didn't exist any longer. At least, not in a form she would recognize. The town was likely hers and her sisters, although that legal fight might still come. He was waiting on the judge's ruling now. They had deeds proving the land, for as far as they could see, belonged to the three sisters. As for Grandfather, … Celeste's old enemy was no longer the same man either. The healing pools had affected even him.

Not fully a normal peaceful man yet, Grandfather had already had enough of a change happen that there was no going back. But no one knew just how much he'd changed, so no one could trust him.

The pools were healing; the forest was healing. However,

still massive electrical storms and system-wide energy outages occurred that no one could explain. Some hypotheses had been formulated. A few of those were downright scary.

Besides those events, some things had happened to Tori that even Matt wondered if their granny had set something into motion before her death. But she had died over a year ago—and had sparked a year of severe trial for the triplets. Matt could only hope that Celeste would survive hers—and that he would be the one she would turn to for help.

He loved her. Always had. Would have given his right arm to not have hurt her. But, after Granny's death, everything had changed for Celeste. And she had gone to pieces. The slightest things bothered her, and slights that would have normally set her off in a small way had devastated her.

Matt was a patient man to begin with, and he'd desperately tried to wait. To be there for her. To help her. To be the one she leaned on to get through this. But she'd been confused and overwrought, and his patience had worn thin. To her, it seemed that everyone had let her down. And perhaps that was understandable, given that fragile state she'd been in at the time.

And then Darbo had chosen Matt, and Celeste had taken it as a horrific betrayal. Matt hadn't understood. He'd so wanted Darbo to be his, understood that Celeste had dozens of other spirit animals to choose from, and had wooed Darbo away.

He hadn't realized he'd crossed a line, until Celeste had disappeared.

That's when he understood the connection between the three of them for what it was.

Darbo had gone into a deep depression. It had taken months for Matt to bring Darbo out of it again. But now,

Darbo was lit up like he was on Glory juice. And his voice? … Well, Matt hadn't seen him this excited—ever. The connection between Darbo and Celeste—indeed, Celeste's spirit pet Silky as well—had been at the deepest level, and Matt had broken it. Something that had caused them all horrific pain.

Matt had no way to atone for this—especially when he couldn't see Celeste to apologize. And, besides, an apology wouldn't cut it. Not now. Even when she did see him, no way she could avoid seeing Darbo, and that wound would hurt her again.

He dropped his face to his hands and groaned.

He knew of no way to make it better.

And now, after all this time, she was back.

Would she forgive him? Or was it too late?

CHAPTER 2

CELESTE DRIFTED IN a half-dream state. The healing pool felt so good that she never wanted to leave. And maybe that was a possibility because the special waters had a lot to work on. Her mental state was dismal, her physical health abysmal. And her emotional state? Well, she might as well just live in here forever if she hoped to fix that. The pool knew her. Knew her body. Her soul. It was a homecoming she hadn't expected, but now that she was in the waters' graceful arms, she couldn't get enough. She'd rolled to her belly and floated for hours, then rolled to her back and floated for more.

The pool wasn't done with her yet, or she would have been lifted out. That such a thing hadn't been presented was her cue to not fight the process. She had a lot of stuff to work on. Even as the pool did its thing, Celeste was supposed to do her thing.

The three sisters had spent days in here at times. Fixing broken hopes and dreams. Lost boy crushes and cruel kids. Growing up, there had always been hurtful words thrown at them; kids were mean and had been horrible to them. They'd hurt for themselves and each other and had always ached for Granny, who'd been feared and, therefore, hated by everyone they knew.

It had been a tough way to grow up. Now Celeste looked back and realized that Granny, at her advanced age when she'd taken in the orphans, hadn't had the energy to deal with the outside influences the way she might had done if she'd been stronger, younger. She'd needed all her strength to just raise three lively granddaughters. And, as soon as that job had been completed, they'd lost Granny.

As if during the last two decades she'd been overdue somewhere else, she'd gone fast—overnight. One moment there, the next gone. A loss so damn permanent.

The triplets should have been prepared. Granny had been incredibly old. They knew she was hurting and spent her days at the lowest pools in the caves. Staying longer and longer each time. She'd needed more rest to work so much less.

She'd hung on as long as she could. Celeste remembered a conversation with Granny only weeks before her passing.

"There's so much I want to pass on to you girls. You have so many trials to come. They will make you stronger, but it will be hard. You need to hold on and to work through the problems."

Granny had mentioned something about the men in their lives too. She'd made the triplets all throw star charts of their own futures so that they might see the world around them as it pertained to their life's direction. See who their partners were.

Granny had smiled and said, *"You three will have to work for happiness, but, once you all climbed that mountain, your worlds would spread out before you in all its glory."*

Ironic that she'd used the word *glory* because, of course, that was the name of this planet.

And, so far, Celeste hadn't seen much glory. She'd seen hatred, jealousy, anger, disdain, envy, and an endless amount of pain and grief. But the glory part? … Yeah, that had been missing. So far.

Celeste had always believed in the star charts. Supposedly

she was the best of the three at throwing them. But Genesis was really. Celeste was the best at *interpreting* the charts. What that really meant was they needed to work together to see the truth of their worlds—and not have everything too easy in their lives. Granny had been happy to see the struggle and the conflict. The sisters had been devastated by Granny's attitude. They'd figured they'd had a horrible-enough childhood as it was, so to think more was ahead? Well, that had been a betrayal too.

"No. You don't appreciate what you don't have to work for," Granny had insisted. *"And, in this case, there is a tremendous amount of goodness out there waiting for you. But you must reach out for it as an equal, as an adult, so that you can handle it all as you should and thus reap the benefits."* She'd shaken her head, adding, *"Not like greedy children to enjoy, then to destroy, moving on, just looking for more."*

The reminder of Granny's words brought grief to the surface once again. The waves from the healing pool washed over Celeste in response. Tears burned her eyes. She missed her granny so much. And her sisters. Why had it taken Celeste so long to come home? Why was she even now avoiding them? Especially now, when they had to know she'd arrived?

Because she wasn't ready of course. She glanced down at her body, seeing the scratches and bruises of the last few weeks melting away under the ministrations of the water. She'd forgotten the power of this particular healing pool. So many of the pools accessible to the public didn't have the same ability as Granny's pool. This one, and those deepest in the caves, were the strongest and most potent around. Granny and the triplets had been blessed.

In many ways.

She'd been given many gifts, and yet did she do anything

with these gifts? No, of course not.

She'd run when the emotional overload had become too much. When she really should have stayed and worked things out. The water bounced gently under her sore aching muscles, making her realize how much healing had occurred already. Not her emotional state yet—that would take more time. But already she felt better. As if she would live a little longer. She couldn't see her future yet, nor sense any star chart tingles inside that she used to feel when it was time to throw one, but she could hope that walking away hadn't damaged that forever for her.

And that hope had been a deeply buried fear, especially over this last year. Had she left her heritage behind too? She sat up and splashed the water on her face, loving how the water eased the burning flood behind her eyelids. The healing water could always see, could always know, where she hurt the most. And her heart? Well, … the pools could try to heal that, but, in truth, the only thing that would heal that was time.

After another hour, she slowly stood and smiled. Her spirit animals had sprawled around the small room. Many knew this cabin as home, so they would be almost as emotional as she had been on their return. It was a homecoming for them all. They had the ability to come here on their own, and likely had many times over the last year, but it would have been empty with Granny gone. And that had to be difficult for them.

Celeste needed to get out for a little while. Check for food. She hadn't eaten in hours. Glancing around, she noted the towels were still stored in the same place. She walked over and grabbed one, and, as she dried off, she had to smile at the silkiness of her skin. She'd forgotten the beauty-treatment benefits of the pool, on top of everything else.

Wrapping the towel around her body and leaving the small pile of dirty clothes on the floor, she walked out to the kitchen. If nothing else, tea should be in the cupboard. If there was actually food, she knew that her life would improve to the point of being seriously happy.

In the kitchen, she put on the teakettle and searched the cupboards. Less well stocked than when Granny was alive, but Celeste found canned and dried goods. She put more water on to boil in a pot and pulled out a package of pasta. It would fill her belly nicely. She hadn't been starving during the last year—at least not all the time—but it had been bad enough that she no longer said anything caustic about people's food choices.

At least they had a choice. Hers had been few and far between. She'd learned a greater appreciation for what Granny had been through, trying to keep three young girls alive and growing in all ways, when Granny herself had been long past the age of working.

In fact, Celeste had no idea how Granny had kept the money flowing to feed them. And then the clothing requirements for three teenage girls. School had been hard enough, but always wearing older secondhand clothes had made them a target of ridicule—when a life just being with Granny had done that on its own.

People had missed out on knowing the most generous and caring person in this town—all because Granny scared them.

Well, Celeste knew about fear herself now and didn't like it one bit.

She glanced down at her leg. It looked better. It felt better. But was it?

Given that the waves of the pool still called to her, she'd take that as a no. Still, it had improved tremendously. Another few hours in the water, and the injury would be a distant memory. She shivered. The pool's euphoria was fading, and now she was tired and hungry. Healing was hard work.

She needed to check her closets to see if her old clothes were still here. The pasta was finally done, so she served herself a bowl and added a few dried herbs for flavor, then took the bowl to her old bedroom. With the bowl of pasta and a fresh cup of herb tea, she stood in the doorway for a long moment, once again the onslaught of emotions washing over her. Was there ever anything more powerful than a homecoming?

She took the few steps inside placing her food down then crawled up on her bed, still wrapped in her towel. She hoped there'd still be the few bits and pieces of clothing she'd left behind. She'd left with much more than she'd returned home with. It was an understatement to say that it hadn't been an easy year. She'd expended a lot of energy to stay hidden. A whole lot more energy to *find herself*, and all for what?

Time to deal with her grief? Her loss? Adjust to her life as it looked now? But did she do any of these things? She'd come home out of desperation for the healing pool, and that in itself said she hadn't adjusted at all.

Placing her empty bowl on the old rickety night table she'd hated all her teenage years, Celeste curled into a ball on the bed, tugged a blanket up over her shoulders, and slept.

❧

MATT PACED. BACK and forth and yet again across his office floor. Damn it. He wanted to rush to Celeste. He knew she'd been hurt. Knew she'd come for the powerful healing pool. He was damn grateful that it existed, that she felt comfortable enough to return for that reason. He wished it was for something else, but he'd take what he could. At least she was back.

Darbo murmured something in his ear. Matt tried to refocus. "She's asleep?"

Darbo nodded.

"Ah, good. That's what she needs. Rest."

So did he, but that wasn't happening. He pulled the files toward him. Since that weird electrical storm involving Tori—almost permanently—Scott, another paranormal investigator and a damn good one, had shown up, asking questions about it.

Good questions. Questions Matt couldn't answer. As to why that storm? What did it need? Want? And, if it did claim people, why?

Devon had been positive that the storm wanted Tori and that Tori had been willing to sacrifice herself to it. Devon was sure that she would have disappeared into the storm forever, if he hadn't been there.

Hence the current case file. How many people had disappeared without a trace in the last decade? There were frighteningly many, but only a few who fit the profile of an energy worker. Scott was making careful inquiries on behalf of Matt and the Center.

But then Scott had an agenda of his own, and Matt suspected that Scott had lost someone, possibly to an energy storm. The man was cagey, private, and reserved. If he was here for personal reasons that was fine, as long as they gelled with Matt's own needs.

Matt had a deep suspicion of what was going on but had no intention of sharing with anyone until he knew more. There'd been enough problems and unrest at this point. Stability was needed. He was already gearing up for an ugly court battle. Grandfather's heirs had mounted a legal defense against the charges, and Grandfather's sister, facing her own extortion and baby-trafficking charges, was going through a health crisis. In order to avoid facing her own crimes? Some thought so.

Matt figured more likely an awareness that she would finally have to pay for her decades of criminal activity was making her sick.

The town was agog with the news of the sisters proclaiming to own so much land here, and, while very little had been made public at this point, it was enough to divide the town. And that made the situation dangerous too.

Matt knew Celeste was needed here to make the sisters' case complete. You couldn't have just two defendants in court and a third lost to the wind—not if you wanted to appear serious. Especially when the charges were astronomical.

They had the proof, which helped, but he'd had to lock down the Paranormal Center and to use extraordinary measures to keep the documents safe. He could hope for the employees' willing compliance, but the issue was too big. Too much at stake to count on it.

And, of course, the big annual social event of the year was happening in a few days. He'd always expected to have Celeste at his side for this. The affair might be social, but it was a power statement too. He needed the others to see him as in charge and capable. The Center was his. Yet, he needed the support of the townsfolk. This was supposed to be a statement that all was well and that he was the right man for the position. Of course, in the last year, while he led the Center, things had gone to hell. … *Sigh.*

He stared down at his big hands, so capable in some ways, and yet too capable of violence. He couldn't shake the feeling that it wasn't just the three sisters going through a personal revelation period but that he would have his own personal shakeup happening as well. His father had died young, trying to control his abilities. He'd slowly gone mad, trying to keep his forces locked down inside, in control. But he'd held a rigid grip on them.

Matt knew that had contributed to his father's death. One had to use one's given paranormal forces, or your life never reached its full potential. Like a flower bud that never opened, it dried up and died—usually taking the person with it.

Unlike his father, Matt wasn't afraid of his powers. But he was concerned. He was strong. Stronger than most people he'd ever met. Stronger than people knew. Not sure who warranted his trust, he'd hidden his abilities for a long time, only letting a few very select people in. Granny was one of them. She'd liked him. Had shared much with him. But she'd been wrong about some things too—like Celeste.

Or rather, his life with her hadn't turned out the way Granny had said it would. But maybe it still would? He'd watched his friends walk through fire for their other half, and, in their cases, it had all worked out.

He knew Celeste was his, but that didn't mean she wanted anything to do with him. Especially with this new problem and the electrical storm.

She'd hate him if he turned out to be right.

But he was pretty damn sure he was. Now the only thing left to do was to prove it. And then find a way to make the others forgive him for what he had to do. It would be done for their sake, but no one ever liked to hear that.

CHAPTER 3

WAKING TO PAIN had to be the worst. Nudged awake by Silky, Celeste realized that she was crying in her sleep and that her leg throbbed to the point where she wasn't sure she could make it to the pool. With Minkel's help, she stumbled to the water's edge, where she collapsed into the waiting coolness. Instantly the water surged over her, enveloping her in its healing coolness. She cried out in joy, as the pain eased. Still half asleep, she let the water work on her sore body and closed her eyelids, willing sleep to claim her again.

Only now worry filled her mind. Why wasn't her leg healing? What could be so wrong with it that this healing pool couldn't fix? She lifted her leg from the water and studied the marks in her calf. A bite? If so, she had no idea when or how she'd received it. For it must be from an animal, and that made no sense. She had an affinity for those. They were all her friends and family. She knew of none that would—indeed, could—bite her. Energetically it wasn't possible.

She'd had a bad fall a week ago, one that had scraped her leg up badly, but that was minor and should have healed within a day or two. As she examined the wound critically, she realized the pool had helped a lot. The swelling was gone; the poison appeared to have leached out, and, although she could see a little damage, it was much better.

Feeling better, she said, "Maybe it just requires more time

to heal all the way."

Silky muttered in her ear.

"I don't remember ever drinking the pool water," she said in response. Yet maybe the lemur was right. There shouldn't be any reason not to. If the injury had such a poisonous effect on her, then, in theory, the poison could be swarming through her bloodstream right now. And internal assistance might be required.

She studied the glowing effervescence of the water around her, then dipped her head and took a big drink. An odd freshness filled her mouth. Hard to describe but seriously addictive—was that because she was badly in need of the water's healing properties? Almost immediately her tension inside eased back, and her fear muted. She took a second drink and assessed her state. Better yet again.

After a third, she figured she'd had enough. She floated peacefully, letting the water do its thing. She needed to be as strong as she could be. Things would go to hell soon enough.

An hour later, more than a little worried, she contemplated her options. Even though the pain had eased dramatically, her leg still throbbed. She had to consider why it wasn't 100 percent better, and she realized a bigger issue must be at play.

The pools could—and would—definitely help, but also chances were good that something inside her leg was stopping it from healing completely. Maybe it was an energy blockage of some kind. And that was scary. She didn't deal with dark energy. Granny had always focused on positive energy. The triplets had been the same.

Everything else was blocked out. Acknowledged, but no more than that.

One couldn't walk in the light without knowing that the dark existed. But she had no dealings with it herself. Until now.

She twisted in the water and pulled her leg up to take another closer look. The swelling on the calf had reduced to almost nothing, the scrape nearly nonexistent, only … She peered intently.

A number of tiny black spots—almost like tiny pebbles—appeared to be embedded deep inside. So maybe this was a physical problem, after all? Maybe they must be dug out, and that would hurt like crazy. She was rather a baby when it came to pain.

Someone else would have to do it. Minkel the meerkat came over and laid a gentle paw on her calf, a tiny whimper escaping from his mouth.

"It's okay. I'll be fine," she said gently.

Silky burst into loud argumentative chatter.

Okay, then. No, she wouldn't be fine, according to the chattering at her ear. Celeste froze, stricken by a thought. "Do you really think it's that big a problem? Surely the pool can fix it, given enough time."

And this time every spirit animal in the room erupted in cries of alarm.

Damn. That wasn't good.

If it was a problem, who could she call on for help? Her sisters, of course, but was there anyone else? She was supposed to handle this herself, but, if so, … how?

Minkel's paw covered the wounds, sending healing toward the injury in his own way. Silky reached a long arm down toward it too but couldn't quite reach it. Celeste stroked the injury with her own fingers. She needed to see if she could dig out the black spots from her flesh herself. She hated the idea, but there wasn't much choice.

Hiking herself up to sit on the edge of the pool, she dug

into her trouser pockets and found tweezers and a pocket knife. The former didn't work at all, so she took a deep breath and opened her pocket knife to cut open her skin, wincing and whimpering against the pain. All without success. Strangely enough, it seemed she couldn't go deep enough. In fact, it looked like her efforts had pushed the objects in her leg deeper under the skin.

With a noisy sigh of frustration, she put her leg back into the pool to heal the damage from her efforts. Instantly the irritated wound felt better. With a groan, she realized someone definitely must cut open her leg and get them out. And she wasn't looking forward to it.

She dried off and limped back to her bedroom. She opened her bedroom closet and smiled to see the clothes she'd left behind. She was damn glad to have them. Funny how time changed one's attitude. Before, she would never have worn these clothes. Now she was desperate to find something clean and respectable. Fashion could wait. And for a long time, given her circumstances.

Pulling out jeans and clean underwear, she searched through the stacks for a clean shirt, crying out in joy as she found over a dozen. A huge haul for her. She would have clothes to go to work in. At the bottom of the closet were shoes. Of all kinds. She'd forgotten about most of them. Happily, she dressed, bending to tie up her walkers.

At the growl of her stomach, she was reminded that she needed to eat. She had no idea what time it was, but the sun was breaking overhead. She warmed up leftover pasta and contemplated her next step, while she ate her meager meal.

The whine of an engine broke the silence. Celeste froze. That was the sound of a hovercraft flying overhead. Had she put the stealth mode back on the cottage? She'd been in so much pain, … she didn't know. Still, she bolted to the door and engaged the energy system to hide the cottage.

But it was too late.

The huge black craft hovered in the front yard briefly, then landed. Pissed, she added another lock to the front door. It was one of the new vehicles from the Paranormal Center. That meant Matt—the last person on the planet she wanted to see.

The hovercraft door opened, as she glared at it.

Genesis jumped out, and Celeste gasped loudly.

And no matter how many locks or stealth modes were available to Celeste, none could keep out her sisters.

Watching Genesis walk toward the cabin's front door, Celeste realized she no longer wanted to hide.

And then Tori exited the craft.

Celeste let out a squeal and threw her arms open wide.

Instantly the locks popped, and the stealth coverage opened up. The front door burst open, and Celeste raced out to the front yard.

Genesis burst into tears and opened her arms.

Like a mirror image, Celeste also burst into tears and hugged her eldest sister. Held tight and secure inside her sister's loving embrace, Celeste realized just how childish her last year away had been. Tori joined them, wrapping her arms around the two of them.

Celeste leaned in close, absorbing the feel and the scent of the two most important women in her life. God, she loved her sisters. She'd been such an idiot. "I'm sorry," she said broken-ly. "I shou—"

"*Shh*. It doesn't matter anymore. You're home," Genesis whispered. "I'm just so thankful you're home."

Tori said, "Besides, I haven't been home long either. It's all got to happen in its—"

"Own—"

"Time …"

They all fell into the same refrain that Granny had repeated all their lives.

Finally, the tears still trickling down her cheeks, Celeste lifted her head and beamed at her sisters. "I do love you guys, you know?"

"And we love you," Tori said. "Now …" She glanced at Genesis. "We know you're hurt. How badly?"

Celeste sighed. "I'd hoped it would be better by now, and the pool is doing what it can, but something is embedded in my leg that I can't get out. Nor can the water get it out. The pool is managing to combat the damage but not enough for the leg to heal fully. It's strange. It looks like a bunch of tiny black rocks."

She heard her sisters each suck in their breath but didn't understand the reason for it. She watched as Tori and Celeste exchanged worried looks.

"What's the matter?" Celeste frowned, her gaze going from one sister to the other. "What did I miss?"

At that, both sisters gave a weary-sounding laugh.

"So much. Oh, my gosh, you missed so much," Tori exclaimed. "And it's not something we can tell you in just five minutes. Let's go inside and have tea."

Tea. Together. A ritual of their childhood. A reminder of all Celeste had walked away from that brought a fresh wave of tears to her eyes.

"And I brought breakfast," Genesis said, with a smile. "There is a little food at the cabin but not much and nothing fresh."

They broke apart, and, for the first time, Celeste became aware of the two men standing strong, arms crossed, behind the women. She knew them both. Connor and Devon. Both had been engaged to her sisters, and both relationships had blown up at the same time as everything else.

She sent a sidelong glance to the women at her side. "Both of them?"

"Yeah, both of them," Genesis said, with a happy smile. "It's been a long road—"

"And not an easy one at that," Tori interrupted, her own smile easy and gentle.

"But we both made it to the place where we were supposed to be," Genesis said.

"And the reward after the pain?" Celeste knew her sisters would understand her question.

"All so worth it, just like Granny promised," Tori assured her. "We did have a little growing up to do, navigating through some trouble, and hopefully we're almost at the end of this mess. If we're lucky, life will get easier from here on in."

"You still have problems?" Celeste asked, startled. "In what way?"

"That's partly what we need to tell you. So much has happened." Genesis turned to Connor, and, with a beaming smile, she asked him, "Can you bring in the basket, please?" Connor gave a curt nod and walked to the hovercraft.

"He doesn't look very happy," Celeste said in a low voice, studying the men's watchful gazes and careful movements. "Neither of them do."

"That's because a lot of serious trouble is brewing," Genesis said. "You're part of it. So are we. Until we get this settled, there won't be lasting peace for any of us."

Damn. But Connor was striding toward them, Devon at his side. And the moment was almost gone.

Before they reached the women, Celeste hurriedly asked,

"And Matt, is he involved?"

Both her sisters reached out to hold her. "Very much so. He's still at the Paranormal Center, but he's also in the center of all this."

Genesis looped her arm through her sister's. "Let's go sit down. There is a lot to explain."

<hr>

MATT STAYED BEHIND, as the others flew to meet Celeste. He wasn't part of the homecoming—not yet. *Maybe not ever.* That thought brought a pang of regret to his heart, yet he knew, at one point, he must face her. And the possibility of that was enough to keep his head buried in his work for the time being. He knew the group would be hours reconnecting with Celeste, and, hopefully by the time they all returned, Celeste would understand the dangers. She might even have valuable information to add to the mess. Her connection to the animals could be a huge advantage, but she must be willing to reach out. That would depend on her health as well. The two sisters had been worried, as the healing pool had been triggered several times. Apparently that wasn't a good sign.

No one knew if Celeste had returned alone either. He damn-well hoped she had, but it wasn't his place to say anything. A knock on his door brought him out of his reverie.

"Matt, we've got something you need to see. Right now." Dr. Mentos, the head of the research lab, stood at the doorway, motioning for him to move and quickly.

Matt reached the doorway in seconds. "What's the matter?" he asked, following Dr. Mentos down the hallway.

"That black rock that Mason stole from the pool and Tori disarmed is disintegrating." Dr. Mentos pushed open the doors, leading to the stairway.

Matt raced down the stairs. "Is that bad?"

"It is if it turns to a powder, yes," Dr. Mentos said. "That can be picked up by the wind and dispersed."

Matt had to consider that, but he wasn't sure he understood the problem. "But, if we've neutralized it, surely the powder is harmless, isn't it?"

"But we haven't neutralized this one. And, besides, what if there are more like this?"

"There aren't." At least, he hoped there weren't. "We caught the guy doing this. Remember?"

"Sure, but did he leave more behind? Mason said theirs had been stolen from Grandfather's estate. But all are accounted for that we know of. If there are more, then we need to find them and fast. They appear to have a shelf life that is very short, before they begin to disintegrate."

When they reached the lab, Matt exclaimed loudly at the sight of the rock contained inside the glass enclosure. The original rock had glowed with power. Now it was nothing more than a pile of dust, but the energy coming off it was dark, diseased, with an unwholesomeness to it that was disturbing. "This doesn't look good. Are you sure it's secure in there?"

"It is, but if there are more, we need to find them."

"Agreed. Yet how?" Matt asked, walking around the container, studying its contents. "Do we have anyone who can track this energy to find other rocks?"

"Not that we know of."

Darbo pulled on Matt's ear. *Right.* "How about the spirit animals? They can work this black energy, so maybe they can find the rocks too."

Dr. Mentos looked doubtful. "That would mean getting them to help us, which, as you know, can be an iffy matter to begin with, and I don't know of any that can. Although dogs are sniffers, so what about Connor's dog? Maybe Devon's cat?"

"*Hmm.*" Of all the spirit animals, that big cat was the least likely to want to help. But if he *did* decide to, then it would be huge. Storm walked with one foot on the dark side. He could handle this energy easily. "I'll have to ask them."

"I'd be more worried about someone using these rock particles as weapons actually." Dr. Mentos's comment was just off-topic enough that Matt was startled. "How would they do that?"

The doctor looked at him in surprise. "Think of a high-powered rifle, firing some of this into a crowd. The particles are that horrid energy. If they were to penetrate the skin, then the person would die. Spray this over animals' feed, and they'd eat it. What if they entered the food chain?" He shook his head at the possibilities. "I'm thinking these are more danger-ous now than I initially surmised." He spun to face Matt. "We must find out if there are more."

Only that was easier said than done. And Matt needed to find someone sensitive enough to hunt down these black rock fragments. He didn't have anyone on staff who had that particular skill. So he'd have to ask the men if their spirit animals knew of any.

Speaking of which … "Darbo, can you see if more of these rocks are lying somewhere?"

Darbo chittered quietly in his ear.

"Right, I didn't think so." He frowned, as Darbo contin-ued to talk. "What? What are you talking about?"

As Darbo continued, Matt's heart and mind froze on one particular sentence. Celeste had several of these particles in her leg. That's why she was in the healing pool. And the pool was having trouble healing her.

He bolted for his hovercraft.

CHAPTER 4

I T WAS TOO much to take in. Celeste kept shaking her head, then gasping and sighing. By the time all the questions had been answered—like that could happen—and the coffee and muffins scarfed down, she needed to go back into the healing pool for her leg. With her sisters at her side, she sat on the side of the pool with her jeans off, and her bare legs dangling in the water.

"How did you get these in your leg?" Genesis asked, studying the injury, worry on her face.

"Not sure," Celeste admitted. "But I fell a week ago, when I was in the woods." She lifted her leg out of the water for the others to see. The water droplets clung stubbornly, as if knowing their job wasn't done.

"It's the blackness I don't like," Tori said. "We've seen way too much of it."

"True, but never this small," Genesis said. "Why would it be this size? It doesn't make sense that the asshole would energize tiny rocks like this. They are almost dust."

At that moment, the door to the pool room burst open, and three men rushed inside. Celeste gasped in shock, as she realized Matt led the charge.

"They are dust. Very poisonous and painful remnants of the rocks you found, Genesis," Matt said, his gaze locked on Celeste. "Dr. Mentos called me to the lab a half hour ago. The black rock they were studying has collapsed into dust. Poisonous dust filled with dark energy."

"You don't belong here," Celeste snapped. "I didn't invite you in."

"No, and I couldn't wait that long for your permission, as that time wasn't likely to ever come, if you had your way," he snapped back. "Genesis, whatever is in her skin is the same nasty stuff that poisoned the pools and killed so many people. It'll leach her life force out of her. We have to remove them."

Genesis gasped and grabbed Celeste's leg.

"Hey, easy," Celeste groaned, as the injury throbbed.

"Sorry, sis, but, if he's right, they have to come out. Otherwise your leg will never heal." She held her hand over the injury and infused as much power as she could into the leg. Celeste watched as Tori joined her energy into the healing efforts.

"The rocks aren't moving," Celeste cried out.

"No. They're not," Matt said, leaning over her. He studied the darkness, watching as the tiny black specks glowed with remnants of power. Instantly Matt leaned over and clamped his hand on her leg.

Darbo added his hand to Celeste's leg too.

Remi, Genesis's rare plumer spirit pet, placed his hand on Darbo's, and damn if dozens of spirit animals didn't arrive beside them to give assistance.

"What on earth?" Connor said faintly. "I've never seen animals collect like this."

"You obviously haven't spent any time with Celeste," Tori said, with a tight grin. "Granny brought every abandoned or forgotten spirit animal home that she could. Celeste is the same. We were raised with dozens of them, always coming and going."

A low, deep howl filled the air, startling Celeste. "Who the hell is that?"

"It's Storm," Devon said quietly. "He's with me."

Celeste stared at the huge cat in shock. "Really?" She studied Devon, her gaze narrowed, as she considered the man in front of her. Who knew he had such hidden depths? "Looks to me like he walks on the dark side."

"He was caught in the middle, but he's with me now," Devon said firmly.

Celeste didn't know if she believed him. She turned her gaze to the large wild shadow cat and called to it. Instantly the cat turned those huge marble eyes her way.

Easy, boy, she whispered to him alone. *We don't know each other, but that doesn't mean I'm here to harm you. In fact, I'm the one who's been harmed. If you can help, then I'd appreciate it. If you can't, well, I understand. And, if you won't, hopefully that's because we don't know each other yet.*

The huge cat stalked closer. Everyone in the room held their breath as the massive animal nosed his way into Celeste's space. In return, she pushed right back until the two of them were forehead to forehead. A huge rumbling purr filled the room.

"Wow," Devon said, his voice full of shock. "I've never seen anything like that."

"Yeah, welcome to Celeste," Matt said. "Her affinity is animals."

"I can see that."

Devon's whisper was just barely loud enough for Celeste to hear, but she didn't dare take her eyes off the huge cat. She understood the cat's connection to Devon. Images of his life up until now, the war Devon and Tori had been involved in, passed through Celeste's mind in a rapid series of still shots.

And his growing respect for Devon. Nice.

She smiled and closed her eyelids.

When the cat moved back, she stayed as she was, enjoying the moment.

"Ah, … what's going on?" Matt asked, as all the animals backed up from where his hand rested. He pulled back too, as if suddenly understanding he was in the way.

Celeste watched. "I'm not sure," she said softly. "Storm is doing something."

Everyone sat back, as the cat sniffed her injured leg, a howl starting in the back of his throat that was both powerful and terrifying.

She tensed, not sure she liked where the cat's thoughts were going. "On second thought, I don't think we need his help, do—?"

And the cat snapped—his powerful jaws taking out a chunk of her leg.

Celeste screamed at the instantaneous explosion of pain.

And blacked out.

HOLY CRAP. MATT had no idea such a thing was possible.

As Genesis and Tori dumped the unconscious Celeste into the healing pool, clothes and all, the water swarmed like a riptide around the now-open wound in her leg.

"Jesus," Matt whispered.

"I'm so sorry," Devon cried out. "I didn't know he'd do that. I didn't have time to stop him …"

Genesis shook her head. "You couldn't have stopped him. He was the only one here prepared to do what needed to be done."

"What? Bite off a chunk of her leg?" Devon asked in

shock. "Is he dangerous? Will he do that again?"

Tori smiled. "I sure hope so." She pointed to the floor. "Look. He took out enough of a bite that he removed the black rocks."

Matt walked closer. Indeed, the organic mess did appear to have the embedded particles within it, but it was hard to tell from all the blood.

Connor raced over to his side. "Here." He held out a glass jar. Using the flipper he'd been handed, Matt scooped up the offending flesh and placed it in the jar.

And sealed it tight.

Inside the container, the rocks looked bigger, swollen, as if having gorged on the tissue around them. Matt felt sick to his stomach. He turned to study Celeste floating in the healing water. She was where she needed to be. And, from where he stood, she looked fine. Decent. Better than that, … she was beautiful to him. Always had been. Covered in mud, or exhausted and in ragged clothes, his heart had always known who she was—his. His jaw worked as he tried to get his thoughts in order.

"Will she be okay?" he finally managed to ask. "This isn't how I'd planned our first meeting to be."

Tori snorted. "Plans never work out. As far as first meetings, none of us had great ones either. However, having those out"—she waved her hand at him and the jar he held—"she should heal fully now. Depending on how deep the gash and how widespread the poison, it will take a little time."

"Right." He stood, helpless, not sure what he was to do.

Genesis smiled up at him. "You did the right thing, Matt. Not to worry. She came home because she couldn't deal with this, and those rock shards were working their way deeper into her skin. Eventually they would have embedded themselves into her bones, and then we would have had a horrible time getting them out." She glanced over at Devon. "Don't feel bad. Storm did the right thing. A little rough, a little harsh maybe, but given the circumstances, it's all good."

Devon nodded but clearly didn't seem to really feel any better. "Maybe I should take this jar of black rocks back to the Center," he said, focusing on something else. "She'll need to stay here for a while."

"She will. And she'll need to adjust when she wakes as well." Genesis smiled gently. "It's okay. We'll take care of her. Go."

"When she wakes up, find out how she acquired these and from where." Matt handed over the jar to Devon. "We need to make sure no other contaminated rocks are left behind." With a last look at Celeste, floating in the water, he turned and walked out.

"Wait, Matt. I'll come with you." Devon raced behind him, Storm loping at his side.

"Fine, you can come, but only if you ditch the guilt," Matt said, as he left the cottage, heading for the small hovercraft he'd flown in.

"That's hard to do." Devon got in the front seat. "I know so little about spirit animals and haven't been connected for very long, but I feel that I *should* know how to stop him and this is my fault."

"Then maybe we should be saying thank you," Matt said. "I don't know that anything else could have done the job."

"I'm sure one of the doctors could have removed the rocks in a much easier, cleaner way."

"Maybe and maybe not. Often a traditional medical doctor can't see what we can see. He might not have been able to extract those things at all."

Matt glanced over at Devon, who looked devastated. "Look. When she wakes up, Celeste won't blame you. She'd been the one to talk to Storm before he acted. She's not that kind of person."

Devon nodded. "Glad to hear that. She's the one I know the least about."

"She's also the one who is the hardest to get to know."

CHAPTER 5

THIS TIME WHEN Celeste awoke in the healing pool, her sisters were chatting away at her side in low tones. Celeste smiled. It was a nice way to wake up. She was also surrounded by spirit animals. Some she hadn't seen in years, and some she had never met before. She presumed they were still finding their way to Granny's cottage. She would set about finding them families to join. She already had a dozen or so that wandered in and out of her life, but three stayed all the time, and another three were here most of the time.

She'd have to ask her sisters if they could connect to any. It was never good to see spirit animals alone. It's not as if they were trouble, at least not until she'd seen that huge one of Devon's. She remembered her leg at that point, and the lunge the shadow cat had made before he snapped at her leg. The pain had been horrific, had knocked her out. But, as she thought about the pain, she wondered if at least part of that hadn't been the damn pebbles fighting back themselves.

Warily, she assessed her leg. It actually felt … decent. As in, much better. Considering she'd had a bite of flesh removed, she felt immensely better than expected.

Now for the visual inspection. She slowly shifted in the water, so she could look at her leg. She gave a happy sigh of relief. It was still brightly colored, but the flesh was filling in nicely. Not fast enough that she was willing to risk standing on it yet, but it was well on the way.

"How do you feel?" Genesis asked, standing and moving closer.

"Better," Celeste said warmly. "Not quite ready to run the Glory marathon yet but getting better."

"Let me see," Genesis said, holding out her hand.

Knowing her sister's persistence was based in caring, Celeste lifted her leg out of the water, fascinated when water wrapped around her injury instead of falling back into the pool. "That's really cool," she admitted. "I don't think I've ever seen it do that."

"I have," Tori said, joining them. "Genesis, do you remember when you stepped on that nail? And Granny had to cut out the damaged tissue?"

"I do." Genesis groaned in remembered pain. "I screamed pretty loudly, as I recall."

"With good reason." Tori studied Celeste's leg wound with her sister.

Celeste let out a quiet laugh. "So? How does it look? Did Storm get it all?"

"It looks like he did," Genesis said, smiling. "Nice and clean."

"I was afraid the spirit animal bite would cause more problems than what he was trying to fix," Tori admitted.

Celeste hadn't considered that. "It's a strange world we live in, when a spirit animal can actually bite us."

"Did anyone consider that maybe spirit animals have abilities, the same as we do?" Genesis asked. "It's not an idle question …"

Tori frowned. "You know I have—often."

"And I'm pretty sure they do," Celeste said in a low voice. "We need to do some research on it, but there's never any time. I've been so busy trying to survive …" She closed her eyelids in relief, as she lowered her leg back into the water. As a test, it was a good one. She was not ready to get out.

"It's tough, isn't it?" Genesis said. "I'm so sorry. I couldn't even return here to the cabin for six months, and I lived in town, trying to keep the herb shop open."

"Is it still?" Celeste hoped so. It was what Genesis had always wanted.

"It is. I hired Vienna away from the coffee shop to work for me." Genesis shrugged at Celeste's shocked gasp. "I am working at the Center with the star charts as well and don't have time to do both."

"And I'm working with Genesis," Tori said. "So we both live at the Center."

"Well, I won't be visiting you there much, will I?" And, damn, that hurt. The Center was where she'd spent so much of *her* time—before. She loved that place. To think of both sisters and their men there without her? Well, that was just painful.

"Matt was here earlier. You remember that, right?" Tori asked curiously. "You can't just ignore it. He came rushing in to warn us about your leg, then left with the damaging pebbles."

Was that where he'd gone? Part of her had been wondering if he was sitting out in the kitchen with the other men. The rest of her had been afraid to think of him at all.

"Devon feels horribly guilty and took off with him," Tori said. "I told him that you wouldn't blame him, but he figures he should have been able to stop Storm before he bit you."

Relieved that she didn't have to face Matt for a while, and hating that she would have to thank him for his part in this, Celeste splashed water on her face, thinking about the spirit animal's actions. "I don't think Devon could have done a damn thing. I'm supposed to have an affinity to them and look, I couldn't do anything either." Then she froze. And laughed drily. "Actually I asked if Storm could do anything to help." She glanced at her sisters. "I'll have to watch how I word things from now on."

They grinned.

"Honestly I don't think I could have stopped Storm either. Not after I requested his help." She shivered suddenly. "I wish I could get out of the water, but my leg isn't ready. I'm getting chilled," she admitted.

Instantly Genesis reached a hand into the water.

Seconds later, the temperature warmed up to make a lovely hot pool. "Oh, thanks. That feels much better." Celeste smiled and closed her eyelids again, before sliding down into the water once more.

"Rest. We'll be here when you wake up."

And, if there was a tone of *We'll always be here from now on* in her sister's voice, Celeste was too happy to take umbrage at her big sister's caring. Celeste didn't want to be anywhere else but here.

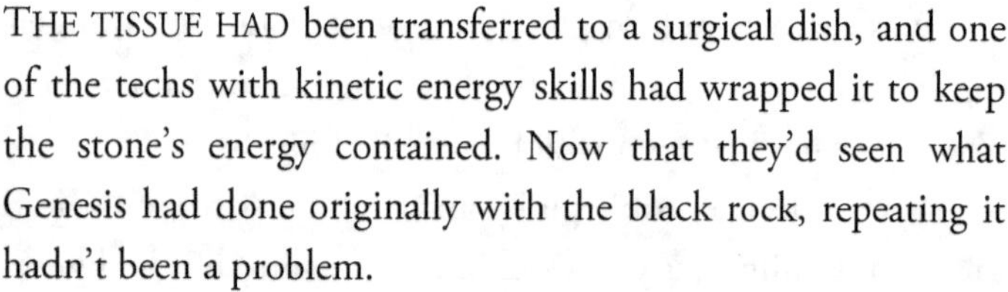

THE TISSUE HAD been transferred to a surgical dish, and one of the techs with kinetic energy skills had wrapped it to keep the stone's energy contained. Now that they'd seen what Genesis had done originally with the black rock, repeating it hadn't been a problem.

Matt and Devon stared at the tissue, watching it pulse, as if the rock was absorbing it—eating it. Matt's stomach heaved. This would be a huge problem, if they couldn't quarantine all the rocks before they turned to dust—and fast.

At hard footsteps behind them, Matt turned to see Scott. But the other man's gaze was locked on the glass box. "What in the hell is that?" he whispered.

"Remember those black rocks we've been hunting down? This is a few tiny particles of the same stuff we just removed from a woman's leg an hour ago."

"They'll be hell to find if they are this small."

"We *have* to find the rest. Mason said they'd all been stolen, but there might be small ones the thieves discounted due to their size. We need to go check."

"I'll go," Devon said. "I was heading there anyway, before we heard Celeste had returned."

Matt nodded and watched as Devon strode off, his fists clenching and unclenching. Devon was still disturbed by Storm's actions. Understandable. Yet Storm had saved Celeste's leg. By removing the poison before it had burrowed in deeper, they'd been able to extract it, before it hit her bones. Who knew what damage could have happened if it had managed to burrow in that far?

Scott walked around the glass jar. "It shouldn't have affected her."

Matt turned to look at him. "What do you mean?"

"It's negative energy. Her positive energy should have neutralized the rocks from gaining hold in the first place."

Matt winced. "Sure, but remember that worry, stress, and fear can have the same effect and can allow anything negative to gain a foothold. She was in a tough place when this happened."

Scott nodded. "Right. We must ensure it doesn't happen again."

Needing to move him off that track, Matt changed topics. "What did you find out?"

"That there is a history of stargazers disappearing into these highly charged electrical storms. Not often and not forever. But somewhere along the line, that balance of having a stargazer available to go and work the storms changed. Then they ran out of stargazers."

Ran out of stargazers? Matt had heard something about there being one per generation, so, in theory, three could be alive at any one time, given three living generations. Plus, given the longevity of the stargazer line, it wasn't unbelievable to consider four or five alive at one time, but there'd been only Granny for so long. And now her three granddaughters. So the system had broken down. Was it repairing itself now? Or was it not repairable? If not, then why three at one time? "Where did you get this information from?" Matt asked in alarm.

"From the archives," Scott said.

Matt studied him carefully. "I don't remember reading any of this stuff in the historical accountings."

"Much of this came from the material Genesis allowed us to bring, and the rest we had but hadn't been translated." He shrugged. "I happen to have a talent for translation."

"Interesting. I hadn't known that. Any translations?"

Scott hesitated.

And that piqued Matt's interest that much more.

"Not all of them, but any old language that I've come up against so far has been relatively easy to decipher."

A useful skill in some ways and completely useless in so many others. Yet, as Matt studied the young man, he realized Scott glowed with power. He just wasn't willing to share those details any further. Fair enough. They all had secrets.

Even Matt.

CHAPTER 6

"**N**O." CELESTE WAS adamant on that point. She didn't dare go back where Matt lived. Too much was wrong between them for that.

"We need you back at the Center." Genesis sat back and stared at her. Then switched her gaze to Tori, as if willing her to help out.

Celeste shook her head. "Still playing the usual games. Ganging up on me."

"It's important," Tori said quietly. "We don't know what's going on. Genesis has been working to stabilize and to heal the pools, and I've been trying to get the forests to heal themselves."

"And, once those two factors happen, then the animals can return. I can't do anything to speed up the process. You both know that." Celeste stared around the small cabin. "Besides, I need time here."

"Time to hide?" Tori asked gently. "Matt isn't an ogre. Even if you have nothing to do with him, other than interacting with him as the head of the Center, he's very involved in this problem."

A snort escaped from Celeste. "Really? You think that'll work?"

"Well, hiding from him won't." Genesis stood. "I need to return. If you don't want to come with us, then I'll come back tomorrow with more supplies. You can make a decision then."

They were leaving. Somehow that hurt. But of course they had to go. They had jobs. Lives of their own. Partners. And homes. Celeste glanced around the cabin. "I need to stay here a little longer," she said quietly. "My leg isn't fully healed."

She'd been out of the water for an hour, and it felt fine, but she could tell that she would need the healing pool sooner rather than later, before the pain built again. "I really don't want to be away from the healing pool, not until the leg is back to normal."

Immediately Genesis's face turned contrite. "I'm so sorry. I forgot about your leg." She dug into her pockets and pulled out her tablet to jot down some notes. "What can I bring you back tomorrow?" She glanced at the food on the table. The basket she'd brought earlier had also yielded sandwiches and salad. "Several sandwiches are left, just for you."

"I have lots of food now," Celeste said. "You'll make me fat if you bring more."

"Oh, I'll bring more," Genesis said. "We all went through this, you know? Stopped eating. Stopped sleeping. Couldn't smile at much anymore. Tired all the time. Not scared but feeling like life wasn't quite right and would never be right again."

Oh hell. Celeste swallowed heavily, as she struggled to her feet.

Tori added, "And we all lost weight. I'm still trying to put on a few more pounds. And you, Celeste? Well, you look gaunt."

"I'm not that bad," she cried out. "Surely?"

"Oh, yes, you are," said Connor from the sidelines, where he'd been the whole time. "Genesis got skinny, Tori became lean, but you're into the gaunt stage. The longer you stayed away, the worse it got."

She stared at him, then down at her arms, seeing the blue veins crisscross the backs of her hands and going up toward her shoulders. "I lost my appetite, then had little in the way of good food to eat. Nothing tasted normal anymore. As if my taste buds had up and left me a long time ago. So I didn't eat," she admitted. "And I didn't have time to worry about it, as so much else was going on all the time. I burned through the food and then the energy. I had so many animals that left home when I did that I struggled to keep them all comforted."

"That's because they wanted to come back here," Genesis said in a firm voice. "To make the energy transfer easier. As you stopped eating your daily requirements, you pulled on more energy to keep going. Where did you source that energy from?" Genesis asked curiously.

"The woods," Celeste confessed. "I haven't been very far away. So I stayed close enough to the forest to stay recharged. However, since I was still hiding, I ran the energy through the spirit pets, so you wouldn't know."

"The black part of the forest?" Tori snorted. "I couldn't figure out why it was struggling so badly. I was pulling from the woods in the same way but from a longer distance. It was in terrible condition, as we were both pulling from the same source."

Celeste stared at Genesis and Tori in disbelief.

Tori nodded and added, "Between us, we damn-near destroyed the woods. Granny has to be rolling over in her grave."

Silence.

Celeste pitched her voice low, hoping Connor couldn't hear. "Did you ever figure that out?"

Genesis stared down at the table and shook her head.

Tori slid a glance over at Connor and said, "No."

Celeste sighed and stared around the small cabin. "We'll have to deal with it at some time, you know?"

"We have lots to deal with," Genesis said, putting away her tablet. She opened her arms, speaking normally. "I'm taking Connor back to the Center. He's been very good, standing watch, but he has work to do as well."

The sisters hugged, and Genesis walked out first, Connor behind her.

Tori asked, her voice gentle, "Do you want me to stay with you?"

Celeste smiled. "Thanks for the offer, but I'm fine. I need to stay and acclimatize. Lots of news to understand too."

"Take your time. And remember to let the healing pool help with that as well."

"Right." She had forgotten about that level of healing. It worked wonders on confusion too. "Will you come back tomorrow?" she asked.

"I will. And I'm warning you. Genesis won't be happy until you're safe in the Center with us. There's nothing like being back together again."

"I know," Celeste whispered, "but I'll have to deal with Matt there."

Tori's smile blossomed. "Enjoy it. Making up is hard, but the end result is so worth it."

"Only if the result is the one you want," Celeste said quietly.

She watched from the doorway, as her sisters hopped into the hovercraft. How life had changed. A year ago, neither had ever been in something so fancy. Now they were living at the Center, working on preserving their heritage. Had partners they'd started out with and had lost but had now regained.

And Celeste? She felt out of sync. Lost. Left behind. As if she'd returned too late to make the grade—again. She bowed her head, then turned and closed the door, replacing the locks and putting up the shield around the cabin. She might be back. But no way she was *back*.

Not yet.

At this rate, maybe never.

As she turned to retrace her steps to the healing pool, she stopped and stared. The room had filled with animals. Spirit animals of all shapes and sizes stood between her and the pool. Why? Puzzled, she slowed her progress and said, "Hello, my friends. What can I do for you?"

The response was a garbled mess of sounds. But the overwhelming answer came in the form of a phrase, bouncing through her head.

Fix it.

"Fix what?"

The forest.

"Are you all from the forest?" They weren't flesh and blood; they were spirits.

That is our home.

"But …"

That is our home, a beautiful deer repeated. *We need to go back to our home.*

"And how can I help you do that?"

Remove the blocks.

Blocks? What blocks?

But even though she'd only thought the words, the answer came anyway.

Your blocks. Your pain. Your fear. Your anger. You denied yourself the full use of the woods and only took the energy you needed, but you didn't give back. Even knowing you shouldn't be doing that. … In so doing, you denied yourself the right to the forest. You denied us our right to the forest. You are us. We are you.

Fix it, said a chorus of spirit voices.

And the room cleared, as they all disappeared.

<hr />

"SHE STAYED?" WHY was Matt not surprised? Not happy about it but not surprised either. He figured she'd do anything to avoid him. He'd hoped, knowing that her sisters were here, that Celeste would come and stay with them. It would be that much easier to keep everyone safe. It would take time, but proximity would help—at least to the point of being polite. Being friendly would come later. Matt wanted so much more too.

"Her leg hasn't healed enough," Tori said. Her gaze flitted to Devon, standing at the window.

Matt nodded. "I'd hoped it wasn't that bad."

"It isn't," Tori said. "At least not because of Storm's incision. Still, the rocks had been there long enough to cause trouble. She could need a day or two yet."

At the term *incision*, Devon snorted. "Is that what you call it?" He continued to stare out the window.

"Celeste admitted that she'd asked Storm if he could do anything to fix her leg, then to please do it," Tori said.

Devon spun to stare at her. "What?"

"She'd been talking to him, just before he acted." Genesis shrugged. "You had nothing to do with it. When an energy worker gives another the right to do something …"

"Surely she didn't mean for him to bite her though," Devon protested.

"Maybe not, but Storm did a job that needed doing. Celeste must have known on some level that it would be out of her hands," Tori said. "At least she was at the healing pool, and it was fast and clean."

Devon walked over and kissed Tori firmly on her lips, then walked out, whistling.

Matt laughed. "Thanks for that. He feels guilty as hell since it happened."

A knock on the doorframe caught Matt's attention.

Matt motioned Scott inside. "Have you any news?"

"Maybe and maybe not. I'm sure Devon told you no rocks were left at Grandfather's place. Storm was doing the tracking, but I want to go to the woods, where Tori found the one in the water. Others might be in that same area."

"Good idea. Take Devon and Storm again. Maybe they can find something this time."

"I'm going with them," Connor interjected. "Kona wants to get out and to do a bit of hunting himself." He followed Scott, leaving Matt and the two women behind.

Matt stared at the sisters to whom he'd become so close. He wanted to ask about Celeste, but didn't know how.

Thankfully Genesis took the first step. "She's not ready to deal with you yet."

"Too much to absorb, too much healing to happen on a lot of levels," Tori added. "Give her time."

He nodded. "Right. I'd hoped ..."

"Keep that thought," Genesis said, "but it might take a bit."

But how long? Matt had hoped that Celeste would have forgiven him by now, but instead she wasn't even ready to see him.

CHAPTER 7

CELESTE NEEDED TO exercise her leg, and walking in the small cottage wasn't enough. She'd been in the pools for hours and felt wonderfully strong. She really wanted to go to the caves and see what her sisters had been talking about. The trip was likely to be long, although plenty of pools were along the way. They'd be easily accessible, and, if she were smart, she'd stop by the string of healing pools on the way there and then again on the way back, so she could heal enough to continue. She glanced around the small cabin. Lord, she loved this place. She wandered into her bedroom, still stunned to think that Granny had owned all the land around for miles. When her sisters said it could get ugly in the courts, they weren't kidding.

Yet what did any of it matter to the triplets? They still had no money. No way they could sell off the land. But owning it all made them gatekeepers. A responsibility they would take seriously and would hand down to future generations. It didn't change the fact that Celeste could stay here for a few days, but afterward she needed a job. Her sisters couldn't be expected to keep handing over food, and that hovercraft didn't come cheap.

No, she'd been independent for a long time; now that she was back home, that wasn't any different. But getting a job also meant needing a place to live. Had Genesis kept her apartment in town? Celeste knew it was small, but, if it had been big enough for Genesis, then it would be big enough for Celeste. Particularly as she might be able to live rent-free, until she got back on her feet.

She opened her bedroom closet and dressed quickly.

Then she straightened to look in the mirror on the back of the door and gasped.

Her jeans needed a belt to stay up, and her generous bosom had disappeared somewhere in the last year. Her collarbone showed above the neckline of her T-shirt, and her cheekbones? … Hollow. She winced. Connor was right. She'd lost more weight than she'd expected.

Turning back to the closet, she rummaged around looking for a belt. She found a thin scarf instead. She threaded that through her belt loops and tied it up lightly in the front. She also felt a chill to the air. Likely a side effect of the weight loss. Her old sweater had dropped to the floor. She loved that thing. It had lost its shape a long time ago and had pulled threads peeking out in various places, but she tugged it on and laughed as it hung loose. "Scarecrow, it is."

Wandering out to the kitchen, she grabbed the two muffins still on the table from breakfast and tucked them into a small bag.

She turned to the empty cabin and called out, "Who is coming with me?"

Instantly the air filled with animal cries.

Silky muttered at her from the table. Celeste reached down and gave him a lift back to her shoulder. As Minkel ran at her side, and Smurg flew overhead, she set off to the back entrance of the caves.

Two other spirit pets raced ahead. There were more here than anywhere else. That was okay. She could remember most of their names. Henkel was the huge rabbit-looking thing with the spines down his back. Rogan was the buck walking at her side. He was souls-old, as in his energy faded in and out every few moments. She had to wonder at the eventual end to them too. Did they die? Not that it was possible, as energy never died. It just changed form.

So what form would Rogan go to next? Or would he just fade to the point of becoming one with the world around him? As in, go back to the woods he came from?

Above, going from tree branch to tree branch, was a tistor. They reminded her of the old pictures she'd seen of squirrels from Earth, only bigger. And meaner. They could hunt all kinds of smaller animals—only, of course, as a spirit animal, no hunting was required. A part she found very satisfying.

They approached the cave entrance in good time.

She took a good look around to make sure she was alone, then slipped inside. This was one of Granny's many entrances. As far as Celeste knew, no one else used it. She noted footsteps in the dirt, but those were likely from her sisters—and their men. According to what they'd told her, there'd been some horrific things going on down here. From evil black rocks to cold-blooded murder. Celeste couldn't take it all in.

Her life when she'd lived here before had been peaceful. Calm. Boring, in fact. Now, since she'd left, the place had come apart at the seams. Who even knew that murder *could* take place down here? These were healing caves. Healing pools. No such thing should be possible.

She walked into the tunnels below, studying the energy of the area. Granny had been big on each of the sisters learning the others' specialties, so they could do some of the same work on their own. Granny had always warned them that just because they'd been born together that didn't mean they would always be together. Granny had been right. Look at what the last year had brought them.

Pain. Loss. Loneliness.

But her mind quickly supplied, *Strength, independence, and a new perspective.*

Right. That was a fair trade.

The string of pools were laid out before her in a cascading string of pearls. Truly beautiful. She went down to the one she'd always been in before and dipped her leg in it. Her injured muscles had started throbbing as soon as she'd started down the path, yet not enough to cause her to want to go home again. The water felt good but didn't appear to help much. She hobbled to the pool below. Same thing. Then she tried the pool below that. In fact, she had to go down four more pools to find one that helped her leg.

How weird was that?

After resting until she felt as good as new, Celeste got up, slipped her socks and shoes back on, and went lower, until she came to the pool where Granny had worn a spot down on the rocks after sitting in the same place for a century. Celeste couldn't help herself; she dropped down and sat in the same place. Instantly she felt her granny right there beside her. Tears came to her eyes. Damn, she missed her.

As she sat here, she realized she'd really come to say good-bye. She'd never had a chance to grieve before. She'd stuffed it all deep down inside and had avoided looking at it over the last year. Now, in Granny's cabin, walking the same pathways they'd taken with Granny so many times before, and sitting here, it was as if Celeste never really had to say goodbye either.

She was still connected to that special woman inside.

Strange. Exciting. Satisfying. Maybe like the spirit animals, Granny had just faded into nothing and become one with everything.

They'd all known the moment she'd died. No one had quite understood what had happened or when or where. They'd found the clothing that she'd been wearing, as she'd only ever worn the one outfit, and it had been at the deepest pool Granny could go. The clothing had been faded and weathered, and it had been left there off to the side, where Granny had likely placed it. But she'd never returned to the pool and had never returned home.

In fact, she'd never been seen again.

They knew she was dead, even if they had no proof.

They'd made a memorial for her and never told anyone.

What could they say? That she was missing? That wouldn't have been the truth, and neither would it have helped anyone. Granny had disappeared, but she'd come so damn close so many times over the last decade that they knew it would happen like that eventually. Celeste had come into the healing pools about a month earlier and found Granny's energy fading in and out. Celeste had known what that meant at the time but hadn't been ready to lose her.

She'd told Granny that too.

Granny had smiled and said that fate had its own time frame, and it didn't matter if anyone was ready or not. Granny's time would come soon enough, and the triplets would know. That they weren't to worry. That Granny would be fine and that she'd keep a watch over them.

But they hadn't really believed her.

Especially not when the rest of their lives had fallen into disarray at the same time. Granny had been the glue, and, with her gone, everything had fallen apart.

Only now Celeste had to wonder. Granny hadn't really been the glue, but she'd been the comfort in their lives. With that gone, the women had to rely on each other and themselves. The problem was, when it came to that, they hadn't known how to deal with it, and they'd splintered. Now they were at a stage of regluing themselves back together—to each other—to the men they'd lost. To the world around them.

Celeste had been the worst. She'd been the glue for the animals, and she'd let them down too. Suddenly unable to handle the heavy emotions flooding her, she jumped to her feet, and ran back to another tunnel, upward to the next series of pools. Where she came face-to-face with a jumble of heavy equipment off to the one side. Shock and outrage hit her. Even though she'd been told about it happening, still it was horrific to see the damage done. It shouldn't be allowed to have such a destructive energy here. This was what her sisters were fighting for. And so much more.

Even though she was hurting again, she felt compelled to see all the changes, all the damage. She walked through the caves and pathways to other pools, other entrances. Finding visual proof of the foreign energy. The negative energy. The evil energy. She came out on one of the smaller entrances on the far side of the tunnels. So much pain was here. So much negativity that didn't belong.

She stepped out into the sunshine and found herself in the woods. The same corner she'd drawn on for her needs.

The black dying trees, the scorched earth, the brittle greenery.

Her throat closed up in pain; her breath—a prisoner inside.

No wonder the animals were upset.

Dear God, what had they done?

MATT STARED AT Darbo. "Where is she?"

Matt understood she'd been walking for several hours. For someone who was supposed to have an injured leg, she'd covered a lot of miles. He didn't know whether to cheer her on because she was doing so well or to be pissed off because she was doing too much. He wanted to go to her, but it wasn't the time. He wasn't welcome.

She's in the dead forest, Darbo whispered.

Matt sat back and winced. That wouldn't be easy on her. That area had been the hardest hit. And the underground pools in there had sustained the most damage. Genesis and Tori had both focused on healing that area, hoping that the healing would then help raise the energy levels of the other pools and forests, but it was slow, hard work.

She's crying. Darbo reached out a paw to stroke Matt's cheek.

Damn. Of course she was crying.

Matt looked outside and sighed. The clouds above looked to be ready to dump rain on anyone unfortunate enough to be caught outside. He wasn't sure any of them had correlated the weather to the triplets' emotions, but Matt had. More secrets that he hadn't shared with anyone.

The triplets wouldn't be pleased with him when it came time to tell them either.

He stood, hating the pent-up energy raging inside, the anger at Celeste for walking away from what they had. They could have worked it out. Should have worked it all out. And, if she'd not just lost Granny, likely they would have done just that. But now? ... Matt had no idea. And he needed to stay close. She was in danger and had no idea.

Until they got to the bottom of this land deal in the courts and whatever evil was still yanking their chains, she shouldn't be alone.

Resolute, Matt stared out the window and studied the weather. Celeste would get caught out there on her own and be too weak to safely get back.

Knowing he was looking for an excuse to go to her, even if she hated him for it, he also couldn't ignore the feeling that she wasn't safe. Hell, Connor and Devon never left the other two women alone either. Unless they were in the Center, the sisters were escorted everywhere. It was common sense.

Then this was Celeste—and she didn't know the meaning of the words.

So he'd have to be that responsible person instead. And, if she didn't like it, then too bad. Better she be angry at him for trying to keep her alive than for him to worry about her reaction and have her die because he didn't want to piss her off.

CHAPTER 8

CELESTE HUDDLED UP against the huge fir tree and let the tears pour. Rain drenched the area in a sudden storm that she hadn't seen coming. Somehow she'd gone farther than she intended. And she was tired. Too damn tired. She should have turned back long before she saw the dead woods, but her heart had been hurting, and she couldn't have turned around and ignored this place for anything. Now she was soaked to the skin, and her body screamed in pain. She was a fool.

She turned to hobble back to the caves, when she heard a foreign sound. Instincts made her stumble back under the tree branches. What was that noise? She peered through the trees but couldn't see anything.

She turned to look behind her, and spotted two men coming in her direction, high-res guns in their hands. *Oh, shit.*

What had she fallen into?

Her sisters had warned her, but she hadn't really understood. As usual, she was the idiot. The one who had to see for herself. Dear God. She pressed herself flat against the trunk, wishing she had Tori's ability to mind control the men to walk away. Celeste had been working on that skill before she'd left but hadn't managed to get it to work well for her.

Now she realized it was a skill she needed, regardless of how well it worked.

"Where is that bitch?"

Were they looking for her? How could they possibly know she was here?

The animal network. Had they told the men? Not if that meant causing her pain. She knew that. They wouldn't do that. They couldn't. She was their master.

But she'd been away, and, if new ones had shown up in the meantime, they wouldn't know her. Or who she was. And maybe someone else had connected.

Her mind reeled with the implications of anyone else speaking to the spirit animals. Or someone who had spirit animals of their own, that didn't recognize her. What if not all animals responded to her? Only the good ones? She'd never met one full of negative energy, but they existed.

"She has to be here. According to the rumors, she's weak and wandering the woods, lost."

Weak? Lost? They had to be talking about someone else. Not on her worst day would she consider herself weak. And how could she, a stargazer, ever be lost? Where the hell were they getting this information, these rumors, from?

"Yeah, but who can trust rumors? Just because we heard that doesn't make it true. It's disgusting out here."

"That makes it perfect for getting rid of her. Dump her in the pool, and she'll drown, and no one will be the wiser."

"Consider they all come from that weirdo crazy lady, they'll think she committed suicide."

"Even better," the first man said cheerfully. "That's one down and two more to go."

"But they're always surrounded. Unlike this one, this time." The second man's voice was sarcastic. "She's got to be ugly, if she can't get a man in this horrible hick town."

They *were* talking about her. Holy crap. For the first time, Celeste truly comprehended the enormity of what her sisters had been trying to tell her. A tale she'd tossed off as being too ludicrous to take seriously. She'd promised to be careful. She'd promised to be safe. She understood that bad things had happened. But nowhere in there had it been brought home to her—as in seeing the reality of the problem—until she'd nearly come face-to-face with two men who intended to kill her.

Somewhere deep inside, she felt her anger fire up. They'd called Granny a crazy lady—again. The poor woman was dead and gone. When would the name-calling stop? When would that beautiful woman get the respect she deserved?

As Celeste felt the anger reach overwhelming proportions, and jumping out into the rain to confront the assholes was starting to look like her best option, lightning cracked overhead. She jumped back under cover at the last minute, as it struck a tree close by.

"Hey, we need to get the hell out of here. It's getting dangerous now."

"It's just a storm. Quit your complaining," the first man yelled, as he stepped into view. Big chest, bigger gut, and bald head. Not what she would have considered the look of a professional killer. A farmer, maybe. Then he turned and pointed the gun right in her direction.

She closed her eyes and held her breath, willing herself to fade into the surrounding elements. *Spirit animals, if you are around, I need help. Badly.*

A flutter of wings whispered overhead. The long grass rustled, as animals raced to her aid.

"Oh, what the hell. Let's go back to the car and wait it out," the first man muttered angrily. "She can't stay in the forest forever."

"*Um*, Jethro? What the hell is that?" Fear laced the second man's voice.

"What?" Jethro turned and saw something out of Celeste's sight that made him shriek in terror.

A SCREAM RENT the air. Matt froze. Darbo squealed in horror. That was enough to unfreeze Matt's feet, and he raced toward the sound.

It hadn't been Celeste. In fact, he wasn't sure he'd heard a woman's voice at all, but someone was in trouble. Dodging branches and leaves, Matt jumped and darted through the woods. A wet brush slapped against his cheek, before he moved it out of the way. He blinked raindrops out of his vision. The lightning storm was stronger in this corner of the forest. Was that Celeste's doing? If so, it didn't bode well for anyone hunting her.

He came to a screeching stop in time to see two men huddled together, terror turning their eyes the size of saucers and stripping their skin of color. They stared, unmoving, to his left. Matt turned slowly to study the woods around them. A shimmer underneath the branches of a nearby tree told him some energy was hiding in there. A second glance reassured him that it was Celeste, and she appeared to be fine. An energy shield surrounded her. Interesting. So whatever terrified the men, it hadn't been her.

Shifting farther, he looked in the direction the men were staring. Nothing. The woods appeared normal. And, given Matt's own energy skills, the woods appeared empty—on all levels. He increased the power so that he could see the energy of what was and what had been. It only worked on whatever had transpired over the last few minutes.

Instantly a dark-gray shimmer filled the woods. He narrowed his gaze and upped the wattage. Oh, very interesting. He had no idea what had caused that. He looked deeper, hoping to see the owner's signature, but if they'd created that energy fog, they could also hide inside it.

The fog layer slowly dissipated, as he watched. So it hadn't been there that long. He closed his eyelids and sent out a probe, looking for the creator. Nothing. The person who'd manifested this had disappeared. And fast.

He crept toward where Celeste huddled, keeping his gaze on the two men, noting the guns hanging useless in their hands. Matt hoped to question these two, but, given their motionless state, Celeste was first.

Her protective shield whispered toward him, as he reached the safety of the tree she hid under. Her energy was checking him out. To see who he was … and who he wasn't. He let it explore his body, let it determine if he was friend or foe.

The energy drifted around him, like a caress, before she abruptly yanked it back.

He grinned. Celeste might not be ready to let him back into her world, but her energy knew him. Cared for him.

She just had to get on board.

"Celeste," he murmured. "Let me in."

The energy stayed stubbornly closed. He could get in on his own, but that would be a violation, and he didn't want to force the issue unless he had to. He shifted his own energy probe to make sure she was okay inside.

Reassured, he crouched near her, as he studied the men.

Neither moved. He studied their features, as if they were frozen in place. He knew they weren't frozen in time, as Celeste's energy had been able to move. How long could the men stay like that? Were they dead? No, their energy, tight against their bodies, shimmered with a little life yet. He had to believe that whatever they'd seen had done this to them. Or the shock was so great …

Either way, his concern was for Celeste.

Unless the men woke up.

He crept out of his dry place and walked over to the men. He retrieved both guns and stuck them in his pockets. Waving a hand in front of their eyes, he realized they were in worse shape than he thought.

Pulling out his phone, he called for assistance. A weird crackling noise echoed through the connection, and he frowned before shaking his head and speaking more loudly. He needed a vehicle to haul the men back to the Center, preferably someone who could heal them. That would be the sisters.

Glory was sadly short on energy workers in the medical field. It should be a mandatory thing really, but so few were around. He figured it was mostly due to the healing pools and their general usage in helping people. But that just led to more problems. How would he get the men to one? Only damaged pools were in this quadrant of the woods.

He ended the call and turned back to Celeste. Or rather, where she had been. "Damn it, Celeste," he snapped. "Stop running away from me."

There was a sense of shock, a rush of anger, then a tiny hurricane battered him, as she raced toward him from behind the tree and beat on him with her fists. "I wasn't hiding."

"Well, I'm sorry." He grabbed her hands to stop hitting him. "I thought you snuck away when I wasn't looking." He glared down at her, wishing he didn't still believe that. But, from the sheepish look on her face, he knew he'd been right. "I won't ever hurt you."

"I know that," she said and made a face. "But I've been in hiding for a year, and it's not something I can stop right away. My instincts say run, and I run. Especially lately."

"Whoa. What do you mean, lately?"

In a wary voice, she said, "I just mean that lately I've been looking over my shoulder a lot more. It feels like I'm being watched." She shrugged. "But then, life was getting a little rough, and I thought a lot of things that weren't true …"

He didn't know what to say. So he backed off. Changed tacks. "First, let's deal with this problem." He motioned toward the two men. "Do you know what happened to these two?"

Her breath caught in the back of her throat. She stepped closer to them, peering into their faces. "Their eyes aren't even moving," she exclaimed.

"I know, but why? They look scared to death, but they are still alive."

"Not by much …" She frowned, studying the men. "I didn't see what they were looking at. The rain was coming down heavy, then the lightning started. Soon afterward, I heard them scream." She shrugged. "Honestly, I pulled in my energy and tried to stay out of trouble."

"And you managed to do that, but it would have been helpful if you could have seen the same thing they had. We know nothing more, yet whatever it was appears to be a powerful weapon."

"Then it's a good thing I didn't see what it was. Otherwise I'd have ended up the same as these two men." She shook her head. "Their energy is so low," she noted.

If her tone was tart, he ignored it. "I've got men coming to collect these two."

"Good, then you don't need me." She gave a quick wave

at Darbo and hobbled as fast as she could into the trees.

"Damn it, Celeste. Don't run," he yelled. "We don't know what's out there."

But she only waved her hand in acknowledgment.

Knowing he couldn't leave the men alone, as they'd never be found without some guidance, Matt had no choice but to stand here and watch her run away.

Again.

CHAPTER 9

WHY WAS SHE running again?

Not very adult of her. But Celeste felt she needed to do it, and to hell with being an adult. She had enough going on in her life. And Matt was just too big an issue to deal with. Besides, she couldn't go back now.

She hadn't a clue what had terrified those men, but, if they didn't have paranormal abilities, then they could be afraid of something she knew to be fine. She'd seen and done things that would terrify many people.

Then again, she knew of nothing that could cause someone to freeze up, like those men had. As a weapon, it was damn effective. Using the spirit animals as an early alarm system, she retraced her steps to the caves, hating the weakness in her muscles, the fatigue coursing through her body. She needed the healing pools and fast. Her leg burned, and she had several miles to go. Not smart of her.

The animals were taking her home the fastest and easiest way. By the time she'd returned to the cave and almost to the first pool, she was shivering. She immediately put her leg in, only to realize she'd have to go to the lower string of pools to get the benefit she needed again. By now, she was cursing her decision to have left the cottage at all. She should have stayed home and worked on healing. She forced herself to keep moving. Past the rock Granny had sat on, and still Celeste kept moving.

Stubborn.

By the time she reached the lower healing pools, Minkel was holding her hand and infusing her body with his energy to keep her going. It wasn't much farther, but she had to walk down the slope, and that was dangerous. It was a narrow pathway, and falling was not an option. Although, without the animals for support, it was a probability.

Her entrance into the pool was a full-on belly flop. She knew she'd be sitting in soaking-wet clothes afterward but couldn't make herself care. Her leg was booming with pain, and tears burned the corner of her eyes. She was such an idiot.

Thank God she'd made it. Closing her eyes, she floated. This pool should give her enough healing energy that she could make it home. Then she would go into her pool and stay there for as long as necessary. Her stomach growled. In all the chaos, she'd forgotten to eat. And remembered the muffins were in her bag, still over her shoulder. In the pool. Shit. She wasn't above eating soggy muffins in a pinch, but she'd really rather not. Although now she didn't have much choice.

She struggled to the side and slipped her bag off her shoulder. She tossed it on the side of the pool and collapsed back.

Closing her eyes once again, she let the healing waters do their job.

Matt was right to be upset about her being watched. She'd put it down to an increased sense of being paranoid. But what if it was more than that? With all that had been going on here, what if she'd been found in the small town where she'd hidden, and they were just waiting for a signal to make a move?

She didn't really want to know what that meant, but something nasty was going on. And it included her.

And that weird blackish fog she'd seen, where had it come from? It had been almost … female in nature. Stupid, really. She couldn't *know* that. But she had sensed it. She didn't know anyone powerful enough to scare a man to death. And two of them at the same time. … Especially not now that Granny was dead.

Celeste groaned as the shivers slowly eased back, and the pain reduced to something more manageable. Only now, her wet clothes were dragging her down. She contemplated stripping off, but having seen men with guns after her in the last hour, she didn't want to be caught in just her underwear. Maybe she could go home now? She tried to stand up and cried out as her leg crumpled beneath her. *Shit. Shit. Shit.* She wasn't going home anytime soon.

"Ready to ask for help?" a man asked from behind her.

She froze. "Damn it," she muttered under her breath. In a louder voice, she asked, "How did you find me?"

"Easy. I can find you anywhere. Anytime, anyplace."

She closed her eyes, realizing what that said about her attempts to stay hidden this last year. Had he bothered to look, or had he found her and left her alone?

"We're joined, in case you've forgotten all those long late-night conversations from a year ago."

Of course he'd bring that up. And why she'd worked so hard to stay hidden. Out from under his watchful guard. Sighing, she rolled over in the water, as he eyed her fully clothed body in the water. He was alone, at least. "Did the men get back safely?"

"They will be at the Center soon, but their prognosis isn't good."

"Can anyone help?"

Matt shook his head. "No."

She nodded. "Right. Healing pools aside …"

"I don't think they will make a difference, but they are being taken to the one closest to the Center. We'll see."

She knew the pools couldn't do anything for the men. They'd had the barest film of energy left in them, but it had already started to disconnect. But, where there was life, there was hope.

"Did you look for me?" she asked abruptly. Then she caught her breath. Damn it. Where had that come from? She deliberately wanted to avoid any discussion of the year she'd been away, and here she'd just opened up the topic.

"No."

Good, right? Wrong. He should have tried to find her. She'd worked so hard to stay hidden and for what? Nothing? That he'd cared so little for her that he'd let her walk away and had made no attempt to find her? She wanted to cry.

"I knew you would come back, only when you were ready. Expending the amount of energy required to find you—when you didn't want me to follow—wouldn't help either of us," he said, his voice cool. Cold, even.

That was her cue. She could be cold too. "Good that you didn't waste your time."

"Not in that respect, no." But he didn't say any more on the topic.

She lay back and gently floated in the water. Come to think of it, how had he gotten this low in the cavern? These pools were too powerful for most energy workers. She and her sisters had taken decades to come down here. And Matt had waltzed right in. Damn. She'd known that he hadn't shared all his abilities with her and that his power was always turned down to a reasonable working level, but she had no idea the amount he had available.

Very interesting.

Not wanting to break the silence, she floated, until the water lifted her up and deposited her, soaking wet, on the side of the pool. Except she wasn't ready to leave yet. That was the thing about the healing pools—each was different and had their own foibles.

With this one, if it felt you were hiding, it would dump you out. She should have made it to the next pool. That pool knew that hiding was often the only answer. She straightened and took two steps, wincing at the excess weight of her waterlogged clothing and the sound of her feet squelching. Only time would dry her out. She would have a very uncomfortable trip home.

She picked up her bag, then gave Matt a small smile. "As you can see, I'm okay. A little wet but fine."

"No, you're not," he countered. "You're weak and injured, and those men were not in the woods by accident."

"I know. They were hunting me. But, as I'm safe here, and they are gone, maybe you should go back and take care of my sisters." She turned and started up the long trek to the surface. She watched the pools twinkle and glow as she passed each one. She wasn't very far down the string of pools. Granny used to go way deeper.

If Celeste hadn't been strong enough to get here today, she would have missed out on the healing. She realized how many people likely needed access to the pools and, because of the physical difficulty in reaching them, lost out. For the first time ever, she understood why people wanted to commercialize the pools.

She didn't agree with charging an entrance fee but could

see that at least one pool needed better access.

"Not happening."

Having been lost in her own thoughts, she didn't understand what Matt was saying. "What's not happening?"

"I'm not leaving you. And your sisters are well protected."

She studied him from under her eyelashes. He looked serious. She'd placed herself in danger. And he wouldn't let her walk away again—not alone.

She really should have stayed home today. "I'm going straight home. You know as well as I do that cottage is safe. No one can get inside."

"Not true. We had a problem with it before."

She nodded. "That's because it was open already. As soon as I get home, I will lock up tight and make sure it's invisible to everyone. I'll be fine." She hoped that would be true but realized the odds of Matt accepting that were rather low. "Besides, you need to go back to the Center. Find out what happened to those men."

"They were scared to death, one way or another. That's the easy part. The hard part is figuring out why. And that's where you come in. You were there."

"I didn't see anything," she cried out. "I told you that."

"I know," he said in a calm voice.

Too calm. She wanted to hit him. "Then why are you here?"

"Because whatever terrified them is still out there. It's an unknown, and too much shit is going on for any uncertainties. I'm not leaving you alone. Regardless of whether it's what you want or not."

She glared at him. "I'm fine. I was fine without you for the last year, and I'll be fine without you for the next year." And she flounced out of the cave into the daylight. Oh, dear

God. Had she flounced? As in, really tossed her head with that nose-in-the-air motion? Oh, good grief. She'd hated girls who acted like that when she was growing up. And she'd just pulled the same stunt.

She picked up the pace and damn-near ran back to the cottage—well, as quickly as she could, considering her gimpy leg and sodden clothing. When she arrived at the heavy wall of greenery blocking the cottage from view, she turned to find Matt standing right behind her. "I told you I don't need you to look after me," she snapped.

"You told me a lot. And most of it was wrong." He motioned to the barrier. "Open up."

"And if I don't want to?" she retorted. "I don't want you here."

"You've made that clear. I, however, know how your sisters would feel if anything happened to you. So don't worry. I'm not doing this for your sake but for theirs."

They were both shouting at each other, nearly nose to nose, when suddenly came a weird popping sound.

They both turned and bolted into the center of the big overgrown barrier.

DAMN, CELESTE WAS stubborn. Matt kept his body between hers and whatever was out there. How had they found her? Had they tracked him? In a way, that was the most likely, but he didn't know. She was so damn stubborn. They could have been safely home hours ago. But, no, she'd worn herself out and had to argue until she was too tired to walk.

Outside the barrier, he watched as she unlocked the energy wall so they could get inside. The most important issue was making sure nothing else snuck in with them. Something large rustled the foliage to his left, but he couldn't see anything. Only Darbo's grip on his ear said something very dangerous was moving toward them at a fast clip.

He pushed Celeste forward and spun around to help close the opening. Together they sealed the protective barrier and doubled the shield. Celeste raced to the front door and unlocked the cabin. "Hurry," she cried out. "Get in."

Matt ran in and watched as she set up the security system. He turned to see dozens of spirit animals inside already, but they were nervous, scared even.

And he realized something he'd never considered before. "How did the spirit animals get in here?"

"They crossed the energy barrier of course." She shot him a questioning look. "Why?"

"What if an evil spirit animal is out there? Can it come in?"

His words stopped her in her tracks. She swallowed hard, then walked back to study her locking mechanism. She quickly made a few adjustments, her fingers visibly trembling. "Not now," she whispered.

"I guess that answered that question."

She shook her head. "This forest has always been one of light. Of healing. The question never arose before because it wasn't possible before. Now a darker element is going on. I don't like it," she said, her voice trembling. "What's happening here?"

"I think it's all part of the same issue. The rocks in your leg were the same black rocks that Portman Junior created. He left a stockpile at Grandfather's place, only they were stolen. We thought we had retrieved them all. Three men searched Grandfather's estate today with spirit animals, looking for more, and it appears one had been crushed by something, and the small pieces were what was left to collect. However, as long as they are out there, causing problems, it creates an opening, attracting, if you will, other animals and people of the same negative mind-set."

"Evil, you mean," she said quietly. "Granny always warned us about that, but, when she was guardian, nothing like that was here. Now that's she's gone …"

"That was likely the window that allowed this dark energy to gain a foothold. Negative energy exists within us all, but, when you get someone like Portman Junior, then it's a huge problem. With Granny around, he couldn't affect the forest, as she was here protecting it. However, with her death, Junior saw an opening and jumped at it."

"Apparently we have a lot to learn as the new guardians of the forest," she muttered. "We suck at it, so far."

"You are getting on-the-job training. A trial by fire."

"That wouldn't be so bad, but there is no training. We're reacting, wandering around in the dark together, with no idea what to do." She looked down at herself. "I'm going to the pool. You can do what you wish. I gather you've been here a time or two lately, so make yourself at home."

And, with that, she walked to the pool room, closing the door firmly in his face.

He knew it would be hard, but this hard? Could she be more frustrating? She'd walked out on him. He hadn't walked out on her. But she blamed him regardless. He glanced down at Darbo. Surely not because of his spirit pet. He glanced around the room at the many other animals sprawled inside the cabin. Were they here because it was safe? Because it was home? Because she was here?

He wanted to ask them, but it was intruding. As if by telling him, they'd be put in a position that wasn't fair. Yet how and in what way, he didn't know.

Darbo squeaked gently in his ear.

Matt nodded. "Right. I know that they are here because it's home. But why did connecting to you become the last straw for Celeste and me? You and I had a bond. Sure it was a bond I really wanted, but she had many other animals. Why did you choosing me cause the breakup?"

Darbo rubbed his cheek against Matt's chin.

"I love you too, buddy." And he did. Always had. Granny had told him about Darbo a long time ago. But he hadn't seen him until after he'd met Celeste. And then the attraction had been immediate, the bond quickly cementing after that. But Matt would have not known anything, without Granny having said something to him first. He'd not been exposed to the world of spirit pets prior to, and even after, the first mention. It had taken months, if not years, before he'd seen Darbo for the first time. The kid in him had been delighted by the tiny sprite, and, realizing that he could be with him all the time, the lonely kid inside had reveled in having Darbo.

Matt still didn't understand why Celeste had been so upset. She had had so many animals in her life.

But it had been bad.

And was still bad—if that closed door was any indication.

He took a deep breath and admitted it to himself. He loved her. He wasn't sure he had ever really stopped. Yet he saw no easy pathway forward. With a several-hour wait ahead, he turned his attention to the small cottage. He'd been here a couple times before but hadn't had a chance to really look around the place. The first time, things had been tense, and he'd only barely gotten a chance to look at the kitchen. The pool room he'd seen this morning only, and it fascinated him. It had to be special, if it had been Granny's personal pool.

That woman had lived well past an ancient age.

Given other circumstances, he could be in there with Celeste. He frowned, realizing that, for all the routineness of the day, he was actually fine. His energy was holding strong. Was that from being close to Celeste? They were grounding rods for each other. Being in the special cottage with the natural healing energy that abounded here helped too.

A special sensation, almost a tingling deep inside, permeated his sense of well-being. In fact, he was delighted to be here. And even though a door separated them, he was glad to be here with Celeste.

He glanced out the window, seeing the wind pick up again. The weather should have been nice and sunny, not hot exactly but warm. The storms had gotten much worse these last few months. This last year, in fact. Scientists had been working on the reasons behind the decline, but, so far, no one had found a cause.

Given the sisters' influence on the weather, Matt had to wonder if they'd been responsible for that as well. If so, they needed to get all three women on track as soon as possible. Agriculture was taking a hit, and, regardless of everyone's personal history, the world still needed to eat.

He drifted around the room, taking a look at ancient paintings on the wall, with Granny's signature. Paintings of scenery that glowed with the promise of so much more. He had no idea Granny had done anything other than star charts. He looked above his head to where the thousands of other star charts were stored in the attic. He wanted them safe in the vault at the Center, but wasn't sure it would happen. Something else the sisters were waiting on Celeste for. The three needed to come to a consensus on some major decisions.

He chafed with impatience. Time was marching forward;

now if only Celeste would too. He wanted to give her time, but so much needed to be dealt with that he couldn't give her much.

Finally he slumped on one of the large overstuffed chairs and leaned his head back. He hadn't had a decent night's sleep in over a year. And now that Celeste was home, rest was tantalizingly close. But, with matters still so unsettled, he knew peace wouldn't happen anytime soon. He yawned and let his mind drift.

"Sleep, Matt."

His eyelids popped open. "Who said that?"

No answer.

Feeling like a fool, he studied each of the spirit animals, but none appeared able to talk to him. At least, not in that tone of voice, like a person.

But damn …

He closed his eyelids, the pull of slumber taking him down, deeper and deeper. Until he let go and slept.

CHAPTER 10

CELESTE KNEW THE moment Matt fell asleep in the other room, sighing as she floated in the healing pool. The energy in the cabin calmed immediately. She'd seen how much older he'd looked today. The last year had taken a toll on him. And her. Apparently on them all. Particularly on her forest. It bothered her to think that the way of life of her ancestors, her granny, was over. But allowing negative energy in was allowing exactly that to happen.

Resolute, Celeste tried to look at it logically. The rift had happened when Granny had disappeared. The triplets, even as her granddaughters, hadn't known how to handle her loss, their lives, or the forest, and hadn't a clue of what was going on. But, like everything in life, windows of opportunity appeared, and, in one, the darkness had crept inside.

But that didn't mean it should stay inside.

If the triplets had enough loving positive healing energy between them to heal the forest, that meant they had enough positive healing energy to kick out that negative energy too.

That was the answer. That negative energy needed to be surrounded by love, by light. Healed in such a way that it was no longer negative. Instinctively Celeste knew that was the way Granny would have dealt with this. In fact, she probably had many times over.

Many times Granny had told them how she had to go to the pools to heal, yet she herself had appeared to be fine.

They'd taken it for granted over time. But what if she'd gone to use the energy of the caves to help her to heal other things—other people, other animals? The world even? Granny was nothing if not capable.

There were other energy workers in other towns on Glory, and Celeste realized that they might have a similar system in place. Maybe not stargazers—but maybe there were some of those too. She only had her granny's word that she and her sisters were the last stargazers here, but maybe it was *here* that was the issue. What if other stargazers were in other parts of the planet? Holding sovereign reign over each one's corner of the planet?

What if the whole planet was suffering, as each generation came along, each new one less proficient in doing what the ancients had done? The population grew all the time, as longevity increased. Fewer people were dying young, which caused a shift in the demographics. There might be more young people, but maybe they weren't as careful about protecting and implementing the old ways. Celeste and her sisters had been the butt of many jokes during school. And partly for that reason. They were old-fashioned. Didn't have the latest and the best.

While she and her sisters had adored their granny, many of the other kids had told horrible tales of their own parents and other relatives. As if respect was dwindling and love fading away.

Such a problem was too big for just the three sisters, but not if they banded together with other healers. They could heal the planet.

Celeste slumped back into the water. Just listen to her. For a moment there, she almost sounded like her granny, when the triplets had been younger. Granny had been full of plans. Always about helping others. Helping animals and plants.

And, with her gone, it was up to Celeste and her two sisters to pick up the reins and to do their damnedest to step into Granny's shoes.

<hr>

MATT WOKE WITH a headache and a shock to his nervous system. A second storm—or maybe the same one—cracked overhead. Lightning flashed and lit the room. Even more spirit animals were in the cottage now, and he couldn't avoid them if he tried. He was desperate for a cup of coffee but knew the sisters lived on tea. He just figured the jolt of caffeine would help combat the physical jolt to his nerves.

He normally loved storms, but nothing was normal about any of the ones happening lately. And that was just crazy. So much power surged outside. Why had they gotten so strong and so weird? And the strangest thing was the colors. In his childhood, he remembered all storms being white, black, and gray. Storm colors. Now they were infused in a green light, sometimes purple shades, as they flashed and danced in the wind. Everyone thought they were pretty, but he was afraid that they meant something ominous.

He knew when Celeste woke in her bed. Heard her as she moved around the bedroom, when she got up and opened her door. He stood and stretched. He'd been sleeping awkwardly in the living room chair. Everything hurt. It was silly, as there were other beds here. Connor and Devon had both spent nights here, and Matt was certain their nights must have been better than Matt's. He massaged the crick in his neck.

"I didn't want to wake you," Celeste said, when she walked out in her pajamas. The first he'd seen her wear. "You were sleeping heavy."

"That's all right …" He narrowed his gaze and studied her face. "How do you feel?" Something was different about her. But what? She looked calmer. More settled.

"I'm actually going back into the pool." She shrugged. "I need to work on a few things."

He wanted to ask more but didn't feel like it would be welcome. "Can I get you anything?"

She shook her head. "I'll be fine," she murmured. She took several steps in the direction of the pool room, when a particularly loud crack of thunder smashed overhead. She stopped and stared. "It's really storming out there."

"I've never seen one like this." He motioned outside. "Is the cottage still hidden, with all that energy going on?"

"Meaning?"

"Will the electrical flow outside affect the energy of your shields?"

"Affect, yes, in that it makes it stronger. It blends with our energy. We are one with nature," she murmured, sounding like she were almost in a trance. "The storm is nature. We are one with the storm." And, on that very odd note, she turned and headed into the pool room.

Matt watched until she closed the door, and even then he couldn't pull his mind away. What the hell was that about? He understood energy was part of nature. He understood that the storm was energy, and, therefore, the two should be compatible, but what the hell did that mean about joining with the storm?

Celeste had been calm, almost too calm, as if she were under the influence of something. And the only thing was the storm. He studied the animals all around him. Most slept or gave the appearance of sleeping. He knew Darbo never slept, but often lay curled up, as if recharging. The others were the same.

As Matt watched the spirit animals, several faded in and out of his sight. Granny had said that was a sign of their fading energy, their fading days on this planet. That they would return to their origins before long. He couldn't imagine losing Darbo and wondered if well-loved animals had a longer life span, since they were connected at a deeper level. Or maybe that was just hope talking.

More lightning. More thunder. This wouldn't end anytime soon. He walked into the kitchen and put on the teakettle. Maybe Celeste would like a hot cup of tea. Given no coffee here, he had to make do.

Waiting for the water to heat up, he stared out the window at the storm. Heavy winds bent over the shrubbery, the trees bowing to a force bigger than themselves. He felt the wind scrape over the roof of the cabin but knew they were in no danger from a rainstorm, no matter how severe. This place would outlast anything in town.

He studied the clouds, squinting, seeing animals in that storm, their faces staring out at him, as if his imagination played games with his mind. Matt blinked several times to clear his vision, and, when he looked again, they were gone.

And then something else appeared.

He gasped and leaned closer to peer through the rain-slicked window glass. Surely he wasn't seeing what he'd thought he'd seen. He blinked and shook his head. When he looked again, the vision was gone. He stared for a long moment. Right. It was just his mind playing tricks. He turned his back on the window, but, unable to help himself, he turned to take another look.

And saw it—her—again.

He raced to Celeste.

CHAPTER 11

T HE MUFFLED SOUND of yelling reached Celeste, as though she were deeply buried under sand or water.

"Damn it, wake up."

She groaned.

"That's right. Listen to my voice. Follow it back to reality, and wake up, damn it."

Matt. He was shouting at her. His words were difficult to understand. Hard to sort out. Her thoughts were thick. Fuzzy. "What?"

"Easy. You were really deeply asleep."

She blinked up at him. "Why?"

He frowned at her. "Yeah, that's the question, isn't it?"

She shook her head, trying to clear the cobwebs in her brain. She was in the pool. When had she come back in here? She remembered being in here last night; then she'd walked through the living room, spotted Matt sleeping, and had gone to bed. She did not remember waking up and coming back to the pool room.

Her teeth chattered suddenly. Also a surprise. She tried to gather her wits about her. Matt stared at her, worry on his face.

"Climb out. I'll get tea. We have to talk." And he disappeared. She stared at the open doorway, then hoisted herself from the pool. The water clung to her, almost pulling her back, but she fought against it. She wrapped the towel she'd laid out for herself around her body, the material rough against her skin, then sat at the edge of the pool, staring down into it. The water swirled, agitated. She reached down and placed a hand in the water. The pool calmed.

"What's going on?" she whispered. She knew one should ever be ripped from the healing waters, as whatever was in process couldn't stop in time, So she slipped her feet back in.

Instantly the warm water climbed up her leg to the injury. She shifted so it was under the water level and glanced at her neatly folded pajamas nearby. She shot a look at the door, made a quick decision, and stepped out of the pool again.

After toweling off and quickly redressing, she rolled up her pajama leg and lowered her leg into the pool again. The water was much calmer now, and her injury had closed completely. But she had a lot of other stuff to heal yet. Some of that took longer, and some seemed to take forever, happening on a different level. She just needed to stay close to home and needed to let her body and her mind do their thing. As for her heart, she had no idea.

"Here's tea," Matt said, placing a hot cup of herbal tea beside her.

He sat down on the edge of the pool, his face easing as he studied her. "You look better."

"I'd be *much* better if you hadn't yanked me out of the healing waters."

"I didn't think I had a choice," he said quietly. "I saw something in that storm out there that scared the bejesus out of me." He studied the water for a long moment, then continued. "Devon said Tori had seemed to be under some kind of control of the storm. Tori admitted she wanted to join with it, become one with it, so when I saw"—he waved his hand at the window—"what I saw, I raced in here to try and save you."

Saw what? *Save her?*

"Save me from what?" She had no idea what he was talking about. "I don't even remember coming back to the pool. The last thing I remember was going to bed last night." She lifted the hot cup of tea to her lips. "I only woke up when you pulled me out of the water."

His breath noisily rushed out of him. "Jesus." He stared at her in disbelief. "I spoke to you a few hours ago, when you came out of your bedroom to head back to the pool. I talked to you about the crazy storm, and you replied, like normal."

Now it was her turn to stare at him. "What?" She shook her head. "I don't remember any of that."

He nodded. "It's true."

She lowered her cup and asked in a low voice, "What did you see in the storm?"

"Your face," he said harshly. "I could see your face."

What was she to do with that? "I don't understand."

"Neither do I, but I know what I saw. First, I thought it was my imagination, as I thought I was seeing all kinds of animals appearing and dancing through the storm, but then, when I looked again, I saw your face. Your eyes were open, staring at me."

"But I'm here," she exclaimed. "And no way I could be in the middle of the storm."

"I know what I saw." He hesitated, then said, "I think you should talk to your sisters about these storms. They are getting worse."

She scowled at him. "So we're to blame for the crappy weather too?"

He took a deep breath and said in a very quiet voice, "I

think so, ... yes."

MATT KNEW CELESTE wouldn't take that well, but he hadn't expected her to shut down. From the look on her face, he knew she wanted him to leave the cottage, but he wasn't going anywhere. She shot him a dirty look and turned her back on him. But she kept her leg in the water and continued to drink her tea.

Back in the kitchen, he washed his cup and set it on the draining board to dry. The storm appeared to be working through its fury. Even as he watched, the clouds broke up and scuttled across the sky. Too fast to be normal. As Celeste's mind was awake and clearing now too, it seemed too easy to relate the calming of the storm to her again.

If this was what one sister could do alone, he was afraid to imagine what three of them could do together. Scary thoughts to let this continue uncontrolled. Her granny had loved the storms. Likely had controlled them herself. But she'd been well into her second century of life. Her granddaughters were babies compared to that. They had so much to learn, and it would take time. Even longer without Granny to show them the way. The thing was, they really didn't have much time. The triplets needed to step up and take their place—now.

He glanced at his watch. It was too early to call for a hovercraft yet. He'd wait a couple more hours. Then he changed his mind with a muttered curse and quickly called.

He ran a hand over his early morning stubble, feeling grizzled. If coffee was out, and sleep was definitely out, then he needed some other fuel to keep going. He walked to the basket that Genesis had packed yesterday. He didn't think Celeste had eaten much. Several sandwiches were still inside.

Loathe to eat one without asking, he walked back to the pool room and asked, "Celeste, do you want a sandwich?"

She jerked, as if he'd disturbed a heavy contemplation, but she turned and nodded. "Thank you. That would be good."

Relieved, he withdrew and plated up several sandwiches and another cup of tea for himself. Back at the pool room, he sat down beside Celeste and offered her one.

She ate it without noticing.

But at least she ate.

He ripped through two, then stopped to make sure she ate the rest of hers. He would have his pilot deliver more food. There was little here for her, and it was obvious she wasn't ready to leave the cabin yet.

Neither was she showing any sign of wanting anything to do with him. "I'll leave as soon as my ride gets here."

Startled, she gazed at him. "Okay," she said, her voice soft, wary.

"I know you don't want to return to the Center, most likely because of me, but I'm not comfortable with you staying here all alone."

"There's nothing wrong with me staying here alone. My leg might be fine," she murmured, popping the limb out of the water to study the unblemished skin, "but I need healing on other aspects."

What did that mean? "So you need to stay here for the day or a couple days?" He was trying to make this work, but he needed her assistance. Something she didn't appear to want to give.

She glanced over at him curiously. "What difference does it make?"

"It determines how much clothing and food I return

with," he said coolly. "I don't know what's going on, but you aren't to be alone, not until this mess is settled."

She lowered her lashes, blocking him out. But she hadn't argued with him. Neither had she said no. So he was making progress.

"I need to be here all day and quite possibly all tomorrow. I don't know. And I don't need clothing. I have things here."

"Good enough. Then I'll bring two days' worth of food, and we'll see how that goes."

"What about your work?"

"I'll bring some with me," he said, a touch of defiance in his voice. She wouldn't dissuade him that easily. "And, while I'm gone, you'll have company."

She raised her eyebrows. "A babysitter? I hardly think I need that."

"Two of them." He smiled, raising his phone. "They already contacted me, asking if they can come."

Her smile, when it finally spread across her face in that long slow movement that made his heart ache, was stunning. She'd been alone for too long. Being home was good for her.

CHAPTER 12

CELESTE DIDN'T KNOW what to think of the babysitting thing or of Matt's refusal to leave her alone. But it was comforting. She was more disturbed by her actions in the night and his comment about her face in the storm than she was willing to admit. Talking to her sisters was the best way to work out these things. Of all the things Matt had said, he was absolutely right about one of them. Something weird was going on—probably been going on for months—and now that she was finally home, they'd hit a crux of some kind.

It needed to be resolved. And fast. Before the next storm, before one of the three of them went in and never came out.

They'd all seen Granny's face in a storm. But that had been when she'd been standing in front of them, not battling the elements but joining with them. She'd been strong enough to do so. Celeste and her sisters weren't. At least, she didn't think so. So far they'd had little experience in controlling the weather. In fact, she'd always thought *it* had controlled *them*.

Only Matt had a different hypothesis. His comments had burned into her mind, where they festered. Making her question other oddities she'd wondered about over the last year.

She needed her sisters to come and quickly. This was a safe place for them to talk, considering someone out there was trying to kill them. Their only saving grace was that, at least, that person couldn't enter the cottage. That was according to Genesis, who had told her about Portman Junior. They had to make sure an episode like that couldn't repeat itself. But beyond that, something was also in the woods. Something that had scared those two men.

"Those men, … who were hunting me?" She didn't want to ask, but she had to know.

"They died overnight."

She nodded. That was what she'd been afraid of. "Not an easy way to go."

"*Is* there an easy way to go?" Matt asked curiously. "Your granny, how did she die?"

Celeste halted for a moment, her teacup in the air, then she said gently, "Old age. She just faded away in front of us." That, at least, was the truth. More than that, she couldn't say.

"Right. I guess that was to be expected, given her age."

She stood and reached for the towel to dry off her leg. "My sisters are almost here. Are you ready to leave?"

"I suppose I am. I don't want to leave, but you need time with your sisters, and I need to check in at work. See if anyone knows those two men who died and see if we can track down whoever hired them."

"That would be good." What else could she say? She needed Matt to do whatever Matt did, while she and her sisters put their heads together and figured this out. "I'll get dressed before they arrive." She walked slowly to the door.

"I don't think they'll get here that fast," he cautioned, following her out of the pool room.

"I can hear the hovercraft," she called over her shoulder, as she walked to her bedroom and closed the door. She dressed quickly. When done, she stepped into the living room. The hovercraft was landing outside. She waved Matt off. "Go."

Indecision warred on his face. Finally he nodded. "I'll be back tonight."

Inside, her heart leaped with joy, but she kept her face impassive. "If you believe it's necessary."

"Oh, it's necessary."

The spirit animals seemed to gather to say goodbye to Matt.

Darbo opened his arms to Celeste, and her heart hitched. She reached out, and Darbo wrapped his long arms around her. The lost look on Matt's face made her realize that he didn't know whether Darbo was planning to stay with her or leave with him. Silky chattered at Darbo in a full-on conversation, before silence descended. She kissed them both, then walked close to Matt, watching as Darbo reached out to Matt.

He swallowed visibly and hugged the tiny lemur, then, with a big grin, settled him on his shoulder.

She was an idiot. She had dozens of animal friends. He had one. With the number needing human interaction, he'd do them all a favor by bonding with a second animal. But, after the fuss she'd made over Darbo, that suggestion wouldn't be well received from her. Better she ask her sisters to mention it to him.

It took longer to open the locks, but finally the energy blocks fell, and she could open the front door.

As she watched Matt walk out into the early morning light, Darbo gently stroking his cheek, it finally hit her why she'd taken such a hit over Matt's and Darbo's bond.

Darbo had been especially close to Granny. Losing Granny, then losing Darbo almost immediately after, had been like losing Granny all over again. As if somehow Matt had been responsible. And that was foolish. She'd been so mixed up. So needy and in pain. She hadn't known which end was up, and she'd reacted badly to everything. She'd refused to go into the pools after Granny's death as well, as they all reminded Celeste of what she'd lost. How damn foolish of her. She'd been given so much, then had let her childishness stop her from gaining so much more.

Her sisters exited the hovercraft, spoke with Matt briefly, then raced toward Celeste, huge smiles on their faces.

Celeste had so much good in her life. Now, if only she hadn't been so selfish to walk away from it all in the first place—and she couldn't repeat it by walking away again.

MATT CALLED A meeting with his investigators—Devon, Connor, and Scott—the moment he got back. "Any news?"

"Some," Devon said. "Smaller rocks were at the water's edge, where we first found the stolen rocks. We used a vacuum and sealed containers to collect every piece we could. We ended up bringing several gallons of water back with us, as it all came with the shards."

"Good thinking. If we can find a way to separate the rocks from the water, we can dump it again."

"The pool did clean up significantly after we removed the rest," Connor said. "The women should find it that much easier to heal the area with the shards gone. And Kona found another area of the smaller black rocks, possibly moved by animals. Likely a large bird."

"I wonder if he was trying to remove the rocks to help out or to spread the poison."

Scott stepped forward. "No way to know. Storm found a small pile as well, that had also been transferred from the original pile."

"So the only way to find these things is to systematically

track them through the woods?" Matt frowned. "That sounds horribly inefficient and slow."

"It's not the fastest process, but at least we're finding them. We were out for hours yesterday. We only came back when the storm hit."

"Yeah, that storm." Moodily Matt stared at the desk in front of him. "What about the two men found frozen in the forest?"

"They used to work for Mason. Now that he's dead, we presume they found a new employer."

"Grandfather?"

The three of them shook their heads. "No, we don't think so."

Scott added, "I'm not sure he's capable of even menial work anymore. He sits and smiles at everything. I don't know what the healing pools did to him, but he's out of it."

Interesting. Matt didn't know if he believed Scott, but it was an interesting concept. How did the pools think that was healing? And maybe the pools had little choice. If he was as far gone as his energy had proven him to be, it didn't leave much left for the pool to heal. Or maybe the healing had required more time, but he'd been pulled out too early. "What are our next steps?"

The men sat down to work out a plan. Devon would check into the two gunmen's bank records. Scott would return to Grandfather's estate to make more inquiries, and Connor would take Kona out to look for more of these rocks. He would also keep an eye out for tracks of where the gunmen had been. Kona had proven to be a decent hunting dog, and they were all grateful.

Storm, the big cat, had a sniffer on him like no one else they'd seen, but he had to want to work. Typical feline.

Whereas Kona was just always happy to be outside. Typical canine.

And Matt? Well, he would collect some of the archive material to study back at the cottage. He needed to figure out this storm stuff, before he lost one or all three sisters to Mother Nature—the same way he suspected the three young women had lost their grandmother.

CHAPTER 13

"I CAN'T BELIEVE someone was hunting you."

"It's not just me. All three of us are being hunted," Celeste interjected. "What scares me is, they seemed to know where I was at the time. And the only way to have known that was through spirit animals."

"Yet that would imply they were people of power, and, if that were the case, what could scare them to death like that?" Genesis marveled.

"We're missing another option," Tori spoke up. "What if someone else, the same person who hired these two, is bonded with a spirit pet, and used the information from that animal to direct his henchmen to the right spot. That's hands-off for them and yet gets the job done."

The three exchanged glances. Celeste nodded. "That makes the most sense."

"I can't believe you had to go through this. Isn't it enough that we did?" Tori shook her head and reached out a hand. "We survived, but it was hairy for quite a while."

"And several of us were injured in the process," Genesis murmured, with a shudder. "So much nastiness."

"That's why we have to get to the bottom of this negativity," Celeste said quietly. "We have to realize that, with Granny gone, we failed to keep things as she did, failed to get rid of the bad energy back then. Now we have to find this negativity and do what she would have done."

Genesis nodded. "I've only recently realized how much Granny did for the townsfolk. Not just the star charts, which are huge," she admitted, "but also the energy balance she kept in check. There were never any murders, kidnappings, or anything so nasty while we were growing up."

"Actually our mother's murder was likely the last act of violence done here," Tori suggested. "And Granny made sure that was taken care of, and afterward she worked herself to the bone to make it safe for us."

"That's the thing, wasn't it? She was less concerned about keeping the townsfolk safe as she was about keeping the town safe for *us*," Celeste suggested. "She needed us to grow up strong and free."

"And, more than that," Genesis added, "Granny needed us to grow up in as positive an environment as she could manage, so that, when we came up against negativity, we'd have that foundation to draw from."

"Maybe she did her job too well," Celeste replied, "as we didn't really understand what we were up against, until long after she was gone."

"Her disappearance," Tori said, lowering her voice, "it caused a hole to open up here. Allowed that nastiness in."

"No arguments there." Celeste studied her sisters' faces. "How do we fix this?"

Genesis shook her head. "We have to heal it. We can only overwhelm the evil with the good."

"How though," Celeste asked, "when we don't understand where all that evil is coming from? We originally thought it was Grandfather, when instead it was Portman Junior …"

"With Grandfather's help," Genesis pointed out.

Tori nodded. "Then it was Mason, trying to take over Grandfather's estate and position in town."

"So Grandfather is likely still at the center of the problem. His family was the thorn in Granny's family's side for decades. They did horrible things to our family and are still trying to hurt us now." Celeste stared at the center of Granny's kitchen table, where the triplets had gathered in the cottage. "I can't see anyone else being in the middle of this. It has to center on him."

"We could throw a star chart and find out," Genesis said calmly. "A triangulated one."

Silence fell over the room.

"We've never done one of those before," Tori said. "Granny wouldn't let us."

"I know, but I was thinking about that. Granny had to operate alone, as she had no choice. Her mother was gone. Her daughter, our mother, was gone. There should have been three generations working together. When we were born, we were never alone. Never really had to work alone. When I threw a chart and had trouble with it, one of you would help me out."

"And vice versa," Tori said, studying her sister. "We learned to work together a long time ago."

The three sat in contemplative silence.

Celeste took a deep breath. "Matt thinks we're responsible for the weather."

The other two stared at her.

"He thinks what?" Genesis asked, her voice full of shock. "The weather? Really?"

"It's not such a far-off concept either," Tori muttered. "I know how I felt when I was connected to the storm."

"Besides, Granny was always working with the storms.

Once she was gone, none of us did. Since then, they've become wilder and more unmanageable."

"Unmanageable?" Genesis slumped back in her chair. "As in, left unmanaged? As in, no Granny, then no one to manage them?"

"We're supposed to manage it?" Celeste cried out in shock. "Oh, my goodness. Granny said that we had much to learn, and we would learn on the job. I just laughed at her because, even on the job, you get training. Often though it's on the rough-and-ready side."

"What are we supposed to manage, in terms of the storms?" Tori asked. "I mean, I stood there and felt it call to me."

"I haven't mentioned it yet, but something weird happened to me last night." Celeste launched into an explanation of what Matt had said. There was an appalled silence when she finished.

"Well, that's proof that we have something to do with those damn storms," Tori said, leaning back in her chair and shaking her head. "This is crazy." She hopped up. "I need more tea."

"I wish you'd brought wine. I could use some about now," Celeste muttered.

Genesis laughed and opened the basket beside her. She brought out a bottle of purple burble juice, made from the local wine grapes, and popped the top.

"I'm still bothered that *you* were in the pool when this happened," Tori said, returning to the table with glasses instead of teacups. "I was outside in the middle of the storm. In nature. My element. If that had been Genesis in the pool, I might have understood."

"I know. Everything is messed up between us."

"Maybe that's a good thing," Genesis admitted. "Lately I've been seeing more spirit animals than ever. It's lovely."

Celeste nodded. "And the pools are laughing, the flowers are talking to me. Everything just seems to be so much more."

"So maybe we're developing a better knowledge of each other's skills, but that doesn't explain the storms. Genesis, have you ever had that happen?"

"Not recently. But I was always the one who walked out into them. Remember? Granny used to run and pull me back inside, saying it wasn't my time yet."

The sisters stopped and stared.

"Not your time *yet?*" Celeste let her breath out. "That implies that, at one point, it will be your time. And likely when she was gone."

"Or when you grew up," Tori suggested. "You could have been the first to go in that direction. Although why she didn't train you, I don't know."

"She was worn out at the end. We were barely adults and still trying to master star charts—something we were a whole lot less interested in than the men in our lives, if you remember?"

That brought wry grins to their faces.

"If I could go back again, I'd spend more time with Granny. Appreciate all she knew and did for us. I know she's gone, but, being here, we're still connected in so many ways." Celeste lifted her wineglass. "To Granny. The best woman ever. I still miss her."

The other two women lifted their glasses in a toast and drank in Granny's honor.

ARMED WITH A stack of copies taken from the archives—all

originals being sealed in a temperature-controlled environment at the Center—plus several basketfuls of food and his overnight bag, Matt settled into the passenger seat of the hovercraft. The pilot sent them skyward and set the GPS locater for the cottage. Although they had the location of the cabin, no one could land if the sisters had the cottage in stealth mode.

For all their fancy gadgets, the Paranormal Center scientists couldn't beat the stargazer security system. If those women wanted to stay hidden, there wasn't a damn thing Matt could do about it. It also meant that, if Celeste didn't want to see him, he was out of luck. So he was going to pick up the other two sisters and return them to the Center, hoping that Celeste let him inside at the same time.

The trip was fast and efficient. Except that, as they circled the correct area, they couldn't see the cottage.

Matt picked up his phone and called Genesis.

The call never went through. His phone was only picking up static. The bars indicated it wasn't sending or receiving.

Damn it.

"Darbo, can you tell Silky that we're here, please."

An audible hum filled the air. The pilot looked at Matt, awaiting instructions.

He was just at the point of directing him to the closest available landing spot, thinking he'd hike over, yet questioning how much stuff he'd have to carry, when the clouds rose above them like a foggy blanket lifting. When they were clear of them, he could see the cabin directly below.

As the pilot slowly lowered the hovercraft and landed in the small yard, Matt had to consider that, as they'd been in the correct spot, if they had just lowered the craft, would the cabin have been there? Or did the stargazer trick actually stop the cabin from being found, even if you were parked right on top of it? He'd have to ask the sisters. It would be good to know, in case something went wrong here, and they needed assistance.

Was that even possible?

He worried that it wasn't. These stargazer ladies had some serious tricks available to them. Except that didn't mean the negative energy hadn't attracted equally talented assholes.

As the pilot shut down the vehicle, Matt got out, his arms full. The pilot picked up the baskets and his overnight bag. Together they walked to the cottage door. But it was closed and appeared to be locked.

"They aren't the most welcoming of people, are they?" the pilot asked in a low tone.

"It doesn't look like it at the moment, does it?" Matt shifted his load of paper and studied the door in front of him. "It looks to be charged with electricity. That if I were to knock …"

"Yeah, you first," the pilot said, with a grin.

Matt studied him. He was a new hire. Ty was his nickname, short for Tyrone. "You're Scott's brother, aren't you?"

"I am. There are three of us here. Six in all but three in town."

Matt nodded. "I remember now. Sorry I didn't recognize you."

"Not to worry," Ty said easily. "I've been all over the place so far. You haven't had much chance to see me."

"The last couple days have been hectic. I should've been more involved. Sorry. I completely forgot your first day was a few days ago already." Matt shook his head. He remembered interviewing the young man. The whole family was an asset to have on board. He'd hired all three of them for different positions in the Center. They were men of power, and Matt needed all those he could get. And had promptly forgotten all about them once Celeste had returned. Not a good sign. She'd always been able to turn his brain to mush.

"Now what?" Ty asked, with a nod toward the locked and protected cottage.

"I'll have Darbo contact them inside."

But either Darbo had already done so, or the sisters had finally clued in to their presence, as the locks fell, and the door swung open.

Only there was still no sign of the triplets. Matt entered, calling out, "Genesis? Tori? Celeste?"

No answer. Shit.

He dumped his armload on the kitchen table and walked through the small space. Spirit animals of one kind or another were on every surface. Then he heard the laughter coming from the back of the cottage. Instantly his panic calmed down.

They were in the pool room. He reached out a hand to open the door, then realized they were likely all nude inside. Not a good way to make an entrance. Especially with Ty at his side.

As much as he wanted to rush in and to confirm that they were safe, he wasn't about to set them off. It was bad enough to have one sister mad at him; he didn't want all three upset with him. Or their partners.

He rapped hard on the door. "Hello, ladies? Can I come in?"

"Just a minute," came the frantic reply, and sounds of hurried movements could be heard on the other side.

When the door opened, it was Tori greeting them, a big grin on her face. "We didn't expect you so soon."

"Really? Then who let us land?" he asked, his gaze zinging

to Celeste's face.

The women exchanged quick glances.

"So, did you let us land? Or did someone else? And the doors unlocked in front of us. Was that you as well?" He followed them to the kitchen, wondering at the expressions on their faces. "If you didn't, who did?"

Genesis brushed past him and checked the security system. "It was definitely released."

"I know that," he said patiently. "I'm asking who did it."

She turned to look at Tori, an eyebrow raised in question. Tori shook her head. They both turned to look at Celeste. Matt's gaze shifted to her and caught her sheepish look. "I knew he was close by but hadn't decided whether I would let him land or not."

Matt's gaze hardened. "Right. In that case, I'll go grab the rest of the stuff now, before you decide to lock me out in the woods, after your sisters have left."

And he turned and returned to the hovercraft. He was trembling now—his panic was gone, but his rage and, yeah, hurt, threaded through his body. Ty had already carried in the stuff he'd brought. He sat on the seat for a long moment, trying to regain some of that control he'd arrived with.

He hurt more than he could imagine right now. She'd known he was here. But she hadn't let him in.

And that begged the question. If she hadn't, who had?

CHAPTER 14

CELESTE HATED TO be wrong. Something about Matt just had her acting like a schoolgirl. She'd hoped she'd grown out of it. Then he showed up, and *boom*—she was acting like a child again.

Her sisters had sent her shocked looks, as they then gathered up their belongings. Genesis had gone out to the hovercraft, while Tori stayed at the doorway. Celeste knew they were stopping her from locking Matt out. As Matt returned, Tori reached up and kissed him on the cheek, then ran to join her sister at the hovercraft. Celeste stole a look at Matt's face. His grim locked-down-and-pissed-off face.

Damn it.

She turned and put on the teakettle. She'd had such a lovely day so far, and now it was ruined.

Not because of Matt's presence because, to tell the truth, she'd been looking forward to his arrival all day. But because of her waffling about letting him in. She'd wanted him to pay, and she still did. But for what? What had he done that was so wrong? Nothing.

She was the petulant child here, and that made her angrier.

Ignoring him, she returned to the pool room and cleaned up the towels the three of them had hurriedly flung on the floor, as they had pulled on their clothing. The pool room was warm and humid at the best of times, but, when the three of them were taking advantage of the healing waters, then it became positively sauna-like.

All day, the three of them had sat at the edge of the pool, stripped to their underwear, their legs in the water and the bottle of wine close by.

The pool had done a lot of work today, as the sisters had healed their own sibling relationships.

Celeste was grateful and felt very much at home.

Until Matt had arrived, and everything had gone to hell.

"Who let us in?" Matt asked.

She winced, but, in a calm voice, said, "I think Silky and Darbo finally decided it was time. For us and for them."

He stared at her in shock. "Say what?"

"I'm not sure though." She walked past him and took out a cup and a tea bag. She'd been feeling a nice rosy glow, and the resounding return to life wasn't so pleasant. When the kettle boiled, she made a cup of tea; then because she knew she'd been a shit, she made him one too.

She placed both cups on the kitchen table and sat down.

"Your highest level of security gets opened by two spirit animals in a trick you've never seen before, and you're calm and laid back, as if none of this matters?"

"I didn't say I hadn't seen this happen before," she snapped. "But, as I know whoever did this—and I presume it was them—they did it for the right reasons, not the wrong ones."

"And just what were the right reasons?" he asked carefully, pulling out a chair and sitting down across from her.

"Because they wanted to be together." There was another reason as well, but she wouldn't tell him that.

He blinked. "What did you say?"

She repeated her comment as if it were a common occurrence. Only it wasn't. And she wasn't sure what to do about it either. If anything. These were spirit pets. Animals. And, as such, they had feelings and needs too. Not all spirit animals appeared when physical animals died. It had taken her a long time to understand that, and it had taken Granny's confirmation as well, but some animals were spirit animals from the beginning, as if born into such a thing. Celeste couldn't imagine, but their existence was proven fact. And, in some cases, they became as strongly bonded to another spirit pet as they did to a human.

And, in her case, Darbo and Silky were one. Part of the reason she'd been devastated when Darbo had left with Matt. It had been a rejection for Silky too.

Now Silky stretched a long finger down her cheek. Right. That had been her human interpretation of a spirit animal event, but, according to Silky, it wasn't true. They were just as close as ever because the two were in telepathic communication, like all the spirit animals. Only stronger.

So although they hadn't been physically close, they'd been close on every other plane.

Silky had said, being in physical proximity was a bonus but not necessary, as they traveled at will.

Now Celeste wondered if she should question Silky's stance on that.

She'd heard the locks release earlier and had understood what was happening but not the reasons behind it, until she'd seen Darbo's and Silky's reunion. Damn, it would be hard to keep Matt out of her life, if her spirit pet wanted to be closer with *his* spirit pet.

So much for distance not being an issue …

Then maybe it was love. And, as everyone knew, love

crossed all boundaries—especially distance.

"That's possible for spirit animals to unlock a physical door?" Matt asked.

"Spirit animals are pure energy. They can do a lot. If they really want something, they can do more than they let on."

She watched, as Matt leaned back and studied the animals all around. Twitch, a tiny field mouse, sat beside her, sniffing her tea. She reached out a gentle hand and stroked his tiny back. "A lot of animals are in need here. I'll have to see if I can find bonds for many of them."

"What do you do with a little guy like him?" Matt asked, pointing to Twitch. "He's hardly going to ride on your shoulder."

"No, but, as they are spirit pets, they can cross distances by thinking about it."

Twitch, as if eager to demonstrate, faded away in front of their eyes and reappeared at the windowsill. Celeste pointed him out to Matt, who stared, his jaw dropped, his gaze round and disbelieving.

"And that means"—she pointed to Darbo deliberately—"that while you are sleeping or busy, Darbo and Silky can and have been visiting each other, without anyone knowing."

Matt's gaze zinged back at her, then down to Darbo, who was slowly making his way across to Silky, who sat in the middle of the table, her tiny lemur body stationary, both her arms out and open. It took Darbo forever to cross the distance physically, but, when he reached her, their arms went around each other and their heads tucked into each other's shoulders, then appeared to fall asleep.

"I had no idea," he said in a shocked voice. "Is that why you were so mad at me for bonding to Darbo?"

"That's one of the reasons," she said quietly. "You took

Darbo away from not just me but also from Silky."

"I truly didn't know," he whispered. "I didn't think such a bond between spirit animals was even possible."

"It took me years to understand it too," she said. "Granny helped explain it all, but I didn't see it for the longest time."

Matt settled back, looking stunned. "And the other part of why you were so angry over Darbo?"

She shrugged and played with her mug handle, as she stared at the tea sloshing inside. She needed to get it out. Explain what she could. It was only fair. "I was a mess," she said softly. "I couldn't think or see anything clearly. It was all so confusing." She paused. Her throat constricted at the thought of saying any more. But she had to get this out. She owed him that much. "And the more we fought, regardless of who was right or wrong, it became something else in my mind."

He leaned across and picked up her hand in his, but he didn't say anything.

She felt his silent urging to get it out. To help him understand.

"I know. I was there. Remember?" he said gently. "You were really struggling with losing her."

Of course he knew. "The thing is, you were there, and Granny wasn't. And I wanted her to be. So, in my twisted state, the more we fought, the more I wished she was there and you were gone. When you took Darbo away, a spirit pet who'd been as close to Granny as he was to me, it seemed I had lost Granny all over again—and so I pushed you, both of you, away." She stared out the window, hating what she had to say next. She took a deep breath and added, "And I couldn't take it. So I ran."

He sat back and studied her.

She dropped her gaze to her cup. It sounded stupid now. How could one explain what it was like back then? All the pain and the pressure and the loss? … Good Lord, the loss had been so difficult. "Instead of letting you be my support system, I *needed* you to leave too. So found ways to push you away."

She heard his strangled exclamation. "That makes no sense."

"I had lost so much." But she pushed on. "I couldn't take more."

"So you pushed me away so you'd have less loss?" He shook his head. "You were losing me then too. Losing what we had together."

"But I'd lose you eventually, and what we had was getting stronger. Getting deeper. And I knew I couldn't handle it when I'd gone to pieces over losing Granny. So I had to make sure you left." She took a deep breath. "To protect myself."

And that made her sound like a weak, silly fool. It sounded stupid now that she'd said it. Yet she meant it. Every word. At least, she had at the time.

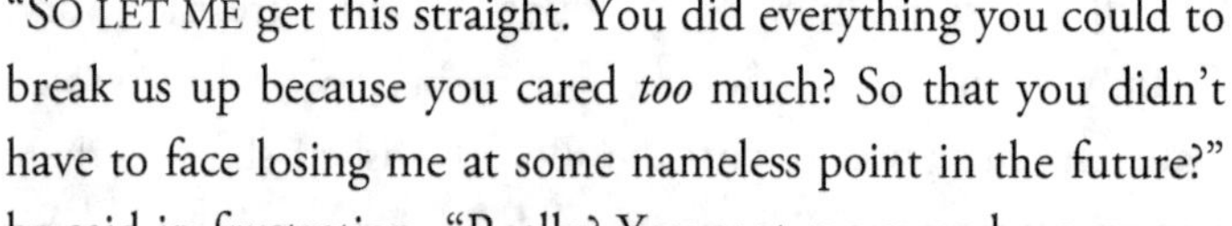

"SO LET ME get this straight. You did everything you could to break us up because you cared *too* much? So that you didn't have to face losing me at some nameless point in the future?" he said in frustration. "Really? You sent me away because you loved me *too* much."

She blinked. Then frowned. "It doesn't sound quite right when you put it that way."

"It doesn't sound right no matter what way anyone puts it," he snapped. He pushed away from the table and got up. Striding over to the kitchen window, he stared at the world.

He was so angry inside, so betrayed. Because she'd loved him too much she couldn't survive if she lost him, so she cut him loose before their love grew any deeper.

He never thought to see the day.

What she'd put him through … Put them through … "I spent the last year trying to figure out what I did wrong. What I could have done better, more of. And instead you're saying that what I did wrong was love you too much." He shook his head. "I don't know what to say."

Inside though, he wanted to say a lot. How could she do that to him? She'd only been thinking about herself. And that was so unlike her. She was the most giving, caring person he'd ever met. It had been partly why he'd been attracted to her. Yet she'd tossed him overboard to preserve herself. He couldn't reconcile those two halves of her personality.

"It's for the best."

Her dismissive tone might have worked, if they hadn't just had this conversation, but he could sense the cracking underneath. Something about all this didn't read quite true. They were close to it. But maybe not all the way. She likely didn't know what was going on here either.

He needed to step back and to let her be. She'd been through a lot. She had a lot more to go through. And then, maybe then, they could get to the bottom of this.

Nothing had changed really. He couldn't let her go. And he couldn't live with himself if he let something happen to her. Maybe they could work this out in time.

He hoped so.

He turned to study her downcast face and her long hair that she was trying to hide behind.

"What's for the best?" he asked, and she glanced up in surprise. He suddenly realized how long his silence had been.

"What did you mean by that?"

"I mean that you're better off without me."

"Are you trying to piss me off?" he asked, losing his hard-won control. "Because talk like that will do it."

She bounced to her feet. "Not everything I do is to piss you off. We aren't meant to be. That's all there is to it. Go find yourself another girl."

His eyebrows shot up at the anger in her voice.

"And if I don't want another girl?" he asked, his gaze narrowed and locked on her flushed face. "What then?"

Her mouth opened, then snapped shut. "Then it's too bad for you." And she turned, as if to walk away.

Only he'd had just about enough of her walking away from him. He reached out and snagged her arm and tugged her backward. She spun and opened her mouth to blast him. He gave her a dangerous smile and interrupted her before she could speak. "That's the last time you'll run away."

Wrapping her up in his embrace, he lowered his head and kissed her—hard. This damn fool woman had no idea where she belonged, and, even though part of her knew, she had let the rest of herself convince her otherwise.

Well, he'd had enough.

He shifted her more comfortably in his embrace and loosened his hold slightly to kiss her again. She wrapped her arms around his neck and stopped him from withdrawing.

Like hell he was leaving. This was exactly where *he* belonged too. Why couldn't she see that? He lowered his head again.

When she sagged against him, he gentled the kiss, before pulling back slightly. He smiled at her unfocused gaze and swollen lips. She lay snug against his chest, and he pressed his lips against her temple. Another on her forehead. He couldn't stop touching her. He cuddled her close, so damn grateful to have her in his arms.

They'd always been good together. The air was electrically charged around them, keeping them in this cocoon of awareness—always knowing where the other was. Thankfully that still existed.

CHAPTER 15

MATT HAD ALWAYS been able to turn Celeste's mind to mush. She wondered if there'd ever been anything else inside her but him. He was hers. Always had been. But she hadn't understood. Why her? Females were falling all over themselves to get to him. He'd been her first. He'd been her only. Yet he'd had many lovers before, and, as much as she hated to think about it, he'd likely had lovers since she had left. Surely he could do so much better than a mixed-up, neurotic stargazer's granddaughter. She knew he could. But, while he was locked on her, he wasn't looking for anyone else.

Granny had said he was hers, if she wanted him to be.

Celeste had tried to question her about that. But Granny hadn't explained. In fact, she'd refused to say any more.

Of course Celeste wanted him. But she really wanted him to want *her*. It couldn't last. Not being under whatever weird spell he'd been under. He must have been under some foreign influence to want her. She almost laughed at that. She didn't want any more pain anyway. So she'd pushed him away and had run, so she wouldn't have to see who he would choose next time.

And he had a lot of choices. Always.

She'd done nothing but make a mess of her life.

And he deserved so much more.

"So what is all this?" he exclaimed softly. "You're mumbling about not being right for me?"

She froze. Then winced. Apparently she'd said that out loud.

He tilted her face up, so he could look into her confused gaze. "I want you. I've always wanted you. I'll never not want you. It's been a hellish long year for me. I'd like to think that you suffered slightly as well." She tried to pull back, and he shook his head. "No. No more pulling away. Let's get to the bottom of the—"

Crash.

The door to the cottage buckled and twisted outward, remaining intact. But barely.

Animals screamed in terror, and the air in the cottage crackled.

Celeste raced to the door, screaming, "Silky, Darbo."

Matt could barely see the energy of the two little lemurs, as they added their tiny bits to hers. All the animals in the room joined their energy with each other's, until a blue streak of twisting winding electrical currents flashed through the tiny cabin.

"Damn. What is it?" Matt yelled across the din.

"Someone is attacking from the outside."

He raced to the door and tried to pull it inward.

"Don't," she cried out. "It's energy work. Way too strong for mere physical strength."

Say what? He stared at the darkness encroaching the cabin. "What the hell is that?"

"Don't look at it," she snapped. "This is likely whatever killed the two men in the woods."

He tore away his gaze to see her sitting cross-legged on the floor, her hands out, joining with the animals around her. "Let me help," he said, dropping to the floor.

"I can do this," she insisted, "but your help is welcome."

He could do more than help. He was an excellent amplifier. He reached out and disconnected her hand from the field mouse and took the field mouse's place, instantly connecting to Darbo on the other side. As soon as the broken links were closed, power surged through the cabin.

"Whoa, nice energy there, Matt," Celeste murmured.

"I try."

"You've been working on it a lot while I was gone," she whispered. "I can do something with that." She was amazed at the power surging through her fingertips because of him. She'd known he was strong. But now, after this year, he was stronger yet again. He'd always been good for boosting her flagging energy when she was tired, but this was so much more. He'd been working on his energy skills. She knew he had.

Now if only she knew what he'd done.

She reinforced the security of the house, then added layers and layers of love to the energy. Negativity was never the way to go, as healing energy always healed, no matter what or who. She just had to stay ahead of the drain. Healing on this scale was hard. Damn hard. But with Matt …

The battle raged on, with her and her animals inside, and whatever controlled that black energy outside. She didn't know how they'd been able to track her down, but they had somehow, and now this was a battle for supremacy.

One she dare not lose.

Too much was at stake.

She could sense the anger. The antagonism of the other energy. It was furious. At what, Celeste didn't know, but it simmered with hatred. For her. There was only one outcome allowed in this case. The enemy wanted Celeste dead.

MATT CLOSED HIS eyes and opened his senses. He was only learning to send out probes, so this experiment could go very wrong.

But the energy behind this black cloud was pissed. And Matt hadn't a clue why, but he needed to find out. He sent the probe sprawling outward, into the center of the black energy.

Then he heard his name. A startled acknowledgment that he was here. Followed by a huge wave of anger, like he'd never experienced before. As a wall of black poured over them.

He heard Celeste cry out.

Holding her hand tight, he opened his eyes to see all the animals now in a big energy circle, wave upon wave flowing outward. And still, this black energy resisted.

Like hell.

He sent more energy probes, keeping his energy neutral and calm, driving them into the center of the darkness. Instantly he was buffeted from side to side, as the energy fought him back. How could it know what he'd done?

Celeste tightened her grip on his fingers "Do it again," she whispered. "I'll cover you."

Surprised that she'd any idea what he'd done in the first place, and not sure what *covering* meant, he sent more energy into the darkness.

This time, his energy was strong, but … weak. What the hell? His probe went in deeper, picking up more energy than he'd ever managed before, and yet the blackness didn't appear to know he was there.

And then he realized that she'd covered his energy with a blanket of the same darkness. Somehow she'd grabbed a corner of the darkness and had wrapped his probe in it to hide it, allowing him to do what he needed to do.

So great was his shock that, for a long moment, he was uncertain what his next step was.

"Move," she muttered harshly. "Now."

Right. Back to business. He collected a sample of the energy, tried to get a signature of the person behind all this, and then slowly, carefully withdrew. He'd learned something for sure. There was no heart to that energy. It was black all the way through, and, as far as he could see, no person was anywhere close by.

Making this the most powerful energy worker he'd ever come across.

CHAPTER 16

C ELESTE CASCADED BLUE healing lights over the blackness. Instinct had her wanting to run and to hide and to let someone else deal with this mess, but her granny, the only *someone else* who could manage this, was gone. So it was up to Celeste. And Matt apparently. She wondered at his abilities and the power behind them. She'd wondered if her abilities might get stronger through her union with him, but they hadn't. It had been a disappointment. Now she wondered if it had been merely because she'd been such a mess back then. And not sufficiently developed herself.

Right now, his power was amplifying her power in a big way. She closed her eyes, delighting in her connection to the animal world, as she heard the tiny murmurs of those in the circle. They were all handing over the same healing energy she would have handed over to her granny. It was as though she now held Granny's power seat. It was such an odd feeling. Celeste wiggled slightly, as if trying to fit into shoes that were too big.

Matt squeezed her fingers. She opened her gaze to see Twitch sitting on hers and Matt's joined hands. Twitch was sprawled on his belly, fast asleep, his little legs hanging off the back of her hand.

She smiled. How special. As she glanced around the room, she realized how purely incredible her life growing up had been and still was today. She'd been blessed in so many ways.

Several animals opened their eyes and squealed in protest.

"Oops," she murmured, realizing she'd slowed the flow of the energy outward, with her lack of focus. She might be sitting in Granny's seat, but it would be a long time before Celeste could fill it.

"Easy. You're doing fine," Matt said quietly.

"Am I?" she asked in a self-derogatory tone. "It doesn't feel like it."

"The energy is abating. As if she's giving up the fight."

"She?" Celeste pounced. "A woman's doing that?" She studied his face, her gaze narrow. Wondering if it was the same energy she'd sensed earlier. "Do you recognize her energy?"

He frowned. "I don't think so."

"*Hmm.*" She closed her eyes again, sending a strong surging energy outward, and realized he was right. The darkness was receding. Retreating. Good. The bitch had damn well better run.

For good measure, she sent another wave of energy outward to keep the darkness retreating. She didn't want it to be gathering up its strength for another charge.

A few minutes later, the tension in the room eased. The animals shifted, some fading out, others curling up to sleep.

Celeste released a big sigh and looked out the window. The darkness was now completely gone, and the electrical static to the air had disappeared. Whatever or whoever had been attacking the cottage—and how had it known where it was?—was gone.

She glanced over at Matt. "What was that probe all about?"

He shrugged. "Something I was working on when I realized the Portmans and Grandfather were such good liars. I needed a way to see who was lying or cheating. For all our paranormal abilities, we were being taken in by those around us. Others with energy skills. Someone needed to find a way to stop it."

"Interesting concept. Why not just have someone read their auras?"

"Do you have any idea how hard it is to find someone who can do that beyond a surface level?" Matt shook his head. "We are in serious need of good talent."

"Not exactly something you can advertise for, is it?" Celeste couldn't imagine trying to word a job ad for energy workers.

"No," he admitted. "I've had to be cagey. I did just hire three brothers, all of power. I'm looking forward to utilizing their skills."

"But no aura readers in the group?"

He shook his head. "We use the term *rainbow reader*, and they tend to be female."

"Well, don't look at me. I talk to the animals, and that's about all I can do."

"Considering how they respond to you and what they can do for you"—he motioned at the circle of animals still surrounding them—"I'd say that's plenty." He looked at her curiously. "But you're also a stargazer. That's powerful without any other ability."

"I'm one of three equally bad stargazers," she replied, with a small smile. "We'll need decades of practice to get as good as Granny."

"And you have that time."

Yes, she did, but somehow that wasn't making her feel all

that confident that she'd hit the same skill level. "Do you think this energy is responsible for what killed those two men?"

Instantly he shook his head. "No, I don't."

She shifted back to lean against the big chair. "Why not?"

"Because there wasn't anything scary in this energy. And neither was there an energy weapon hidden inside that I saw."

"Maybe it wasn't turned on you?" she suggested. "Maybe it wanted to keep you alive?" She caught a whisper of something odd flash across his face. It was gone before she had the chance to decipher what it meant. "What aren't you telling me?"

He turned to stare out the window. "I think it called my name."

She gasped. "What?"

"Yeah." He shrugged. "Don't think it knew I was here before either. It's as if, it suddenly saw me, then gasped my name."

"And is that when it receded—because you were here?" she asked cautiously. "As if the energy didn't want to hurt you?"

"No, the opposite. She gasped my name, then slammed on the power, as if she were in a rage over my presence here."

"Very strange. And how the hell did she know to come *here*? That's what I can't figure out."

Matt shook his head. "A huge pulsing beacon of energy is collected here. It wouldn't be hard to track."

"So that energy was searching for energy, not this cottage?"

Matt shrugged.

"So then, by tracking the energy, she would have found me anyway." She pursed her lips. "That makes sense. And something else we never considered *could* happen."

"Right. But, if she could find this place, what are the chances she can get at us inside?"

At that question, several animals raised nervous glances her way. She smiled at them reassuringly. "It's okay, everyone. Even if she was here, specifically looking to hurt us, she can't get inside. As long as we continue to roll warm loving energy over this person, then she'll be powerless to hurt us. Remember that," she added gently.

Soft murmurs filled the cottage, as the animals settled back down again.

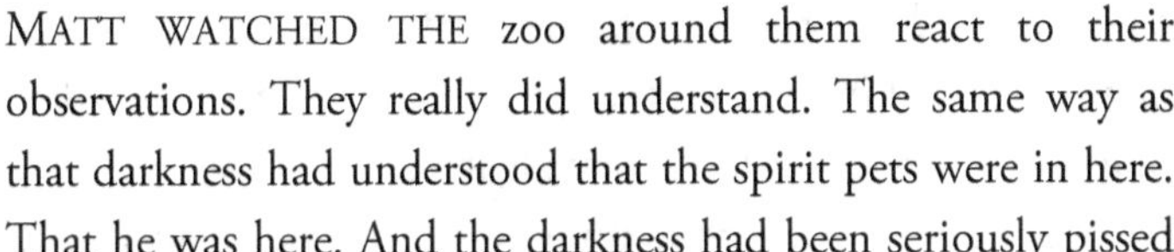

MATT WATCHED THE zoo around them react to their observations. They really did understand. The same way as that darkness had understood that the spirit pets were in here. That he was here. And the darkness had been seriously pissed at the idea.

Matt didn't recognize the energy signature and hoped he would recognize it, if he ever saw or felt it again. Was this someone in his everyday world? He couldn't forget the flash of anger at recognizing him. Seeing him? Or sensing him? He wasn't really thinking that this person could see him from inside the darkness, was he?

Turning to Celeste, he asked, "When you are pushing your healing energy out there, can you see what's happening on the front edge of that? As in, really see what's going on?" He'd seen her face in the storm too. "Or when you are part of a storm? I saw your face. Your eyes were open. Did you see me?"

"I don't think so," she said. "I was in the pool room." She stood and said, "I'm going back there now too." She stretched and yawned. "Then bed. I know it's early, but this wore me out."

"Dinner?" He hopped to his feet. "Before the pool or after?"

She stood, undecided, wavering on her feet.

"Or dinner while you're in the pool?"

She grinned. "That's perfect. Give me ten minutes." And she walked away.

He watched her go, feeling a peace he hadn't known for a long time settle deep inside. They weren't sparring verbally. She wasn't fighting his presence here. She'd accepted his help, treated him as an equal. That was progress. He walked to the kitchen table and opened up the special heated containers his chef, Henry, had packed. A bottle of red wine sat on the side of the basket. He checked the age and smiled. So Henry had understood what this dinner was all about.

Matt carefully distributed the hot curry, rice, and vegetables onto plates and opened up the package of fried bread that had been packed separately. This was a decent meal. And several other meals were still in the baskets. They certainly wouldn't starve.

He waited another couple minutes, then walked to the pool room. "Can I come in, Celeste?"

"Yes," she called out.

He pushed open the door to find the pool room lit with candles, giving the atmosphere a soft romantic look and feel. The gentle rippling sounds of the water added to the magical ambiance.

He glanced outside. Although the angry darkness had dissipated, evening was now descending. He smiled at her. She floated in the pool in a bathing suit, her hair streaming out behind her. A beautiful mermaid. Scratch that—a very sexy mermaid. He shifted the small side table closer to the edge of the pool, then returned for the food and drinks.

It took him a couple trips, and, by the time he carried the wine glasses and the bottle with him, she sat on the side of the pool, studying their meal with interest.

"This looks great. I haven't eaten like this in …" Her voice broke off.

He'd done this a lot when they'd been together. Henry had a soft spot for Celeste. Actually, at this point, he was pretty much over the moon about all three of the stargazers being around the Center. He'd been busy in the kitchen, whipping up specialty dishes for weeks. When he'd heard this meal was for Celeste, well, Matt flushed at the memory. Henry's last words were, "Don't mess it up this time."

Right. Well, Matt hadn't planned to last time either, and look what happened.

"I'm really hungry," she confessed, and, as soon as he sat down and poured the wine, she took her first bite. And moaned. "Henry still works there, doesn't he?"

Matt laughed. "He does, and he says hi, by the way."

"He's a sweetheart."

"He's also an energy worker with a talent for cooking. And I'm blessed to have him."

She nodded in agreement but didn't say a word, as she worked through her plate. The silence around them was peaceful. Happy. Matt couldn't remember the last time he'd felt so content.

"You know, I was thinking …" Celeste began.

He looked up from his plate. "Thinking what?"

"I'm thinking that the energy might have had a personal vendetta here."

"That would make sense," he said cautiously, wondering

where she was going with this.

"She was angry that you were here."

"Sure, but she had been attacking you and this cottage before she knew it was me too."

"*Hmm.*" Celeste nodded. "That's true. But I still think it's important that she knew you. I've just returned. No one knows that yet, outside of a handful of people. But the energy almost raged when it realized you were here."

"So it attacked an empty cottage?" He frowned. "That doesn't make sense."

"Not necessarily. It would have sensed the energy and just wanted to destroy that. Or the animals might have had something to do with it."

"Or someone else heard you were here. Don't forget. Someone sent the gunmen into the woods after you. That's hardly guessing on their part. No, someone had to suspect that you were here. No way they didn't."

Her shoulders slumped. "Damn." After a moment, she suggested, "They could have tracked the hovercraft from the Paranormal Center."

"Then why the surprise to find me here?" he asked in a reasonable tone. He finished the last bite of his food and laid down his fork. He reached for a piece of fried bread and wiped up the sauce on his plate. "No, the dark energy was after you and was angry to find me here with you. Either not expecting us to be together or not expecting you to be with anyone."

"I was thinking it could be an old lover of yours."

He froze. "What?" He stared. "Why would you think that?"

CHAPTER 17

"**S**HE TARGETED ME, and she's angry you're here. Sounds like an ex-lover who is hoping to get you back. Indeed, she may have thought she had a good chance to get you back."

"That is a bit farfetched, isn't it?" Matt said in a calm voice. "I haven't dated anyone since you, so this person must have been harboring a grudge for a long time."

"But not impossible, considering a woman scorned," Celeste murmured. Still, she had to marvel, as her insides danced in joy. She'd been through a roller coaster of emotions after walking away a year ago, knowing that he was free to find someone else. And it seemed like she'd been in a state of waiting ever since. And hoping.

"That's not likely. I'd bet it was more about the huge inheritance you and your sisters are getting."

"But the land wouldn't have gone to anyone else," she exclaimed. "It was always ours. And there's no money."

"But it makes the most sense. Besides, no one knows the details of what you are inheriting."

"Hell," she said in disgust. "Neither do I."

He laughed. "Nothing has changed. You are keeping what you already had, and, if there was no money before, there's no money now."

"Now that part is too bad. I could use some money." She polished off the rest of her dinner and handed the plate back to Matt. "That was delicious. Henry is a genius."

"I won't tell him that part. Life is tough enough with his rather large ego in the mix."

"He deserves it all," she said warmly.

"He's looking forward to seeing you again. He always had a soft spot for you."

She wrinkled up her face, not sure when she'd be at the Center again. Yet Henry was a rotund male who lived for food. The magical offerings he could prepare in that kitchen of his, … well, they were nothing short of perfect. "He's a wonderful person."

Matt stood and took the plates from the table and returned them to the kitchen. It gave her a chance to figure out if Matt meant something deeper with his comment about Henry seeing her again. Of course she'd see him again. Only not for quite a while. She wasn't living at the Center, had few reasons to go there, and Henry never left. As in *never* left. His groceries were delivered to the Center, and he refused to leave the kitchen under the watchful eyes of his staff. They were all good too, but Henry just couldn't let go of the control of his kitchen. Besides, that was his home.

"You could move back in." Matt leaned against the door jamb, staring at her, a glass of red wine in his hand. She set down her wine and let herself drift back into the water. Physically she'd healed. Mentally she was on her way, as the stress and the trauma of the last few days—hell, the last year—calmed down. Emotionally and spiritually? Well, she still felt bruised.

The reason for that disconnect stood in front of her. Matt had always been the problem. He placed his wine on the table and proceeded to unbutton his shirt. He pulled it off, then sat and unlaced his shoes.

She stared at him in alarm. "What are you doing?"

"It's hot in here," he said, pulling off his socks. "I feel like crap."

Oh no. She paddled closer. "Did you get hurt?"

"I've been hurting for a long time," he said, standing and opening his belt, then unzipping his pants.

Her heart pounding, she watched as he stripped down to his boxers, grabbed his glass of wine, and swung his legs over and into the water.

"Ah, that is so nice," he exclaimed.

She watched in fascination, as the water surged up his heavily muscled legs and went to work. When she glanced at his face, he slid all the way into the pool. The water surged over his body, hungry to help.

"This is an incredible pool," he whispered, letting his head drift back, so the water worked into his scalp.

She knew how this worked and reached out to take the glass from his fingers. Instantly the water surged down his forearm and over his fingers. He closed his eyes and let the healing pool do its thing. She moved to the far side and watched in wonder.

He'd always been hard to read. She'd never understood why he would want her. Granny had said that a lack of self-confidence had been Celeste's downfall, and she needed to pull that ego of hers up around her chin some more. But she hadn't been able to do it.

However, she'd reveled in her relationship with Matt. Yet she always feared that he would wake up one day to realize he wanted someone else.

"We were good together." She winced as the words slipped out of their own accord.

He stilled, then said in a soft voice, "We were very good together, and we will be again."

"Will we?" she asked in a small voice. "It seems like I

screw up everything I do."

"Except that, in this case, you're not alone." He studied her as he slid upward, until he leaned against the pool wall again.

She'd floated ever closer, until she was almost on top of him.

And unbelievably he opened his arms.

She never questioned her actions. Never let herself think about them. She didn't dare. And stepped into his arms.

He held her close.

She rested her head against his chest and smiled as the healing pool surged around them, over them, between them. And she realized what the water was trying to do. Heal her. Heal him. Heal them.

A huge ugly sigh worked out of her chest, her body shuddering, as she let go of the pain and grief she'd been hanging on to for so long. She couldn't do anything about her granny, and, indeed, Granny had been ready to go. She'd been in so much pain. She'd held on for so long. But now she was at peace.

And the sisters' job was to find their own level of peace with that.

In Celeste's case, Matt had just added to her pain and loneliness. And walking away had added to her grief.

Maybe Granny was right. Maybe everything did have to happen in its own time. And maybe Celeste had to go through this last year in order to appreciate what she had. She'd had several big epiphanies about her life here. About Matt. She just didn't know where it would all lead.

She and Matt were healing the past, but that didn't mean they had a future. He seemed to think so; she wasn't so sure.

She didn't know what she wanted.

And she didn't want him to assume they had more than

she was willing to give.

"Turn off your thoughts, and let your mind rest," he whispered against her hair.

"I wish I could," she said quietly. "So much has happened, and so much is still going on that my mind keeps reaching for answers and getting nowhere."

"Then stop reaching," he said in a reasonable tone. "Rest."

"Easy for you to say …"

He turned her suddenly in his arms and pulled her up against his chest. "Not easy to do, I know. But no decisions have to be made right now. We need this." He squeezed her gently. "Time to be together."

She smiled and closed her eyes. In that, he was right. She just wanted—needed—to be held by him. To know that he forgave her for her part in this last year of pain.

*

CELESTE WAS THE sweetest, most confusing, … damnedest female Matt had ever met. He'd loved her since the first moment he'd seen her; he knew their energy had clicked within seconds, and it had cemented over time. And yet she kept backing off. Early on, she'd been the same, and he thought he'd finally gotten her over that. But, when she had walked last year, he realized she'd just been shoving all the issues deep inside. He should have done his best to reassure her more. That he was in the relationship for the long haul. Not just that moment in time. But he'd thought she'd gotten it, had understood how perfect they were together. Except she'd had no relationship experience to go on. And, as such, had nothing to compare it to. And didn't understand how good a thing they had.

He'd never explained it to her. Had never really shared his feelings, thinking it was a given. But he'd failed her there.

He should have made sure she understood.

That had been a mistake.

In the last year, it had bothered him a lot to think she might have found another partner. He'd never even looked. He couldn't. *She* was his partner. That she needed a year away sucked, but he had to know she was there 100 percent for him. And when she'd walked, he realized that she hadn't been at all. That had hurt. In a big way.

He also missed Granny. She'd been a character but an honest straight shooter. He'd come to her for advice more than a few times. He'd seen her devotion to her granddaughters, to her energy work, to her star charts. When she died, a hole in his life appeared, and it had ripped into a huge crater when Celeste had walked too.

Holding Celeste close, he stared up at the ceiling in wonder. Granny had produced thousands of star charts in her time. Matt remembered the documents that Genesis had found. And the letter to her from her granny. They hadn't even had a chance to look for more. And were there letters for the other two triplets? He knew how Genesis had cherished hers.

Maybe, when this hell was over, he could convince Celeste to do a full-on search, to see what other paperwork was hidden in the cottage. Bring all the sisters in on it. Honor Granny at the same time. Make it a point to move on from here.

Hopefully with everyone together.

He glanced down at Celeste to see her almost asleep. Only in a healing pool could one float and sleep without any concern for drowning. The water looked out for her every need.

With a happy sigh, he leaned over and kissed her gently. "God, I missed you."

CHAPTER 18

CELESTE LOVED THAT about Matt. He'd always been that way. Easy with compliments, easy with words in general. He was a man who loved to hug, to just hold her. She missed that. She hadn't thought she was the type to want to be touched all the time, but, as her relationship with him had progressed, she'd craved it more and more. That one thing had brought tears to her eyes during all those long nights of sleeping alone in bed this past year. She'd wished for his arms to hold her. That easy confidence of his to say life would be okay.

It hadn't been okay for a long time. She'd cried buckets for weeks, until the need to make a living had reared its ugly head, and her pride had set in. Somehow, after a few weeks, she hadn't been away quite long enough, but, at the same time, she had been away too long to easily return at that point. She refused to come home as a failure. A child returning from a reckless act. She couldn't reconcile her newfound independence with her contrition.

Her small step of independence didn't prove anything, as if she'd truly grown up. Instead she'd come home to make peace and to apologize. Of all the things she'd done wrong, leaving Genesis to clean up behind Celeste was the biggest mistake. And walking away from Matt was the one that hurt the most.

"I hurt Genesis badly when I left," she said quietly. "I wasn't thinking of her or what she'd be going through when I walked. I knew things were tough for Tori, and, when she left, it seemed like a perfect solution. But, when Tori disappeared, she did so believing that Genesis and I would have each other. I don't have that excuse. I ran to get away and left my beautiful sister behind."

"Which is also what Connor did to her."

Celeste winced. "Yeah, we all have baggage from a year ago, don't we?"

"We do. Whether it's baggage we understand or not."

"Connor and Genesis appear to be fine now," she said in a hesitant voice.

"Yes, they are." Matt smiled and stroked her head. "It took a bit. Same for Tori and Devon."

"Yeah, that reunion was different too."

Matt's laughter rumbled through his chest, making Celeste smile at the noise under her ear. "It doesn't matter how or what it's all about. It's getting to the bottom of why. Then working to heal that issue."

"How come you're so smart?" she asked in a flippant tone, expecting a joking response in return. When he didn't answer, she lifted her head to study the grim lines around his mouth. "What's wrong?"

"Well, I'm not very smart, am I?" he said, his voice distant. "I always thought I was. I always thought I had the answers. Life wasn't terribly easy, but I would set a goal, and I worked until I got it. I was determined and used intelligent actions."

"You are intelligent," she repeated. "Where is this coming from?"

He slid a sideways glance her way but wouldn't say anything more.

"It's because of me, isn't it?" She straightened, brushing back strands of wet hair. "How? I don't understand."

With a shrug of his shoulders, he slid deeper into the water. "What's there to understand? I messed up."

His tone was harsh, a complete contrast to the look in his eyes. The insecurity she caught a glimpse of was stuffed back down inside. It took a moment for her to put it altogether. "You can't blame yourself," she cried out. "You aren't the reason I left."

"Neither was I a reason for you to stay, was I?" he said, bitterness in his voice. "If I'd understood how insecure you felt or knew what else you needed from me, … maybe then you wouldn't have run away. You didn't just leave, but you left me." He ran a hand down her face. "You left us. What we had together. It wasn't enough for you. *I* wasn't enough for you. I would never consider such a thing being possible, as I was so damn happy with what we had. But you weren't …"

"But I was—" she cried out.

"Obviously not."

Yet he wasn't listening.

He leaned back and closed his eyes, as if to say the conversation was over and done with. Judgment rendered, and he'd been found wanting. His fault.

"Oh, good Lord," she whispered. "I never considered your feelings like that either. Never thought it would matter."

At that, he rose out of the water and stood glaring down at her. "Never thought it would matter?" he asked incredulously. "We were together damn near every moment of the day. We were not an item. We were *the* item. One. The two of us together. What did you think would happen when you ripped that apart and walked away?"

She swallowed hard. "I didn't think. I was hurt and react-ed. Instinct said to run, so I ran."

He stared at her, then looked around blindly, as if not sure how they'd come to this point, and then he didn't know where to go from here.

But his words reverberated in her head. "I'm so sorry," she whispered.

"Whatever." He reached for his towel, and, with his other hand, he snatched up the wine and tossed back the remaining liquid.

She knew that he was building up his walls right now. Higher, bigger, stronger. He hadn't ever opened up like this before. And, if she didn't do something, he would close that opening and lock it down, never to be mentioned again. He'd always been good at compliments and saying things that made her smile. Just as she'd thought earlier.

But he'd never been good at talking about his feelings. And that's what she'd missed. All his conversations before hadn't been superficial, but they'd been built on that founda-tion that said he thought she'd been on the same wavelength, and she had been, but without the words to confirm it. To give her the confidence she needed. Who knew she needed the words?

Jesus, what had she done to him?

As he wrapped the towel around his shoulders and lifted his leg to step out, she realized she had to fix this somehow. The only thing that came to mind was the truth. "I love you," she whispered. "I always did."

He froze, but he didn't turn around.

"But I didn't *know* that you loved me. You never said so. You never shared your feelings. You always said lovely things to me but never those words. We never talked about a future.

You were all about living in the moment, and, to me, that meant you were only looking at today, and soon today would be over, and you'd move on to tomorrow."

She stood and looked down at herself, watching as the water flowed off her body, the healing pool backing off, letting this next step take place. Maybe they were ready now.

She certainly was.

She continued. "I had just lost someone I'd known couldn't stay forever but hadn't been ready for Granny to leave. When I considered going to you for support, not consciously but on a subconscious level, I knew you wouldn't be there forever either. There is no tomorrow in today, and the future is all about tomorrows. I couldn't handle it. I figured that, while I was dealing with the adjustment, a clean break would be the easiest way. And I left. Left you behind. Left my beautiful sister behind. Left my animals behind." She stared at him, realizing she could barely see him for the tears filling her eyes and spilling out over her cheeks. She swiped them away. "You weren't ready for a commitment, and I couldn't handle temporary. Not when I'd just lost someone very long-term."

She sank back into the water and let the tears come—for her granny, for her sisters who'd suffered. For Matt, and then for herself—the young woman she'd been back then. She was much older and wiser now. Hell, they all were.

The tears wouldn't stop though. Until Matt's strong arms pulled her up against his chest and cradled her close. "Easy, Celeste. Calm down. We'll get through this."

"No," she whispered. "I ruined it all."

"I think we need to split that blame fairly between us," he said in a wry voice. "We both made mistakes. Both suffered. Maybe we needed to. Maybe it's the best thing for us."

The tears slowed, as she stared up at him hopefully. "Do you think so?"

"I have to think so." He tilted her chin up higher. "I couldn't imagine that the words needed to be said, as what we had was such a perfect connection that I knew you *had* to know."

She opened her mouth to say something, but he closed her mouth with a fingertip and added, "But I should have. You needed to hear them."

"And, if I'd had any experience in the world, with relationships, I would have known that, but I didn't," she said, with a smile. "You were and still are my only lover."

A light shone inside Matt's deep gaze that had melted her heart the first time he'd turned it on her. She'd fallen instantly back then too.

"I do, you know."

"You do what?" She'd lost track of the conversation when he turned her insides to mush with that gaze.

"I LOVE YOU. I saw you and fell instantly and forever in love with you."

He snatched her in his arms and kissed her breathless.

By the time he raised his head, she had more tears running down her face. He frowned and gently stroked her cheek. "More tears?"

"Tears of happiness." She beamed at him. "Not pain."

"Thank heavens for that," he said, dropping a kiss on her nose, her cheek, then on each closed eyelid. "I never wanted to hurt you. I know I probably will at some point without realizing it, but I would never do anything to hurt you on purpose."

"Ditto," she said, resting her forehead against his chin. "I'm so sorry for all the hurts I inflicted on you."

He held her tight. "I know why you did it, and that's what's important, so that we can stop hurting each other in the future."

She shivered in the water.

He stepped back. "Do you want to swim more?"

She shook her head. She knew the pool gave one an appetite—hence keeping food stocked here all the time—but besides the hunger for food, when people stayed in the water for longer periods of time, other appetites surfaced. One in particular. It was actually the primary one, but it hadn't ever been an issue before. From the look in Matt's eyes, it was an issue now—for both of them.

"No, the pool is cooling to move us out. It's healed us to the extent it can, and the rest we're to do on our own."

"Really?" He glanced down at the cooling water. "It actually drops the temperature?"

"Yes." She disentangled herself from his arms. "I need to grab another towel."

"I have one—" He found it now lying half in and half out of the pool. "I guess I should say 'had.' I lost my grip on it apparently."

She laughed and climbed over the edge of the pool, grabbing several towels from the shelving on the side.

Accepting another towel from her, he stepped out beside her and whisked off the water. His skin dried off quicker than expected. He looked over to see Celeste hanging up the towel he'd dropped in the pool and her own. Her skin had also dried, but her swimsuit hadn't.

"Does the water dry faster too?" He handed her his towel, studying the water on the floor that was seeping through the wooden slats and into the ground below.

"It does. Dries faster, doesn't hurt your skin, and requires no PH testing."

"Even though it doesn't have running water from the other pools in it?"

"It does actually. It's connected at the far end to the same natural spring system."

He walked over and studied the natural rock formation, noting a small bubble of fresh water trickling in. Minkel sat up from where he'd been sleeping. He yawned, then slipped into the water and floated on his back, almost instantly asleep.

The two lemurs joined him, completely at home in the water.

Fascinating. "Any idea how old this pool is?"

"Older than Granny. *Her* granny used it all the time."

He nodded, not surprised. Secrets were here that they would likely never understand. And maybe that was okay too. "You're very blessed," he said.

"We all are." She held out her hand. "Come on."

He grasped her fingers gently. "Where are we going?"

"To bed."

CHAPTER 19

CELESTE COULDN'T BELIEVE that she and Matt had gotten this far this fast, but she couldn't wait any longer. The last year had fallen away like it had never happened. He was right. She was very blessed. More so because she had him.

Opening her bedroom door, she led the way to her bed. It was slightly bigger than her other sisters' beds, as she'd inherited it somewhere along the line, but it was barely big enough for two of them.

"I figure it's small but could work," she said archly, giving him a raised eyebrow look.

"I think we'll manage just fine." He held his clothing in his arms and turned around, looking for a place to put them down.

"The chair is empty," she said. "Put them there."

With his back turned, she stripped off her bathing suit, and stood, waiting until he turned back and saw her.

She loved the catch of breath in his throat, his widening gaze, and the jump of his erection in his wet underwear.

She smiled. "I think you're overdressed."

He stripped off his boxers and kicked the garment back to the chair, where he'd left the rest of his clothing. "Darbo? Silky?"

"They're in the pool room," she said. "As are the dozen other animals, lying around."

"The living room was full when I last saw it too." He walked toward her, his arms open.

She smiled and stepped into his embrace, loving the feel of his heated skin against hers. "That is life in my world. See what you're signing up for?"

"I do, and I'm fine with it." He smiled down at her. "In fact, I can't wait."

She tilted her head back and whispered, "Show me how much."

And show her, he did.

Like a step back in time, or maybe it was the present wiping out the past, his touch was familiar and yet new. Each touch poignant with memories.

This wasn't the same as before. Similar but so much better. She'd wanted this. Been afraid she would never have it again. His hands stroked and caressed, sure and knowing, as if their last time together had been just yesterday. Her response was instant, as always—more so, as it had been so long. She'd missed him so much. Emotions swamped her, as she realized she was here in his arms. Finally.

Where she'd always wanted to be.

He walked her backward until her knees hit the bed frame. He pulled back enough to reach down and grab the bedding and throw it back. Gently he lowered her to the bed. She shifted under the covers and moved to the far side, so he could join her. It would be a tight fit.

Seeing the look on her face, he smiled and said, "It will be fine."

She laughed. "If you say so."

"I'm not that big." When she pulled the covers over her body, he protested, pushing the bedcovers down to their feet. She squealed and complained about the air being chilly. He laughed and said, "You won't notice soon."

And she didn't. Moments later, a raging inferno simmered inside, as he gently caressed her body with such attention, as if he were trying to remember each and every part of her. He'd always been a caring lover. Always seemed to enjoy touching her skin, as if that alone brought him pleasure. She certainly loved it.

Reaching up, she slid her fingers into his hair and down his scalp. He lowered his head and kissed her gently. "I missed you," he whispered. "Every damn night when I lay in bed, I thought of you. Of this. Of how good we were."

"How good we are," she said, changing it to the present tense. "We're both here now. It's our time."

His gaze smoldered down at her. Then he lowered his head and kissed her hard, his touch possessive. Loving, but letting her know in no uncertain terms that she was his. That this was a point of no return. They would be together now and for always.

She couldn't wait. She tried to tug him closer, but he wasn't having any of it. He dropped kisses on her collarbone and down to the top of her breasts, his hands gently gliding across her belly and wrapping around her hips. Long fingers slipped down to her bottom and squeezed gently. She shifted restlessly under his hands, wanting him closer and closer. When he slid his all-too-knowing fingers down the back of her thigh and around to the top, she twisted, but he held her firm.

"Oh no," he whispered. "I waited too long for this."

She smiled, then moaned, as he tangled his fingers in her damp curls. Those damn teasing fingers. How could she forget that part? She gasped, as he pushed apart her legs. Tugging at him, she tried to move him over her, but he wasn't budging. Then he touched her intimately. Shudders rippled down her spine, and, when he slid first one finger, then a second, inside her tight passageway, she arched, crying out. "Matt. … Come to me," she demanded.

But he refused. Instead his fingers stroked her again and again. When he slowly withdrew them, then entered her again, the tightness inside released, and she cried out in joy.

He rose over her, replacing his fingers with his erection, and waited at her entrance.

She lifted her hips and wrapped her legs around his waist. "Come to me," she said.

And he surged deep inside. She groaned as he filled her, coming to rest at the entrance to her womb. So damn special.

Then he started to move.

And it started all over again. Small eruptions built, as he moved faster and faster and deeper, until he jerked hard above her. As his seed spurted deep inside her, Celeste's climax ripped through her. She cried out and rolled her head to the side, shudders rippling over her skin.

MATT COULDN'T STOP cuddling her. He'd been so afraid this day wouldn't come. That Celeste had meant the split to be final. So much stuff had risen between them that he knew it would take time to sort through. But the bottom line was, they were here now. Together.

Thank God.

He shifted so he could look down on her, but her eyelids were closed. Asleep? He knew she was still healing, but he didn't want to end this now. He wanted to go on loving her all night long. But maybe a little rest would be good for both of them. He pulled the blankets up and over the two of them and moved to get comfortable, tugging her half over his chest.

She never made a sound. He smiled. Good. Maybe now she'd get the rest she needed.

He sighed and relaxed. He wasn't sleepy, but he had no intention of moving again. His gaze shifted around her room. She'd spent her entire lifetime in here, short of the year she'd been away. The insight into her younger years was too tempting to ignore. No teenage posters were up on the wall—not that she'd been a teenager in a while, but still her bedroom was that of a young woman's. Except for a star chart on the back of her door, the walls were plain, unadorned.

Had she had pictures up and had ripped them off when she knew she was leaving, or maybe when she came back? Or maybe she'd left her walls bare growing up. They'd had such an unusual childhood that he couldn't imagine. Glancing over at her night table, he saw Silky and Darbo, sitting with their arms around each other, staring at him.

"Right. We're bonded, and you need me as much as I need you."

Silky moved to perch on Celeste's shoulder, her head lying across Celeste's cheek. They were special, these two. He glanced up to see several other animals in the room now as well. Did they stay out while Celeste and he were otherwise engaged, or did they read the energy to know that all was calm again? He had a lot to learn. That reminded him of the paperwork he'd brought to study. To see if he could figure out what was happening with the storms.

He glanced down at Celeste, confirming that she still slept soundly. He snuck out of bed, easing a hand on her shoulder when she murmured in protest. "I'll be right back."

While up, he used the bathroom, then stopped in the kitchen to stare out at the world outside. The night appeared to be clear, with bright stars twinkling in the black sky overhead. Peaceful. Quiet. But he didn't trust it one bit.

He snatched the paperwork and returned to her bedroom. It took a bit of maneuvering, but he managed to get back into the bed without waking Celeste. Leaning up against the headboard, he opened up the files he'd brought. Scott had translated several of the texts. He selected the first one and buried himself in the world of stargazers.

Several paragraphs in, he frowned. By the end of the page, he was damn-near terrified.

He wanted to wake her up and to ask her if she knew about this. Was it still a common practice? But, as he studied the lax look on her face, he realized that she was lucky she was sleeping. After what he'd just read, he wasn't sure he'd sleep ever again.

CHAPTER 20

CELESTE WOKE SLOWLY, as if coming back from the dead. With her eyelids barely open, she assessed her surroundings. It was her room. Her bed. But the big hulking male sprawled out across the mattress hadn't been hers in a long time. She was grateful to see him here now.

He slept heavily, his thigh across hers, pinning her down. As if, even in sleep, he wanted to make sure she didn't leave him. She didn't plan to ever again, but she knew it would take time for him to trust her.

Wiggling out from under him, she took a quick shower. As she dressed, she realized he didn't look to be waking anytime soon, and so she wandered out to the kitchen. She frowned at the weather outside. Apparently last night's calm, clear sky had been only temporary. Even though it was early morning now, dark roiling clouds filled the sky. What was that all about? She'd not seen this many ugly days in a row in a long time. They would hit a couple weeks of dismal weather now. At least, she'd assumed it was weather.

With Matt's questions in that area, she had to wonder. Then, if that were so, what was this weather all about? Her sisters were all fine. Neither had mentioned bad weather in relation to their reconciliation with their men. So why Celeste?

It wasn't as if her affinity for animals made a difference.

Did it?

She turned to look at the spirit animals. Even more of them were inside the cottage now, and Celeste didn't remember this many being inside all the time. Of course this ugly weather was a new thing, so maybe they were staying in because of it.

Was staying inside for an extended period also affecting the weather? Was this a cycle that was doing itself in the longer it went on? If so, how to stop it? She made quick work of the locks, opened the kitchen door, and walked outside. Instantly the wind whipped her hair behind her and buffeted her body. She stared at the storm building on the outside of the safety zone. Below was a black low ground-hugging fog. Could it be the same darkness they'd seen before? The energy wasn't angry or aggressive.

It shifted restlessly back and forth on the outside, waiting, watching. Maybe it couldn't do anything else in daylight. There were people whose abilities were especially fine-tuned for the night. And then others needed the daylight to function at the highest level. She studied the energy and called out, "Why are you here?" The energy shimmered in place. "What do you want?"

No answer. Then what had she expected?

Wondering how far to push, she took a chance and said, "Matt is mine. Forever. You can't have him."

Instantly a surge of darkness washed over her protective dome. Making her realize just how defined this zone was. She didn't remember ever seeing this.

Overhead came a mechanical sound. A hovercraft approached. The darkness retreated to the edge of the dome. Interesting. Then she understood. Whoever controlled this darkness now waited, assuming the energy shield would have to open to let in the hovercraft. Then, while it was open, the darkness would make a move.

"Not while I'm here," she announced. "Not sure who or what you are, but I do know one thing. ... You can go to hell."

And she turned, walked back inside, and slammed the door shut behind her. She reset the locks and checked the protective layers outside. Everything was on. She didn't understand how this energy knew she was here, but it did. And now it had no intention of leaving. Well, that was fine. Once her sisters arrived, they could get answers.

Because this couldn't go on.

She wanted to stay here but not as a prisoner.

That meant she needed to go back to the Center with Matt, where he could help protect her. Funny, yesterday she would have bitten his head off over the idea, and yet now she was all over it.

There was something about that black darkness though ...

She turned to the kitchen and let out a light shriek. Matt stood in the middle of the small room, still rubbing the sleep out of his face. He croaked in a hoarse voice, "Coffee. I brought coffee."

She grinned and walked to the baskets of food he'd brought with him. As she studied the contents, she realized he'd come prepared for a siege. Or planned to leave her well-stocked for several days. Either way she appreciated it.

In a second basket, she found the coffee. It took just a few moments to set the boiling water on the stove and to measure grounds for the pot. "It will be ready in a few minutes," she said. "Just in time for our company to arrive."

"Who is it, and can they get through?"

"It's my sisters and yes. Minkel is talking to Remi right

now. Telling them about the problem."

"What problem?" Matt asked, suddenly wide awake, his voice hard.

She waved out the window. "That problem."

"Good Lord," he said, studying it. "It's sitting and waiting, ready to pounce."

"That's exactly what it's doing."

"Can we leave?" He hesitated. "Although I don't know if you're ready to venture out of here yet."

"I'm not, but I will be." She motioned to the black energy. "We need a solution to this and fast."

He nodded. "Good. Then instead of your sisters staying, I suggest we all get back on and leave. Providing you think that it will let us leave?"

"We'll have to find out." She gave him a tight smile. "At least with my sisters here, we'll have a lot of energy to help cloak the hovercraft. Once we do that, we should be able to escape."

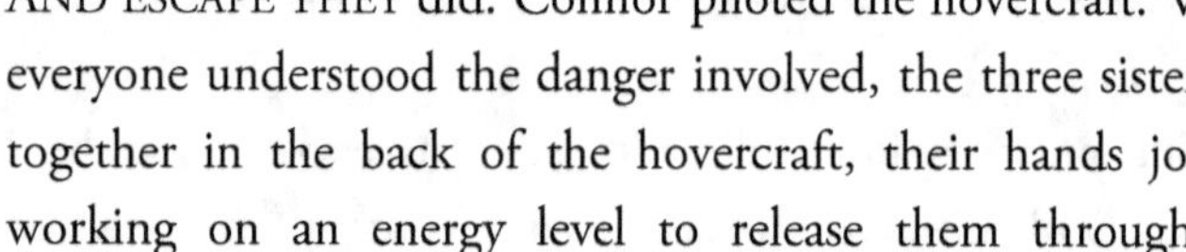

AND ESCAPE THEY did. Connor piloted the hovercraft. When everyone understood the danger involved, the three sisters sat together in the back of the hovercraft, their hands joined, working on an energy level to release them through the protective dome without opening it—something Matt didn't understand. He sat in the front passenger seat and studied the dark fog, as they passed over it. It didn't appear to register that they were leaving. "Looks like it's working," he said to Connor.

"Too early to tell," Connor said, "but let's hope so. What the hell is going on? We've had nothing but trouble these last few months."

"I think we're coming to the end of it," Matt replied. "Think about it. Each sister has had a trial to go through. Now it's Celeste's turn. Maybe if we can get through this one, we'll be good."

Connor looked at him. "Each is getting more complicated too."

Matt nodded. "It started with Granny's death and was compounded by the inheritance she'd left behind. I can't see anything else that would be a big enough motivation for all this evil. We have to find who is running Grandfather's show, now that Mason is gone."

"I vote for his sister," Connor suggested. "She's the witch who sold the triplets in the first place."

"We definitely need to look into her," Matt agreed. "She had the business sense to take over—and the lack of morals to handle Grandfather's corrupt life."

"Right. I'll check it out when we get back."

Just then, the hovercraft was hit by a strong blast. Connor struggled to handle the controls. "What the hell?" he cried out, his hands busy on the controls.

"I'm afraid"—Matt studied the air around them—"that our escape has just been noticed." He twisted in his seat. "Ladies, we've been seen."

The low hum from the back of the hovercraft immediately picked up in both noise and tempo. He studied the three women, still sitting with joined hands and bowed heads. He was about to turn back to the front of the vehicle, when he caught sight of the energy around them. It was more out of the corner of his eye, but a huge vibrational circle of blue glimmered around the triplets. He frowned as the wave washed wider, bigger, stronger. He felt it moving toward him and Connor but in a gentler motion.

As he opened his mouth to say something, he was twisted and placed firmly back in his seat. It was done gently, yet with no option for resistance, and all done by gentle hands.

"Hey," Connor said. "What is going on?"

"It's the women. I can't move either," Matt said, quietly fascinated. Did the sisters know what they were doing?

"I'm trying to fly a plane here …" he snapped.

When Connor's hands were forcibly removed from the controls, and that wave of energy washed through the cockpit, Matt didn't know what to think. When would they have to jump for the controls before they crashed? He glanced out the cockpit and froze.

"Jesus," Connor whispered.

"I see it." Matt stared out the window in shock. In that split second, they'd gone from flying over the forest in the Center's direction … to suddenly appearing on the landing pad. At the Center.

They were just … here.

He spun around, realizing the shackles of energy that had held him down had been released. Connor unbuckled his seat belt at the same time Matt did. But the stunned look on Connor's face made Matt feel better.

"I'm not sure what just happened," Connor said in a low tone, "but I didn't fly or land the hovercraft here."

"I think the operative word here is *fly*. I don't think we 'flew' at all," Matt responded quietly. "I think these ladies pulled a spirit pet trick and transported us here."

Connor shot him a horrified look. "They did what?" He spun around to stare at the three sisters.

Matt snorted. Three bland faces stared back at them.

Genesis murmured, "Connor, could you open the doors for us, please?"

"Really? You can't do that all on your own too?" he asked, an edge to his voice.

Matt understood. What else could these women do that they hadn't told the guys about?

"We can, but we might fall on our faces," Tori said gently. "Not sure any of us can walk at all actually."

Enlightenment struck Matt instantly. The sisters weren't being demanding princesses, they were drained of energy.

At that moment, Celeste reached out a hand toward her sister. "Help," she whispered.

Then she collapsed to the floor of the hovercraft.

Unconscious.

CHAPTER 21

N OW WHERE THE hell was she? Celeste stared wide-eyed at the ceiling above her and then studied the bed where she had slept. After the year on the run, she'd never lost that instant awareness when she woke. And this moment of awareness said this wasn't her room, Granny's cottage, or any other place she recognized. She frowned and slowly rolled over. Matt worked on a small desk on the side of the room. Floor-length windows were on the side wall, offering glimpses of a garden on the other side. Light shone in long rays, barely hitting the bed, telling her it was late morning.

She yawned and slowly sat up. She'd spent a lot of time at the Center with him before, but he'd had a small room back then—nothing like this.

At that moment, she remembered.

The blackness. The panicked flight away from the cottage. That energy reaching for them and the rush to escape.

Then euphoria struck. Look what they'd done!

She hadn't planned on transporting. It was as if, in their hour of need, the energy had understood and had shown them the way. It had to do with raising that vibrational effort to the point of connecting on a different plane. Something spirit animals did subconsciously.

She didn't think any of the triplets could do it alone. As if the three of them had supplied the necessary energy to make this happen—and probably needed that emergency situation to push it to this level.

Regardless, she was ecstatic. What an accomplishment.

"How do you feel?" Matt asked, striding toward her. "You collapsed inside the hovercraft."

She wrinkled up her face. "Thanks for that reminder. Would have been nice to have made it off and then a graceful swoon instead."

"Nope, sorry. You face-planted on the rubber mat."

"Great." She stuck her tongue out at him and tried to stand. Only her legs were wobbly. Matt's arm shot out to hold her steady.

"Easy. You're obviously not back to normal yet."

"My sisters?"

"They managed to get off the hovercraft with help, then had to be carried inside. They were asleep before anyone made it through the door."

"Oh, good," she said. "It wasn't just me."

"No." He grinned. "You were pretty cute though."

She snorted. "Yeah, I'm all about class."

"Glad to hear that. I forgot to tell you that we have a big social happening at the hall tonight. Hundreds of guests are expected here. And I would like you to attend at my side."

"Is that safe? We could be asking for trouble doing that."

"And I figure it will be the opposite. We can flush out the asshole who is terrorizing us, right?"

She shook her head. "I'm too confused to work through that right now." She turned to look around the room. "Bathroom?"

"Right there." Matt spun and pointed to the door behind him.

She attempted a few steps and found herself gaining in

strength. She dropped his arm and made her way to the bathroom. She closed the door firmly in his worried face. After using the facilities, she washed her hands. Glancing up, she caught sight of her face in the mirror. And the dirt on her nose. Really? She'd really face-planted onto the dirty floor? She groaned and washed her face. Why couldn't she be the classy sister for once?

And that just reminded her of the upcoming social event tonight. How could he have forgotten? Or had he deliberately avoided telling her? She would have been perfectly happy to stay at the cabin and to avoid the public event. She had only been back a few days; no one knew she'd returned, and she'd been out of crowds for the last year. She really didn't want a big production going on tonight. Neither did she want this to be an announcement between Matt and her and the rest of the world. She might have returned. They might have renewed their relationship, but she was a long way from wanting to tell anyone.

When she realized she'd taken long enough, and Matt would likely bust down the door to check on her, she opened the door and walked back out. Matt's worried expression caught her attention before he managed to hide it. "I'm fine, Matt," she said, making her way back to the bed, where she lay down again.

"Do you need to rest more?"

"Not sure. I'm not tired but not quite 100 percent yet." And she yawned.

"Sleep," he murmured.

"Can I sleep through tonight?" she muttered. "Because I'd be happy to miss it."

"Not happening." A light blanket was tossed over her shoulders. She closed her eyes and dozed. She heard him on the phone behind her. She heard the odd knock on the door, and voices sounded, but always in the background, a long way away. She smiled and snuggled in deeper, feeling cozy and content. Maybe she could use a little more sleep.

When she woke the second time, she felt much stronger. She managed to get up on her own and could walk around the empty room. Somewhere in the last hour Matt had left. Then again, he had a Center to run and a big event planned for tonight, so he couldn't stay with her at all times. She, on the other hand, was contemplating returning to the cottage. She obviously needed more healing time, if she'd done nothing but sleep so far.

Besides, she had nothing to wear. In fact, she had nothing here at all. She couldn't even change into clean clothes. Frustrated, she searched the room, but none of her belongings had come with her. Not that she had much to begin with …

A knock came on the door. "Celeste, you awake?"

Genesis. Celeste walked to the door and opened it to see Genesis pushing a tea cart. With a happy cry, Celeste opened the door wider and said, "Food. Yum."

Genesis laughed. "And tea. And I brought a change of clothes for you. They're mine but should fit."

"We always shared clothes before, so I presume that hasn't changed. Although I've lost a lot of weight…" She grabbed the clothes her sister handed her and quickly got dressed. As she pulled the shirt over her head, she asked Genesis, "How do you feel?"

"I'm much better. Remi helped to balance out my energy, so I'm back to normal. You?"

Celeste stopped. "Well, if I'd thought to ask one of my spirit pets to help, then I'd probably be doing much better, but it never occurred to me." Instantly Minkel the meerkat showed up and held out his hand.

She smiled and accepted it; immediately the energy worked up her arm and throughout her body. "Why is it I never think of the very basics to keep myself healing?" she asked sadly. "You two were likely healed enough that you didn't have to nap."

"We both napped but only about twenty minutes." Genesis poured her baby sister a cup of tea. "I think the problem is, you have too many spirit pets that you don't connect with one or two in a way that could help you. You see yourself as a guardian for them all, and that's a different story."

"I see myself as Granny in that aspect," Celeste said quietly. "As a caretaker, not an owner."

"I'm not an owner of Remi. We are friends, bonded partners."

Picking up her tea, Celeste wondered if it were that easy. She certainly felt better now as Minkel's energy moved through her body, and, if she had Silky's energy as well, … but, then again, she wasn't anywhere to be found. Staring into her cup, Celeste wondered if Silky had forsaken her too. And, if so, how did she feel about that?

As soon as the question crossed her mind, Silky appeared on the chair beside Celeste, Silky's arms still wrapped around Darbo. Maybe that was the real issue here. The pets didn't belong to anyone. They could belong and appeared to have bonded to more than one person. She'd never seen that before. Of course that didn't make it wrong. Maybe in this case, with Darbo and Silky bonded together as the primary bond, it was to be expected.

"That shirt never looked that good on me," Genesis said, with a touch of envy in her voice. "Although you need a few more pounds back on you."

"My coloring is different," Celeste said. "And I'll gain the weight back soon enough." She held her arms out and twirled. "My dark hair is picking up the midnight-blue in the weave."

The two women studied the shirt for a long moment; then Celeste finally brought up the topic sitting in the back of her mind and bugging the hell out of her. "Matt wants to me attend the social event this evening here, at his side."

"Excellent." Genesis reached across and picked up a scone and placed it on her plate.

Celeste watched her, nonplussed. "That's all you have to say about it?"

"What's to say? You two are back together. Yes, you have things to still work out. Yes, the future isn't settled. And, yes, you need time. But you have time, and Matt wants everyone to know that you—all of us—have the protection of the Center. Considering what we're up against and that this woman is after you, then I have to agree with his strategy."

"I hate to be a *strategy*," she muttered, except her sister was right on all accounts. "I have nothing to wear," she admitted. Only she knew what her sister would say before she got the words out.

"You can wear something of mine. I don't have many fancy clothes either, and this is the first social event any of us have ever attended, but we need to go. We also need to make sure the others see us for who and what we are. Women of power, who aren't afraid to use it when we have to. You have to realize, Celeste, that we own all this land. And Granny might have been happy sitting in the cabin and raising us, but we can do so much more."

"I was trying to figure out what to do," Celeste admitted. "I need a job. Even with owning all this land, we have no money."

"True," Genesis said cheerfully. "But we have so much more."

Celeste laughed. "All right, so what the heck are we supposed to wear to wow the crowd tonight? We've never done anything like this."

"And now we have to do it for ourselves, not just for the men."

"We can't do it *for* the men," Celeste agreed, "but it sure won't hurt to knock their socks off."

And the two women put their heads together to discuss clothing.

MATT STUDIED SCOTT. "We need to double the security in the main hall. I want energy blocks throughout the Center, allowing the guests to only pass through certain hallways. Everything to do with the Center's business, research, and the personal quarters of those living here must be blocked off."

"I can do that." Scott motioned at the huge lop-eared rabbit at his side. "I know Mopsy doesn't look like much, but he's a speed demon when he gets going."

Matt studied the oversized fluff ball doubtfully. "You're right. He doesn't look like much. How can you use him here?"

"He'll monitor the doorways."

"We still need to block them with energy."

"No problem. That's what Mops specializes in."

"Not that I don't believe you, but how about a demonstration, so I can see him in action?"

Scott laughed. He turned to Mopsy, and the air around them buzzed. Mopsy looked at the doorway.

Just then, Connor walked in through the door and fell to

his knees. "What the …?" He struggled to get up but couldn't.

Matt was impressed. "He's good. Does he do that at your request? I've never seen any spirit animal do that."

"He does it because he loves it. I think he sees himself as a guard dog," Scott confessed. "Regardless he's great at handling about a half-dozen entrances, so I figured we'd put him to work tonight and keep the elevators to the upstairs apartments and the downstairs research labs free from unwanted guests."

Matt grinned. "Okay."

"Hey, you guys want to tell floppy here to drop his guard, before I have to use energy to get back out of here?"

Scott grinned and said something to Mopsy. Matt was still shaking his head, as Connor then stood up and stared at the rabbit.

"I know I'm new to the world of spirit animals but rabbit doormen?" He shot a glare at Scott. "Really?"

"Hey, he's the one that loves it. Not me. I've got better things to do." And, whistling happily, Scott and Mopsy walked out of the room.

Connor approached Matt, his head still turned to watch the two leave. "Can we trust that rabbit?"

"If nothing else, crossing him will trigger the energy at the door and will alert the rest of us that someone is trying to access the restricted area."

"That will work then." Connor looked like he wanted to say something else.

Matt waited. When the other man didn't speak, he asked, "What's the matter?"

"How big a deal is tonight?"

"Big, why?"

"I don't think any of our ladies have clothing that will

work," he said. "Genesis said Celeste could wear something of hers, but they haven't ever attended a formal evening affair."

Matt slouched back. "You could be right." He considered the matter. "And tonight is important. Damn."

"And it's late. As in, too late for custom fittings," Connor said cautiously. "I know Genesis would wear the best she had and would raise her nose in the air in apparent unconcern but …"

"Right."

Just then, Celeste entered behind Tori, Genesis at her heels. "And three of us need something appropriate," Celeste said. "We might have been able to find something at home, but we are no longer at the cottage."

"Why would you have formal wear at the cottage?" Matt asked in confusion.

"It's where we grew up. And Granny had some beautiful things there."

Matt managed to keep his expression bland but not bland enough.

"We need the right clothing, Matt," Celeste said, spearing him with a pointed look.

He nodded. "Of course you do."

"Good. We want to go back to the cottage."

"No way."

She glared at him. "We have to."

Genesis stood beside her sister. "Celeste, what's at the cottage?"

"Cloud dresses."

Tori gasped and Genesis blinked. "Yes," they shouted in unison. "Those would be perfect."

The three women grinned at each other, then spun to Matt and said, "We have to go back."

He shook his head. "No."

They smiled. "We're not asking," Celeste said gently. "We're going."

"You would risk your safety for the sake of a few dresses?" He slowly rose to his full height. "We barely escaped this morning. No way in hell I'm allowing you to go back there now."

"Allowing?" Celeste said, even more gently.

A soft hum filled the air.

Matt turned on Tori. "Don't bother. Your mind control won't work."

She shot him a disgruntled look. "It wasn't mind control. It was an autosuggestion."

His glare deepened. "Same thing. If you must have the damn things, find another way to retrieve them. I'm not sending you back, escort or not." Surely the triplets would listen to common sense. Then he caught sight of the look on Celeste's face. Suspicion bloomed. "What did I say?"

The three women beamed at him. "Nothing."

And they disappeared, practically running from the room.

"*Uh-oh*. They're up to something," Connor said, staring at the empty doorway. "It might have been easier to escort them to the cottage for a simple retrieval. This way, there is no telling what they are up to."

"Whatever it is, it had better involve them staying here, safe and sound."

"Are you forgetting how you got here this morning? They moved the entire hovercraft. What if they only try to move themselves?"

Matt stared in horror at Connor, his feet already moving toward the doorway. "Shit," he cried out, as he stared down the hallway, but the women were long gone.

CHAPTER 22

"ARE WE GOING to try to move ourselves back to the cottage? Surely that will take more energy than we can afford, considering we'd have to do it twice. Not to mention, this is hardly an emergency situation." Celeste saw her sisters' faces, broke off, then amended her words. "Okay, so it is kind of an emergency. What about just asking Remi to get them?"

Genesis frowned. "I don't know if he can."

"We won't know until we try," Tori said. "I'll ask Jessie and see if he can retrieve them."

"But they must know exactly where the dresses are."

"They're in Granny's closet. That big box on the left. I think." Celeste shrugged. "Maybe."

"Granny was making those for years. Did anyone consider why?"

"They are power dresses," she said. "However, we were never allowed to wear them."

"That's because we never had any occasion to wear them."

"Until now."

In agreement, the three women continued discussing options. "I'd rather go in person," Genesis admitted. "It seems like the right thing to do."

"Except for the danger involved," Tori said in dry tones. "How is that the right thing for any of us?"

"We'll take you," Matt said from the doorway. "If it's that

important, we'll go, but we need to take every precaution to keep you safe."

"Then let's go now," Celeste cried out, jumping to her feet, a huge smile breaking over her face. She wanted to race over and hug him for joy. She needed to go back; she just didn't know why. Instead she said, "We can be back in an hour." She walked over to Matt and said in a quiet voice, "Thanks. It is important."

He rolled his eyes. "Fine, let's go."

They were back in the hovercraft within minutes, and, with Connor piloting again, they raced back to the cottage.

About a mile out, Tori gasped and grabbed her head.

"What's the matter?" Celeste reached over to hold her sister's hand.

"The forest. Something is wrong with the forest."

They were almost at the cottage, when they could see a swath of black where trees had once been. A paintbrush stroke of charcoal, as if someone had wiped out a long stretch of trees on a canvas.

They all stared in shock at the woods below.

"It's terrible," Genesis whispered. "Who could do this?"

"And why?" Celeste wondered. "Being as close to the cottage as we are, it was probably that energy we saw this morning."

"Maybe it was because we escaped," Matt suggested. "It looks like someone had a terrible temper tantrum and lashed out in anger." The ladies looked at him. He shrugged. "Well, it does."

Celeste stared down at the black streak that managed to completely wipe out the woods on one side of the cottage, the building thankfully remaining protected and safe. Celeste stared at the destruction, tears filling her eyes. "How horrible."

"Horrible, yes, but it will regrow," Tori said, anger in her voice. "It's senseless. The animals would have escaped though, having recognized the terrible energy before it was unleashed here."

"Now that she's lost her temper, she'll be drained," Celeste noted. "She'll be calm, making it that much harder to figure who she is."

"We also can't know for sure that this energy is a woman," Matt added. "It has a feminine tinge to it that does not necessarily mean a woman. It could be a man, with a lot of feminine traits. It could be a man who carries a lot of his mother's or his wife's or even his daughter's energy with him. It could be a woman hiding behind a man. No one can know for sure at this stage."

"So make no assumptions. Right, got it." Connor set the machine down outside the cottage.

"Let's get what you need and get back," Matt said at the open door to the hovercraft. "You have ten minutes, and that is all."

Celeste was the last one inside the cottage. The other two headed to their bedrooms. Celeste went to Granny's room, looking for the box Granny had told her that they could have when they needed it. She opened the flap to make sure that the contents were what she was expecting. And winced. Lord, she hoped these were them. Her first glance wasn't encouraging.

She didn't know if her sisters even understood what these dresses were, but Celeste didn't want to explain here. And, besides, she might be wrong. Her memory was less than perfect. She carried the box to her room and gathered up the little bits of jewelry she had. She had no idea what might go with the dresses, so packed it all. Shoes were the real issue now, but again, without seeing the dresses, then she had no idea what would go with them. She did have tiny thin ballet slippers, and, in a pinch, they might do. They might also look like the stupidest thing possible. But again, not the time or place to make that decision. Besides, as she stared into the dark corners of her closet, she didn't really have a choice. Dress shoes were not something she had a reason to own before.

She carried the box out to the living room to find her sisters waiting for her.

"Is that them?" Tori asked.

Celeste nodded. "It is. Are you ready?"

The other two nodded.

"Let's go, ladies," Matt said impatiently from the front door. "A storm is building out here."

The women exchanged worried looks and ran outside. "That's not a normal storm," Celeste cried out. "That's what Granny would call a cyclical storm."

Matt ushered them into the hovercraft. "What is that?" he asked.

"One that needs our help."

He shot them a surprised look, then slammed the door closed. "You're not helping with any storms. Not today."

"You don't understand, Matt," Celeste said. "It's not a choice. If the storm needs us, it will get us, no matter what. It always came for Granny, asking for help."

Connor lifted the hovercraft into the air. "Not today, it won't."

He was just rising up above the cottage, when a huge crack of lightning directly struck the hovercraft.

MATT REACHED OUT and grabbed the stick shift that Connor was struggling to control. "I'll handle this. You steady the craft."

A loud din overtook the cabin.

"I'm trying," Connor yelled.

"Hang on," Matt called to the back of the hovercraft. The vehicle lurched sideways and slid down toward the ground, a weird screaming sound filling the air.

"Go back," Genesis yelled. "We have to go back."

Matt shot her a disbelieving look. "There's no way. We'll never make it."

"You don't understand," Celeste snapped. "We have to. We return willingly, or we are returned by force, but we have to go back."

He glared at her, but just then, a screech ripped across their voices, and the shuttle swerved and lurched to the side again.

"I can't control it," Connor shouted, his hands busy on the controls.

"There is no controlling this," Genesis shouted back at him. "Take your hands off."

He swiveled, as if to look to see if she meant it, and then, with a disbelieving look at Matt, he slowly lifted his hands off the shuttle console. Immediately the hovercraft leveled off, before descending at a normal, albeit slightly faster, pace.

"What the hell?" Matt whispered, as everything in his belief system took a jarring step back. How was this possible? He'd been blown away when the women had managed to transport the vehicle with them in it this morning, but to think an electrical storm was taking over and controlling this vehicle and doing so in a safe manner? Yeah, he didn't think anything would be the same again.

How could it be?

The vehicle landed, a little roughly but safely, in front of the cottage. Leaving everything onboard, the three sisters hopped out and walked to the edge to the yard.

Matt and Connor raced behind.

Celeste reached up an arm and held her hand out to stop them. "No closer. You'll get hurt." She turned to look at her sisters. "We haven't played the storm game in forever."

"Years," Tori said, her gaze on the storm racing toward them. "I never connected that game to this though. Nothing is playful about this."

"It can't be anything else," Genesis yelled above the din. "I think everything we did, including the games, was training."

"But for what?" Tori asked.

"To take Granny's place. To do whatever was needed to heal the woods and to keep us safe," Celeste cried out, her arms instinctively going back, her face lifting to the dark sky, the wind whipping her long blue-black hair around her face.

Matt wanted to get closer, to tug her back toward him, to safety, but he couldn't move his feet. "Connor, can you move?"

"No, my feet are stuck to the ground somehow," Connor cried out. He raised his arm and pointed to the mass of dark-blue clouds almost upon them. "Look!"

Matt froze. "Oh, dear God. What is that?"

"It's the cyclical storm," Genesis whispered in awe. "We haven't seen one in a long time. And never one this big. We used to play a game with the little ones but nothing like this superstorm."

Play games? Matt couldn't begin to comprehend the idea. He'd held Granny in such high regard, but to put her

granddaughters in danger with a storm like this? And now? …
Now he had no idea what to think …

The storm whipped forward and rolled right over them. So much for the cottage and the surrounding area being safe.

The wave of clouds struck, so dark and dense that Matt couldn't see, and he couldn't move. He raised his arms to protect his head, as the wind raged on. Through the darkness he watched all three sisters stand, their hands joined and raised in supplication to the elements.

And then Celeste rose off the ground.

CHAPTER 23

CELESTE LET THE old nursery rhyme roll through her head, seeing the child she was, remembering her granny's constant reminder to learn the chant by rote. That the woods needed her. That the sky needed her. That the world around her *needed* her.

She felt the power surge through her, as her body rose higher and higher. She was still connected to her sisters. Still connected to the world around her, but no longer to the ground beneath her.

She heard the storm work inside the thick clouds. Energy twisted, weaving and repairing the world around her. Now she understood. It wasn't that the storm was different than the others she'd seen, but that it was working to repair the damage that had been done below, and the damage done was worse than before.

Celeste was a stargazer. This land was hers to protect. That someone had damaged it meant that the energy had to be repaired immediately. And it wasn't just the energy. It was the water. The land. The animals.

At that moment, she realized something else as well. She didn't have just an affinity for animals but for all things. She glanced over at her sisters and saw the same awareness on their faces, as the cyclical storm healed and regrew the world below. The stargazer cottage was so special that it could never be destroyed, but the outlying areas that worked to camouflage the cottage operated at a lower level. It had been sacrificed to keep the cottage safe. The cottage and everything in it.

Sacrificed because it could be rebuilt.

She smiled and felt great joy surge through her. This heritage that she'd been gifted with, … it was a huge responsibility, but with that came the power to do what was necessary.

She *was* powerful. Her sisters *were* powerful. They belonged to a special line of great women, and maybe, just maybe, they could do damn-near anything they needed to, if it was for the greater good of their home and their lineage. Healing the land around the cottage was just one more part of the whole special ecosystem. It had been injured. That inner call prompting her to return to the cottage was less about the dresses and more about the cottage calling them home. They'd escaped this morning, but there was no escaping their fate now.

They were destined to do this. To be the healers of their world. To heal themselves on the inside, thus healing everything else.

She laughed, the sound joyous, as it rippled outward into the midst of the raging energy. She stared at the world, her gaze taking in the roots regrown, the dirt no longer blackened and charred. The tiny critters inside the ground were back again, as the ecosystem restored itself. Small saplings regrew bigger, better, stronger. She watched as that vast wasteland turned back into the lush forest she knew and loved in no time. One area was slower to fill in. She pointed a finger at it, showing her sisters. They joined hands and sent energy flying in that direction. Instantly growth happened.

They were really doing this.

Celeste grinned at her sisters. "Who knew?"

Tori, in a soft gentle voice, said, "Granny knew. She must have known. She did this all these years, until we were big enough to do so ourselves."

"She hung on for us," Genesis said. "And I, for one, am so damn grateful. We would have struggled to do this even a year ago."

Celeste nodded. "I'm not sure I could have done this even days ago."

"No, you had to heal with Matt first," Tori said, a beautiful smile on her face. "We all had to. The men are part of that balance. As always, the world needs us and the men. And we need them."

As suddenly as it started, the storm eased back. The three sisters stared into the darkness. Celeste smiled, as the atmosphere lightened in front of them, turning from deep darkness to a wonderful golden glow. The air itself was healing, replenishing the atmosphere with not only healthy air but joy and peace, replacing the darkness with light and the evil with goodness.

As she slowly lowered to the ground, Celeste looked at the flowers around her. They flashed and smiled with colors again. Buds and butterflies flitted around. Beautiful. Normal.

"Look," Genesis said urgently. "Look!"

Celeste raised her gaze and gasped. "Granny!"

And there she was.

In the middle of the clouds, more beautiful, younger, more at peace than they'd ever seen her before, was Granny's face. Celeste didn't dare breathe or blink, in case her beloved granny disappeared.

"Are we imagining this?" Tori asked. "Seeing her face in the clouds like another game we played as a kid?"

"No," Celeste whispered, tears rolling down her cheeks. "It's her."

"Why? How?" Genesis asked. "Granny, why are you in there?"

Celeste waited, hoping to hear Granny's voice once again. To have confirmation that she truly was there. Granny tilted her head back, her gaze going to the top of the clouds, and she smiled, a beam of golden joy that touched them all.

A voice whispered across the sky, "I'm here because I'm on my way to the stars. We're stargazers, beloved children. When our time comes, we return to the stars, where we can then gaze down and protect those who are below."

With that, Granny lowered her gaze and gave each of them a breathtaking smile, matching her smiling eyes. "I will always watch over you."

And she was gone.

The storm clouds disappeared.

The air calmed.

And finally, as if a string had been cut, the three women collapsed to the ground, unconscious.

MATT RACED TOWARD Celeste, his mind still arguing with what he'd seen, what he'd thought he'd heard. Surely that hadn't really been Granny up there, had it? And the words he'd sworn he'd heard her say to her granddaughters—was such a thing possible? Was she not only a stargazer, as in threw and read the star charts, but also a *stargazer*, as in stargazing down on this world below?

Again his mind shifted through the things he thought he knew. To some place where nothing was as he'd first known. He had so much to think about. So much to consider. To study. How? Talk about mind-blowing. This changed everything. All this needed to be recorded. That was what the Paranormal Center was, at its heart. It was intended to preserve the nature of the paranormal world. The truth behind so many lies. The knowledge behind so much that was unknown. The secrets kept for future generations.

He studied Celeste's face. Such joy filled her expression, a sense of peace. There was more to all this, he knew that, but how long until she shared this truth with him? They'd come so far, and yet, in many ways, they hadn't gotten anywhere. He couldn't imagine the games she and her sisters had played growing up, if this was an example. It didn't bear thinking about. No wonder Granny had fought so hard to get and to keep the triplets.

He wondered, if they had not succeeded on their own, would that storm have swooped down and shifted life as they knew it, until the triplets were returned to where they rightfully belonged? And had there been a price paid by those who had taken the life of the triplets' mother? Not enough of one, he believed, given that a stargazer had been murdered.

And, if that had been Granny in the storm, where was the triplets' mother? Had she gone into the sky above, ahead of Granny? He couldn't help it; he looked up at the bright sky and stared hard at the deep blueness. Did Celeste's mother exist as a twinkling star? Really? It blew his mind.

"Matt," Connor said at his side. "I think we need to get the women back to the Center."

He nodded but didn't make a move to pick them up. "They look …" He shrugged, feeling stupid, but added, "Happy."

"I know. At peace. It's really amazing. But right now I'm more concerned with getting away. That might have been normal for the triplets, but no way that will ever be normal in my world."

"I hear you. It changes everything."

"And yet nothing." Connor stood, Genesis in his arms. "How many more times will we have to do this before we get to the end of this mess?"

Matt scooped Celeste up into his arms. "I don't know. I suspect things will get really ugly now."

"What?" Connor gave him a startled look.

"Think about it. What happens when this person realizes that all her destructiveness was wiped out in a moment? That she is powerless to permanently destroy these women?"

"Shit." The word came out more as a whispered prayer.

"Yeah."

The two men stood, set the women into their seats, and buckled them in securely in. Matt returned to carry Tori back to the hovercraft. "Is this vehicle capable of flying after that?"

"I don't know," Connor said, from the pilot's seat. "I'm running it through a safety check right now."

"Good." Matt scrambled into the passenger chair. He glanced back at the cottage. "And then the cottage. Is it locked down? Secure?"

"That's the last of my worries right now," Connor said, flicking switches. "That place has more guardian angels than we will ever have."

"True." With a final glance at their unconscious and so-damn-precious cargo, Matt turned to Connor and said, "If you think it's safe to fly, let's get home."

CHAPTER 24

THIS WAS BECOMING a bad habit. Celeste had woken to the sight of Matt's ceiling once again. And once more, she was atop his bed, a blanket thrown over her body. She was tired but buzzed. Energized but fatigued. Silky and Darbo curled on either side of her neck, snuggled up tight. Minkel the meerkat held her hand, and damned if Smurg the owl wasn't perched on her other arm.

To top it off, Twitch lay on her chest, snuggled up between her breasts. She marveled at what she saw. She'd never really had this much physical contact with them. She had held them, had cuddled them, and had even kissed them, although that didn't work very well without their acceptance, but to choose to lie here with her like this? ... Well, ... that was special.

A whole day of special events.

She smiled, remembering the storm. The hovercraft being taken over. Granny. Quiet tears slipped from the corner of her eyes. Granny had been in that storm. Controlling it. Wielding the power. Showing the triplets what they could do. What they would at one time be called to do.

"You feel okay?" Matt's caring voice rolled over her.

She let her head fall to the side, so she could see him. His face was wreathed with worry. She smiled. "I'm fine," she whispered. "The tears are good tears."

His face cleared. "If you say so," he said. "Although I doubt Connor and Devon will believe that from your sisters, any more than I believe it from you."

She laughed lightly. "I got to see Granny again. That was bittersweet," she said. "So tears because she's gone, but good tears as I had that last moment with her and know she's okay. She's in a good place now."

"Is she?"

She studied his searching gaze, realizing how much he had to adapt. "I guess that was a bit much for you, wasn't it?"

"It was out there," he agreed. "I saw Granny's face in the clouds, heard her voice, but believing what I saw …?"

"And since you're back at the Center, farther away from the event, with the passage of time too, the more disbelieving you have become." At his shrug, she smiled. "That's okay. Just know that you saw what you saw, in case of a similar future event."

His face twisted in alarm.

"And the fact that, down the road, we—my sisters and I—will also go into that storm as we travel to the stars above."

He sat down, hard. "Is that really what happens? What she said?"

"It is." Now the tears fell in earnest. "I never realized what I'd seen before. Missed my chance to experience that at a whole new level."

"Before?" Matt pounced on the word she'd let slip.

"It happened once before, like this, but with a different face." She sighed. "One I didn't recognize."

He reached out and cupped her cheek. "Your mother?"

She gave him a sad smile. "Yes, my mother. Only I didn't understand what I was seeing. I was just a child. And now the opportunity is lost. She's gone, and Granny has taken her place."

"But at least you know she's okay, like your granny," he said in a quiet voice. "That is worth so much."

She nodded. "I know. And you're right. It would have been nice to have seen her at least once. I never knew her. Granny was our everything. She kept our mother alive inside our heads, but that's not the same thing as seeing her, knowing who she is, deep inside."

"True, but having the assurance that she has moved on to where she belongs has to be worth a lot."

"Even if that's in the sky with the other stars," she said, teasing him gently, knowing that he had to fight with all that knowledge he was so proud of.

"It appears that everything I thought I knew about star-gazers and Granny—and, indeed, the reality of life around us—needs to be discarded and relearned," he said in a slightly sour voice. "And new records to keep track of for future generations."

"And maybe that's why you are in charge of the Center," she said. "Granny made sure you got that position."

"Maybe, but I can also lose it," he warned, wondering at the sense of an inner-knowing.

She shook her head, her gaze intense. "No, it's yours for life. Your abilities will grow to keep up. As will Connor's and Devon's. We are all linked, the six of us. There can never be any going back."

"Good. I don't want to go back. There is only one direction to go from here, and that's forward."

His phone rang. He glanced at the number and stood. "I have to go. Things are still being set up. You have time to rest and relax. The event doesn't start for another two hours. Then I want you at my side for the duration of the evening."

She smiled up at him. "I'll be there."

He leaned over and kissed her hard. "Forever."

He walked to the door, leaving her feeling damn lost already.

"You sure you can't push them off for a half hour or so?" she suggested, her voice smooth as silk and suggestive as hell—at least, she hoped.

He turned back, a frown on his face.

She kicked off the last of her clothes, before walking over to him, naked. She reached up, her arms around his neck. "I need a shower. Thought maybe you did too." She gave him a quick kiss and walked away into the bathroom. She turned on the hot water and stepped under the spray.

The door opened right behind her. She shrieked with laughter, as an equally nude Matt stepped in and reached for her. "I told them ten minutes," he said, with a grin.

"Well, guess what? You'll be late." She chuckled. "But I'll see what I can do."

He lowered his head and kissed her, her slick body pressed tightly against his, from breast to hip. Heat flashed between them, instant and powerful as always. And Matt was damn inventive with that bar of soap. When he lifted her against the shower wall, she was more than ready. When he slid deep inside, her body erupted in instant joy. She cried out and hung on, as Matt surged into her again and again. When he shuddered in her arms, she held him close, a smile on her face.

"I have good ideas," she murmured against his neck.

"You have wonderful ideas," he whispered back. He slowly withdrew and turned down the water temperature.

She shrieked, "It's too cold."

But he was already laughing, as he quickly showered off. "Now I'll turn it back up for you."

She grinned, as she heard him whistling in the bedroom. She'd done that for him. She ran the washcloth over her sensitized skin and realized she'd done the same thing for herself. She felt wonderful.

Later, after she finally shampooed her hair and finished her shower, she walked through the bedroom and saw the box sitting in the corner of the bedroom floor. She stopped and stared at it, the memories hitting her hard. She was a little girl, watching Granny at the sewing machine, but she didn't sew traditional cloth but something that shimmered like moonbeams.

She shook her head. What if these cloud dresses weren't for tonight? That would be horrible to feel underdressed at an event where so many people would be staring at them.

She wanted to open the box but turned and grabbed the hair dryer instead. If they were still in the cottage, her hair would be dry in one-third of the time. Here, not happening. She closed her eyelids, wondering how her sisters were faring, when she heard a noise outside the bedroom door. She quickly pulled on her underclothes and dressed in casual pants and a shirt. If she were going to have company, she wanted to be dressed for it. It could be her sisters though. But she thought they still had well over an hour. Not that it was very long.

She walked to the door and opened it.

The hallway was empty. She frowned. Had she only imagined someone there? Closing the door again, she picked up her phone and called Tori.

No answer.

Maybe she was still asleep.

She called Genesis next. Again no answer.

What the hell?

Dialing Matt, she quickly explained the situation. "Is

something wrong with them?" She had a hard time keeping the worry out of her tone.

"They were both up and walking around a little while ago," Matt said. "I'll send Connor and Devon to find them."

She put down the phone, wondering if someone had been foolish enough to try and harm her sisters. Could anyone already know about what had transpired at the cottage this afternoon, or did they know and not care—but had planned to target the sisters regardless?

Worried, she wandered the room, walking past the box several times. Finally she picked it up and carried it over to the bed. Opening the flap on the top she studied the drab-looking contents. Her heart sank. Damn these things were ugly. And not at all as she remembered.

Wincing, she dug into the body of the fluffy material and realized several envelopes were in the bottom. One had her name on it. She slowly sat down on the bed and opened it.

It was from Granny.

Of course it was. Celeste sighed with heavy memories. Granny had thrown the triplets' star charts many times. Said it helped to guide Granny's actions to know what and when her granddaughters would need something from her. That's why she'd made the cloud dresses so long ago, she'd said. Yet why make them so … ugly? Celeste turned her thoughts from the dresses and pulled out the single-page letter inside.

Dearest Celeste,

I'm gone, if you are reading this. Don't be sad, child. You saw me today …

Shivers rippled down Celeste's spine. Good Lord, it was as if Granny was sitting beside her and speaking to her out loud.

You now know I'm fine. You should tell Matt. And let your sisters tell Devon and Connor. Your lives are inextricably entwined now, so there should be no secrets.

At least you weren't afraid of me this time. Your mother had tried to contact you when you were little, but it was too early for you, and that connection was lost. But not forever. You should know by now that forever can't happen in our world. We are always one. Your mother's blood runs in your veins, as much as mine does.

You will always be protected, but you must be aware of the danger you and your sisters face. Tonight. At the ball. Matt says it's a low-key event. It's not. It's a chess game, and you need to know who your opponents are. And that will happen, but I fear not without more trouble coming to the three of you.

Be careful, listen to the man of your heart and know that life is unfolding as it's meant to. You will survive. And you will thrive. I rejoice in your growth and that of your sisters. I'm always here. And I will always be watching over you.

Sometimes I might be too strong. Sometimes I might be too protective. Have patience with an old woman who only wants to see you three do well. You all enriched my life, and I hope that you remember me as fondly as I do you.

My love to you forever,
Granny

At that point in time, Celeste lifted her head to realize she wasn't alone.

Matt stood in front of her. She walked into his embrace. Gently he took the letter from her hand and read it over. His features turned grim, as he read down to the bottom. He held her close to his heart. "I will protect you," he said. "I'm so glad you have this letter."

She nodded. "Me too. There's one for Tori and Genesis in there as well."

"They can read it later. After we find them."

"Tori's missing?" she cried out in horror, tilting her head back to stare up at him. "Genesis? Is she missing too?"

"*Shh*. Everyone is on the lookout for them."

"Wait." Celeste took a step back and closed her eyelids. *Smurg, can you hear me?* The response was instant. She said to him, *My sisters are missing. Find them.* Then she called to the tiny mouse who could go places the bigger animals couldn't. *Twitch, did you hear that?*

Twitch muttered quietly, then came a tiny rustling sound, before he disappeared.

Minkel? she called out.

On it, Minkel whispered.

Contact Remi and Jessie.

She opened her eyelids, her gaze wide as she stared at Matt. "We'll have answers soon. The animals are searching. Twitch is inside the Center. Minkel is tracking Remi and Jessie."

He raised his eyebrows. "And if they are outside?"

"Even better," she said, with a smile. "Smurg is out there. And no way that the pools and the forest will let anything happen to them."

He nodded in relief. "Good." He glanced down at the letter in his hand. "Granny really was in the storm, wasn't she? And your mother long ago?"

"I was terrified when I saw my mother," she confessed. "Granny tried to get me to go out into a different storm, and I refused," she said quietly. "One of my greatest regrets."

"You were young. It's all understandable."

"That doesn't change the fact that I wish it had been different."

He held up the letter again. "And what are you supposed to share with me?"

She frowned.

"Even Granny said to tell me."

She sighed. "It's something all three of us should say as a group."

"Good, we'll go over it again, when we have them back." His tone wouldn't accept being pushed off much longer.

"It's just we never found Granny's body." Celeste stared outside, hating the pain and loss still hurting her at the memory. "She just didn't come home one day. We went to the springs to find her, but only her clothes were there. The physical body of Granny, as far as we know, became one with the world around her. She just faded into the framework of our existence." She shrugged. "We knew she was dead. Yet we had no proof. No physical body to prove her passing."

"Nothing to prove she's dead?" He stared at her. "We have laws that govern things like that."

"Sure. How about we stand up and say we saw her in the clouds?" She laughed at the look on his face.

"Damn."

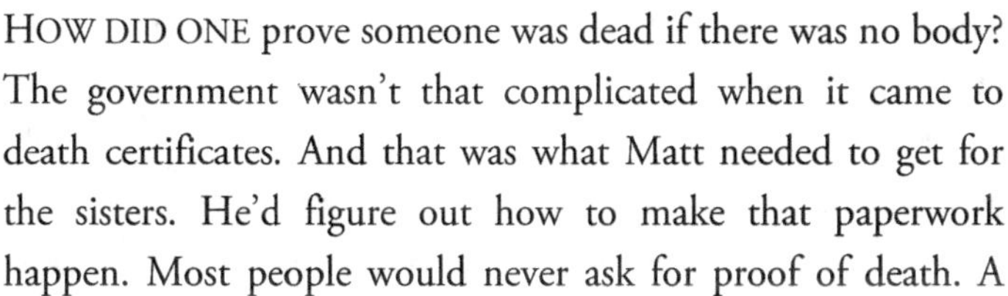

HOW DID ONE prove someone was dead if there was no body? The government wasn't that complicated when it came to death certificates. And that was what Matt needed to get for the sisters. He'd figure out how to make that paperwork happen. Most people would never ask for proof of death. A grave in this case would suffice. He hadn't spoken to many people about Granny's death, just the triplets. As for the rest of the world, they just hadn't cared enough to notice. Granny had done so much for everyone, and they didn't know. She'd been good with that. The triplets were good with that. Matt wasn't so sure that he was.

Surely someone should know.

Back to the record-keeping again to inform the public.

And his job to set the record straight. Inside, he understood that something had changed. He had a new sense of what his purpose in life was. Why he was here, with Celeste. What had Granny wanted him to understand? This was important, and life was changing. Society was changing. And someone must ensure that society never forgot who had saved their way of life all these years and why. Ensure that the sisters were no longer despised because of Granny. That Granny had an honored place in the archives, whether she wanted one or not.

He would see to that.

He smiled down at Celeste.

His expression fell away when he saw the envelope she held out to him. Similar to the envelope she'd opened earlier, this one had his name on it. "Why?"

Celeste shrugged. "Granny. She knew everything. Remember?"

"Everything?"

She nodded. "What she didn't know, she only had to throw a star chart to find out the answers. And she threw star charts constantly."

He flipped the envelope over several times, as if it would give him the answers he wanted without opening it. He wasn't sure he was ready to take that step. What had Granny needed to say to him so badly that she'd left him a letter to open a year after her death? "How did she know when we'd find and open them?"

"She just knew." Celeste nodded toward the letter. "Are you going to open it?"

"No, not right now. We have to find your sisters first."

She bolted to her feet, as if just remembering. "Any news?"

He pulled out his phone. "Nothing yet. What about the spirit animals?"

She closed her eyelids and called to them. She heard several answers but nothing affirmative. "Nothing yet."

"Damn."

Then Twitch responded. With jerky movements, she paced the bedroom. "Twitch is following a scent downstairs," she cried out. "But it's not as if they can be spirited out of here. Not without being seen." She spun around to gaze at him. "The tightest security here used to be down in the research labs." She narrowed her eyes. "Is that still the same?"

He nodded.

"And does it still have the emergency exit, in the event of a bad accident?"

He froze. Then burst into action.

CHAPTER 25

CELESTE RIPPED DOWN the hallway behind Matt. She called out to the field mouse, "Twitch, how far did you get?"

The faint voice rippled from the lower levels of the building. He was working deeper into the basements, where the research labs were. "Twitch has tracked them down to the research levels. Not sure where after that."

"We'll be there soon."

Matt avoided the elevator and raced down the stairway, taking the steps two at a time. She struggled to stay close. He blasted through the double doors ahead of her.

"Hold up, Matt," she warned. "The kidnappers could still be there."

"Good," he snapped. "Let me at them."

He was at the security check and through it before she had a chance to see what security checks he had in place. She watched as he twirled in a circle, studying the empty lab. She stopped at the doorway and stared. Where could her sisters be? Her gaze caught sight of the storeroom off to the side. And Twitch sitting on his back legs, sniffing the air outside the door. "Matt," she called softly.

Matt turned to look at her. "What?"

She pointed at the doorway, where Twitch stood on his back legs, nose in the sir, whiskers moving rapidly. "Look."

Matt raced over, Twitch darting out of his way. Matt tried the handle. Locked. He pulled out his security card and used it to unlock the door.

As he pulled it open, Tori fell out.

She hit the floor hard and lay there, emitting a low groan.

Celeste cried out and raced to her sister's side. She crouched down beside her. Matt stepped into the closet and bent over another prone body. Genesis.

"Is she okay?" Celeste asked, her voice trembling.

"She's alive."

Matt pulled out his phone and called for help. In the background, she heard him speaking to Scott, ordering a lockdown on the Center, until security could do a complete sweep of the premises. Celeste doubted they'd find anything. As she sat on the floor beside her sisters, waiting for help to arrive, she connected Jessie's spirit energy to her own, and used Tori's spirit pet's energy to heal her sister. Celeste poured her energy into her sister, and Tori's body pulsed, as it gained strength. Soon Tori's body hummed with health.

She groaned quietly and opened her eyelids. "Celeste?"

"Yes, it's me." She smiled down at her sister. "Stay calm, and don't try to move yet. I have to help Genesis."

She shifted to Genesis's side and repeated the healing motions, transferring energy for herself and her pets to her eldest sister. Remi was already there, pouring his own loving energy into Genesis. It took a little longer, but soon Genesis woke up to stare at Celeste in surprise. "What happened?" she whispered, her hand going to her head.

"We believe you were both kidnapped."

Her gaze opened wide, as she understood Celeste's words. "Really?"

Celeste nodded.

The research lab doors opened, letting in a dozen men. Devon led the group. He gave a shocked cry and raced to Tori's side. "Who the hell did this?" he roared.

Tori reached up and stroked his cheek. "I'm okay."

"You are now, but what if we hadn't found you?" he cried out. "And who did find you?"

Celeste spoke up. "Twitch found them."

Devon looked at her. "Who?"

Tori smiled weakly. "Twitch." She pointed to the side of the chaos, where Twitch sat, staring at them all, his whiskers trembling.

Storm had arrived with Devon, and he paced the room, anger vibrating over his sleek frame. He pounced on Twitch.

"No!" Devon cried out.

Tori gasped.

Celeste sucked in a sharp breath.

Twitch ran up over Storm's nose to sit on top of the huge cat's smooth head. He perched there happily, now high enough up to see everyone, and twittered.

Celeste let out the breath she had been holding. And, of course, no one would touch Twitch with Storm as his protector. "So, Devon. I know you have Storm as your bonded pet, but Twitch could use someone too."

Devon turned to look at her in shock. "Surely they don't belong together."

"They do now," Tori said, with a shrug. "You might as well give it up already. If you think you have a choice, you clearly don't understand how this works."

"How does that work?" he asked, studying the two spirit pets in wonder. "What is going on?"

"Our family is growing," Tori said in dry tones. "It looks like Storm has found a friend. Twitch found me. Now Storm has found him, and they have bonded."

The group stopped to watch, as Twitch raced up and down Storm's back, the big cat sitting there, unconcerned, a contented look on the predator's face.

"If I hadn't seen it with my own eyes …" Connor stood and stared. "Unbelievable."

Matt shook his head and gave a short dry laugh. "Only with this group."

MATT NEEDED SEVERAL more hours to get through everything that had to be done in the next hour. The triplets were resting in Genesis's suite, none of them wanting to be separated at this point. The guests would be arriving in twenty minutes, and the security, although always on alert, obviously should have been doubled up earlier. Fool him once and all that. No way he was signing up for another nightmare scenario like the one he'd just been through.

Thank God they'd found the women. Too bad the two didn't remember anything.

He still couldn't logically understand why they'd been stashed in the storeroom, unless someone planned to move them out later during the celebration. And that might have worked. The storeroom was only a few feet from the emergency exit. Except this evening's event would have been canceled, if they hadn't found the sisters. No way it would have gone on without them. They were an integral part of tonight.

Whether they knew it or not.

He ran his hands through his hair. Connor walked over, already dressed for the night ahead, overseeing the last of the arrangements. "Matt, go get changed."

"Right. Still haven't done that." He looked around, his

mind still buzzing.

"The first of the guests will be here soon. You're not ready."

"I'll go now. Check with Devon and Scott. They are co-ordinating the rest of the security."

"I'll see to it. Go." Connor pushed him toward the elevators. "Go."

And Matt went. His mind whirled, mentally compiling a list of the things that still needed to be done. This evening was important for a lot of reasons. His first event as the Head of the Center. He needed Celeste at his side. A pang of guilt hit him. He knew they'd had a shock tonight. It shouldn't have happened in the first place. But it had, and he had to deal with the fallout. The women had reassured him several times that they were fine. And *they* might be.

But he was not.

Devon and Connor were on his side on this one.

Tonight they were bringing this to an end. In as big a way as possible. A lot was at stake. And the women had been kidnapped tonight on purpose. Whoever was doing this wanted to undermine his position. His power. Do away with the most powerful women on the planet and steal their inheritance.

Good timing on their part.

Well, he'd make sure whoever was doing this was ruined. Preferably tonight. And preferably as publicly as possible.

Scott had set the traps. Mopsy had shifted his focus to watching the traps. Matt could only hope Mopsy was as good as Scott swore he was. A lot was at stake.

Inside his suite, he stopped for a moment and swallowed down that pulse of panic when he realized that Celeste wasn't here. It was quickly followed by the reminder that the sisters were together now and would arrive together a little bit later.

It was all about the big entrances and all that power stuff.

He stripped off his clothes, wished he had time for another shower. The ghost of a grin crossed his face. He'd love another shower like he'd had earlier with Celeste, but regretfully he was alone, and time was of the essence.

He quickly shaved and washed the soap off his chin. He dressed carefully, aware that this was a power session for him. He had to give that impression that he was in power on all levels. And that he planned to stay in power.

His fingers slowed, as he thought about that. The thing was, he *would* stay in power. Regardless of what anyone thought. He knew that. This was where he belonged. This was where he *would* stay.

The pressure eased when he shrugged on his jacket, then walked out to meet the first guest.

He couldn't wait to see the reactions from his company when they saw the sisters here, whole, healthy, and together. As they would always stay. Scott had doubled up the available cameras, so that they could record everyone's expressions, as the triplets walked in.

At least that way, they'd search the films tomorrow to see who'd been shocked and dismayed to see them arrive.

Not that he was looking for answers tomorrow.

He would end this tonight.

CHAPTER 26

"ARE YOU SURE you feel okay?" Celeste asked Genesis for what had to be the fifth time in the last hour.

Genesis took her sister's hand and squeezed it. "I'm better than okay. Stop worrying."

"Yeah, like that'll happen," Celeste said. She waited a moment, then said, "Are we ready?"

"Hell, no," Tori said, with force, "but we have to do this." She shuddered. "Why are the dresses so ugly?" she wailed.

"I was thinking the same thing." Morosely Celeste stared at the stack of potato-sack-looking dresses on the bed. The three so-called cloud dresses weren't even close to the image she had had in her mind from long ago.

Genesis frowned. "Maybe they'll look better when we're wearing them."

"Not possible." Tori glared at them. Then turned her back and walked away. "I just can't do it. I'll go in jeans before I go in this."

Celeste agreed. Why had she expected the dresses to work? Had she really thought they could pull a crappy dress out of a box and make it beautiful?

So not happening.

But she couldn't let it go. She'd seen Granny make these. A memory she would always hold dear. There had to be a reason. Shuddering, she said, "I'll go first." And she picked up the dress that had her name on it. "Why did Granny feel she had to identify these?" she wondered out loud. "They're equally ugly."

She stepped out of her pants and pulled her shirt over her head. Taking a deep breath, she gently lowered the incredibly light material over her head and let it settle in place on her shoulders. "I'll say one thing—it's so light, I feel like I'm wearing nothing." She held her arms out and pivoted slightly. The dress had a handkerchief bottom, so it flared and twirled as she turned. She loved that. It just looked … She sighed. "Damn, it's still ugly."

The look on her sister's faces brought tears to her eyes.

"I'm so sorry," she cried out. "I thought these were special. I was sure they'd work."

Minkel sat on the bed, beside both Darbo and Silky. They beamed up at her encouragingly.

"Sure," she said resentfully. "You're not going to be put on display tonight, wearing a potato sack."

Jessie showed up just then. Now lime-green, instead of the bright-purple color she'd seen him in last. Celeste stared at him. "How is it your spirit pet can change his colors, yet this dress can't?"

Genesis sat upright. "Do we know they can't?" she asked cautiously. "Granny said these were cloud dresses. Power dresses of some kind."

"And we're women of power," Tori said excitedly. "Celeste, do something."

Celeste stared at Tori. "Like what?"

"Anything that uses your abilities …"

Genesis jumped to her feet. "Or focus energy on the dress. Like this…" And she reached out a tiny pulse of healing energy. But there was no change. Dismayed, she tried again.

"Damn. I thought for sure that was the answer."

"And maybe it is." Celeste stared down at the dress, cut too large for her body, and, in a soft whisper, she said, "Dress, tighten up." And she zapped it with a little energy.

Instantly the dress clung to all the right places.

"Whoa!" she cried out.

"What did you do?" Tori asked, walking around her. "It fits like a second skin."

"Yeah, is that a good thing?" Celeste said. "I'm not sure I want anything quite so revealing."

With a whisper of sound, the dress relaxed on her bosom slightly and draped across her chest instead.

"Oh boy," Genesis said, awe on her face. "Is this really happening?"

"I'm not sure," Celeste said. "I want long clinging sleeves to match."

Instantly the material unrolled to her wrists.

The women stared at each other; then, in a flurry of activity, the other two stripped down and reached for their own dresses. "That's why the names are on the dresses. The dresses are tuned to our energy," Tori said in a whisper, as the dress floated over her shoulders. "But the color is really ugly."

"No," Celeste said, with a quiet laugh. "It's the absence of color, not *the* color." She closed her eyelids and envisioned a beautiful midnight-purplish blue with a shimmer. She opened her eyes and gasped. "Oh my."

The sisters screamed. "Holy crap."

"So do we really have dresses that change shape, style, and color at our whim?" Genesis asked in delight. "Is that really possible?"

"And possibly affected by our energy," Tori warned. "If we get angry, our dresses may change on us too."

That was a sobering thought.

They stared at each other, wondering at the possibilities.

Tori stood in front of the full-length mirror and changed the color of her dress from flame-red to deep-purple. "There's so much choice," she marveled.

"Maybe too much, considering we don't have any time." Then Celeste whispered with quiet joy, "Oh, thank you, Granny."

"So let's help each other right now, and we can try something different next time." Celeste turned in a pirouette. "What about this?"

"Schoolgirl, lacking self-confidence," Tori said instantly. "Honestly that first dress that clung was a power dress. Get the right color, do the hair, and you're all set."

In a blink, Celeste turned the dress back to the one she'd started with. She winced. "It's awfully revealing."

"And Matt is your mate. Don't you want him to see you in that outfit?"

Celeste flushed. "Oh, I do." Then her face fell. "What about shoes?" she cried out. "No way we'll wear ballet slippers with this."

Genesis dove for the box. "Granny wouldn't have let us down on that item." She pulled out three ugly pairs of slippers from the box and shook her head. "If I'd seen these while cleaning up the cottage, I'd have tossed them." She placed hers on her feet and ordered them into stilettos. With a laugh, she held out her foot and said, "Look."

"Oh my God." Tori grabbed hers and put them on. "We are going to knock them dead."

Celeste was a little slower to put on her shoes. "Does it come with the ability to walk in these suckers? 'Cause the last thing I need is to fall in front of everyone." But even as the words left her mouth, she felt the power surge up and down her legs.

And she realized they really were power shoes. She stepped with confidence and strode across the room, her steps strong and sure. "Wow," she said, with delight. "Who knew this was even possible?"

"I know," Genesis said in a low, reverent whisper. "I hope by the time our daughters are fully grown, we know how to make these."

The mention of daughters brought tears to Celeste's eyes. "I would love nothing better."

"Me too." Tori danced and laughed, as her dress kept changing color to match her shoes. "I can't decide."

"We're out of time," Genesis warned. "We still have to do hair and makeup."

That sobered them up, and they got down to the business of adding the finishing touches to their outfits.

A half hour later, when the knock sounded on the door, with Scott calling out to them, they were ready. With last glances at each other, they reached out and grabbed each other's hands.

"We can do this," Celeste said softly.

Her sisters nodded.

Genesis walked to the door and threw it open. She smiled at Scott. "We're ready."

Scott's gaze widened when he saw her, his mouth falling open. His shocked gaze traveled to the other two sisters, and he shook his head. "Good Lord. You three will shock everyone tonight."

"Good," Celeste said archly, although inside she was still worried. "This town hasn't seen us for who we really are, until now."

Scott motioned for them to proceed him. "There won't be any doubts after tonight, ladies. You are doing yourselves proud."

Celeste smiled up at the man she barely knew but already liked and admired. "That's why we're a little nervous."

"Don't be," he said seriously. "You three have got this."

On that note, Celeste smiled and nodded her head. He was right. They had this.

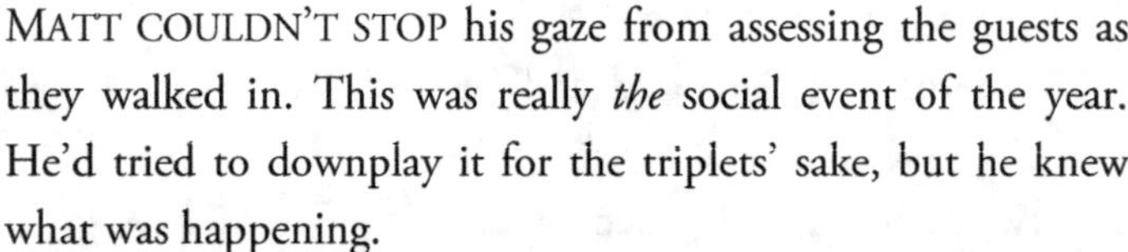

MATT COULDN'T STOP his gaze from assessing the guests as they walked in. This was really *the* social event of the year. He'd tried to downplay it for the triplets' sake, but he knew what was happening.

It was all about power tonight.

He shook hands and smiled, his gaze always assessing, his probe always working. He would be completely exhausted after tonight. It took a lot to keep that probe moving. Darbo had wanted to come tonight, but Matt had put his foot down and had said no. Now Darbo was helping Mopsy. Matt couldn't imagine. But as Twitch and Storm appeared to be a matched set now, Matt wondered if anything could surprise him anymore.

"Good to see you, Steve." He shook hands with the new Head of the Cantrell Paranormal Center. Cantrell was the closest city to them, and, of course, the new head there was interested to see how things were done here.

He smiled at Steve's wife, Cynthia. A middle-aged couple, they wore their power like a comfortable mantle of longtime use and acceptance. He hoped he could consider them allies. He would know after tonight. Matt moved on to greet three board members of the new business consortium that had moved into town. They were looking to build here. And Matt might even let them, if they were decent and honest. He had his doubts, but who knew. It was too early to tell at this point.

He scanned the crowd again. A number of wealthy landowners and absentee businessmen had returned for the occasion. And then, at the doorway, standing and staring with that same haughty air that he always wore, stood Grandfather, his gaze a little sharper than Matt had seen lately. His sister, her husband, and several other family members stood supportively behind him. Including Chelsea.

Matt studied her. She appeared subdued, with downcast eyes and a slump to her shoulders. As Mason's wife, she could be grieving or possibly hadn't wanted to attend after the last dustup. She might even blame Matt for her husband's death.

He studied her, sending out the probe. Couldn't find anything wrong. Satisfied, he turned to greet Grandfather. "Glad to see you're well enough to be here tonight, Grandfather," Matt said, reaching out to shake his hand.

The old man stared at Matt's hand, refusing to offer his own. So it would be that way, would it? Fine. Matt shoved his hand in his pocket, nodded politely at the rest of the group, and then deliberately turned and walked away. Only good manners dictated good manners in return.

He heard Grandfather's sister's shocked gasp at the insult, but Matt had no patience for that drama crap. He walked over to see Scott, waiting at the entrance to the ballroom. "Are they ready?"

Scott nodded. "Are you?"

Matt checked out the ballroom full of company. The atmosphere was social but with an air of expectancy. And he could see why. He strode up to the front dais and held up a hand.

Immediately silence fell on the crowd.

"Good evening, everyone. Thank you for coming."

In the back, someone muttered, "Did we have a choice?"

Immediately he went on the offensive. "Of course you have a choice. This isn't a game. Feel free to leave right now, if this isn't where you want to be. I invited you here to share in a special celebration."

He ran a hard gaze around the room. Not a soul moved.

"I didn't think so. Let's be clear. This is my Center. This is my house. If you have any doubts about my position, feel free to stand up now and say so." He waved a hand in a negligible manner but made sure that a ripple of power wafted throughout the room. "And, of course, I'll be happy to listen to anyone you feel is the best person to supplant me."

Once again, there was silence.

"Before we move on to the real reason you're here, a few things need to be mentioned. These last several months have been brutal, as murder and mayhem have raged, unabated, turning our peaceful city into an unchecked nightmare. And it's going to stop." He paused. "Most of this has happened since Granny died."

A twitter ran through the room.

Matt held up his hand, and instantly a massive power surge slammed to the back wall and bounced back to hover over the audience.

The room hushed.

"Let's take a closer look at Granny. The woman—someone most of you mocked, laughed at, and in general made fun of while she lived—was very special. And, in spite of all your horrible treatment of her, she did her damnedest to keep the woods, the town, everything you take for granted, safe for you all. I don't expect you to understand the very nature of how she did that, or the extreme efforts she went to, to keep it this way," he stressed. "But I will be doing a full historical accounting, so that she and her life might be better understood."

Several people shifted uncomfortably in place.

He nodded. "You all know who you are. What you've done. Be assured that Granny did too. So speaking behind her back, then smiling to her face, didn't hide your actions. She knew. And she helped each of you anyway."

Now that he had everyone's attention, he walked across the podium. "Why am I bringing this all up when she's gone, you might ask? Because there is much about her that you do not know. And, no." He held up a hand again, as he caught sight of several odd looks on people's faces. "This isn't a wake for a woman dead for over a year, but it is a clearing of the air." He smiled. "And also a reminder. So that you don't make the mistake again."

"Again?" someone asked. "How would we do that when she's gone?"

"She's gone, but her granddaughters are not," he said smoothly. "And, in their own way, each of these three woman are more special and more gifted than their granny."

The crowd parted, as a path opened up, letting Scott through, as he led the three sisters in a row behind him. They walked, heads high, toward Matt.

He would have smiled if he could, but the women were so breathtaking, he couldn't breathe. He caught sight of Celeste, and his heart threatened to burst. God, she was unbelievable. Connor stepped up and offered his arm to Genesis and led her at his side to stand beside Matt. Devon stepped up next, and Tori slipped her hand through his. Carefully, she walked up to stand on the other side of Matt.

Matt walked down the steps and held out his hand, completely mesmerized as Celeste—her dress of the deepest purple that he'd ever seen, with shimmers of dreams and stars dancing as she moved. Matt stepped up to place her hand in his, then led her back to the front of the dais.

"I'd like you all to formally meet the three official stargazers for this quadrant."

He felt the glances of the three women but didn't dare break contact with his rapt audience. "They have been attacked, shot at, kidnapped, and hurt in many ways, and it stops now. These three women, together, own the entire town center, all of Grandfather's estates, and the woods. That's over seventy square miles of land. It's theirs. Legally and aboveboard. As it was their granny's."

The room erupted with cries of shock.

Matt glanced at Celeste. She held her poise, with the casual elegance of someone who was used to power, who wielded power with a careless surety.

Perfect.

"I'd like to introduce you to Genesis." Matt motioned to Genesis, in her fiery-orange dress. "Tori." Who'd chosen emerald-green with red highlights. "And, of course," he said, with a huge grin, "my fiancée, Celeste." He squeezed her hand.

And the room erupted in cheers and applause.

CHAPTER 27

"THAT WAS A hell of an introduction," Celeste said in a low voice, when Matt finally helped her down the stairs again.

"It was. And you deserve it," he said calmly. "Hang on now. Here they come."

Her gaze widened, as she spotted the line to meet her forming. She turned to see her sisters getting the same treatment. Both hung on to their men, as if, without their support, they'd be crashing to the floor. They might be wearing cloud dresses, giving the impression of being in control, but inside, they were still the three young granddaughters who lived with their crazy grandmother.

When there was a break in the greetings, Celeste turned to Matt and said, "Thank you for what you said about Granny."

"It needed to be said." He smiled and shook hands with yet another farmer, who grew acres of wheat outside of town. The man's expression seemed worried, and Matt knew just what was on his mind.

"Do you really own my land?" asked the man named John, in low, worried tones. "I've been paying Grandfather, since I took it over from my own father."

Celeste nodded. "We do. Plus your brother's land and, indeed, your sister's clan's land as well."

The breath rushed out from John's mouth as his lips

worked, clearly unable to say what was on his mind.

Celeste reached out a hand and touched his. "It's all right. I won't take it away from you."

He searched her gaze intently. "But I'll have to pay rent?"

She looked surprised. "I'm not even sure how that works, or how much money I owe to the city for the land on an annual basis myself. I won't be asking you to pay more than you can. I'd like to say that I won't be charging you at all, but—"

"But she can't do that until we figure this out," Matt interjected smoothly. "Rest assured, John. Your farm is yours. We'll come to some mutual solution, once we sort out Grandfather's books."

Celeste could see that John wanted to look relieved, but something deeper was bothering him.

She studied his face. "You owe Grandfather still?"

He nodded. "I couldn't pay as much this year 'cause we had a bad season."

"And he still demanded the same payment, even though you were having trouble?" she asked in low outraged tones, her gaze assessing the truth of the matter.

When John nodded, shamefaced, she shook her head. "Trust that we won't have that same issue. And, indeed, we'll need to take a serious look at just what Grandfather has been doing with all this money."

Matt squeezed her arm. "Easy. There is much to sort through."

She nodded, but inside she was furious. Had Grandfather done anything at all to help these people? This was not an age of slavery or serfdom, like on old planet Earth.

"John, we'll speak later," Matt said quietly. "There is a lot to sort out."

"And you'll be fine," Celeste whispered to him. "That land has been in my family for many generations. We've never come after you yet."

He brightened and reached out to grab her hands. "Thanks," he blurted out, before rushing away.

She watched him, as a woman of similar age stepped up to him, worry on her face. He bent down and spoke quietly into her ear. She brightened, then realized that Celeste was watching.

Shame washed over her face.

With difficulty, she left her husband and walked toward Celeste.

As the woman reached her, Celeste instinctively understood what the problem was. And could see this would be the first encounter of many, if she and her sisters were lucky.

"I'm sorry," the woman said. "I'm guilty, as Matt said." She winced. "I never imagined that Granny was anything other than a cra—"

Celeste tried to take a calming breath, but her emotions flared, causing her dress that had been lying close against her body to whip about her small frame.

The woman's eyes widened, and she caught the words back and closed her eyes for a long moment. "I can only say in my defense that I was raised with that attitude, and, to my shame, I carried it forward."

"And now that you know differently?" Matt asked curiously, showing he'd been paying attention to the conversation and, as Celeste looked around, so were many other people.

"I will have a talk with my children," she said immediately. "And make sure they understand. My parents have both passed away. So I can't do anything there, but I can make sure no one in my family perpetrates the problem." She gave a small nod and stepped back. "Again, my apologies." And she rushed away to join John.

Celeste watched, as the two headed toward the exit.

Minkel, tell Mopsy to tell Scott that the couple heading for the door should stay and enjoy the food and drink, Celeste said. *They don't have many nights like this. And tell them it's a special invitation from me.*

She watched as Scott approached the couple and motioned toward the heavily laden tables of food. She caught their glances her way. She nodded at them. They both smiled, their shoulders relaxing, and they allowed Scott to hand them champagne flutes and to direct them to the food.

"I saw that," Matt murmured at her side.

Her lips quirked. "Did you now?" She turned to glance at him. "I couldn't let them leave like that."

"I understand," he said, a lot of pride in his voice. "And so does everyone else."

"You don't mind?" She studied the warm glow in his eyes.

"Mind that you are gracious, inside and out? Never." He tucked her up close. "I'm the luckiest of all men."

"You are, indeed," said another man, standing nearby, beaming at her. "Honored to meet you, Celeste. My name is Josh. Your granny was a special woman, and we are delighted to hear that you three are stargazers in your own right."

"Just nowhere near as good as Granny was, not yet," Celeste said, with a warm smile. "I recognize you. Didn't you meet Granny somewhere in the last couple years?"

"I came often," he said. "She helped me solve several problems in my corner of the world. And, of course, paired me to my beloved wife, Melinda."

The two women shared delighted smiles. Celeste turned to smile at Josh. "I'm happy to hear that," she said sincerely.

"Granny was a special woman."

"And powerful in many ways, which is rarely under-stood." Josh added to Matt, "I'm grateful you will be looking at the record-keeping of Celeste's family. It's a story that needs to be told."

Matt nodded. "I agree. Much has been lost over the last few centuries, and I'll do my best to restore what I can."

"Too bad you can't tell the truth while you're at it," Grandfather roared beside him. "How dare you say that the land belongs to these upstarts? We are in court over this."

Well, at least some of Grandfather's old personality lived inside. The healing pools obviously hadn't finished their job. Grandfather was still an asshole. This split in his personality, with this part only showing up in anger, did explain why the rest of the time he appeared simple. The pool had taken away much of Grandfather's negativity but hadn't finished, and, therefore, hadn't replaced those pieces with anything, leaving much of his personality a void.

"No, we *were* going to court over this, but, as the land registry does have the documents going back since the time the land registry began, there is no dispute, and the judge has thrown out your claim. Or did you not check your messages today?"

"*Bah*, that judge," Grandfather snorted. "I'll just pay him more, and he'll reverse that decision again. I have more money than you ever will …"

"And apparently you stole that too, so we'll be reclaiming that money at the same time," Celeste said in as haughty a tone as she could manage. "Charges are pending."

Grandfather's sister gasped from where she stood just be-hind Grandfather.

Celeste eyed her balefully. "And you for child trafficking.

Did you really not expect Granny to keep a record of what she was required to pay to have her grandchildren returned to her? Then we must come to justice for my mother's murder." Her voice rose, as anger rolled through her. "And the people who paid to make it happen. The people standing before me …"

The room fell silent.

Immediately Genesis and Tori stepped forward, so they could stand beside their sister. They tossed out disdainful looks at the audience. "We have not forgotten all the injustices done in the name of greed. That your family murdered a pregnant woman—our mother," Tori snapped.

"Now I suggest that you and your family return home," Genesis said, her gaze glacial. "Your lawyers are waiting."

Grandfather's head reared in anger. The members of his family grouped behind him gasped in shocked horror.

And damn if Tori's autosuggestion waved over him and his group, the whisper audible to Celeste.

Go home peacefully. You cannot hold your head high any longer. Everyone knows who and what you are. And all the horrible things you have done. Go home now.

Yet the wave of suggestive energy dissipated in the air around the group, instead of forcing them to act. Was the autosuggestion not working or was it slowed by the various strong energies?

"You cannot speak to him like that. Anything done to your family would have been our father's doing. Not my brother's or mine," his sister cried out.

"You sold us," Genesis said coldly. "Or how about the money you demanded from the people who worked your land, while you do nothing but steal and lie and cheat?"

Grandfather's sister's face blanched.

"That's not fair." Chelsea spoke up for the first time, cold dark anger in her voice. "My family is not responsible for the wrongs done to you."

"Really?" Celeste snapped, studying the woman who'd arrived looking tired and cowed, but now stood in front of them in righteous anger.

"We'll make allowances that you might be a little more emotional after your terrible loss," Genesis said in a calm voice. "But do not make the mistake of thinking that we will do so forever." She upped the wattage of her smile and raised her voice. "We are well aware of Mason's attempts to kill my sister Tori. We know Mason had help. We're just gathering proof of the others involved, as they will be charged accordingly."

"Except, by your own actions, Grandfather has been in your very powerful and very private healing pool, and not only couldn't do such a thing to anyone, he has no recollection of such a dark history either anymore." Chelsea tucked her hand into her grandfather's arm protectively, adding, "I'll take him home now, so he can rest." She gave a poisonously sweet smile to the room around them.

"After all this stress and accusations, I'm sure you can see he needs to recover. Such a shock to a man who has done so much for so many of you." Her gaze landed on several successful businessmen, who stood close enough to hear the conversation. "We'll be sure to follow up with all of you."

With those veiled threats, she led her grandfather out of the room.

Minkel asked Celeste, *Should Scott let them go?*

Absolutely but place a tail on them, so we know that all of them have left and that they go straight home.

MINKEL, DON'T WORRY. Scott has this one handled, Matt said to the spirit pet.

"Glad to see you're not being taken in by all these lovely personalities at play here," Matt said in a low voice only Celeste could hear. "But we have tails already set up."

She smiled. "Nice to know you aren't missing anything."

"Not if I can help it." He motioned her toward a tray of flutes, presented to her by a young server. "Care for a drink?"

She stared at the wine and was about to accept, then saw an odd glow coming from in front of the glasses. "No. And not only do I not want one, no one should be having any of this bottle." She glared at the server. "Matt, the ones in front are poisoned."

Matt grabbed the entire tray, as the server bolted through the crowd. "Damn it," he said in a hoarse whisper. "How that hell did he pass through here?"

Connor appeared and removed the tray from Matt's hands. Matt explained what was going on. A dark look settled on Connor's face, when he realized that Genesis was also one of the targets. He stepped back and reassured them that the champagne would be disposed of properly.

"It had tiny dust speckles in it."

Matt nodded. "We'll take care of it."

Devon raced through the crowd, with Storm leading the pack, as they chased after the server.

"Shall we go to the food then, my dear, if you don't want anything to drink?" He placed a hand on her lower back and nudged her toward the buffet table. "If nothing else, maybe we should check to make sure that it is all safe."

The crowd parted, allowing him and the three sisters, staying close, to pass. He had to appreciate the impact of the beauties at his side. Even as worry over other attempts to harm them dominated his thoughts.

He couldn't believe the server had managed to infiltrate the staff. They'd all been vetted and checked by him personally. Then Matt realized that the server could have been any young man with his jacket off. He hadn't recognized him. The servers were all wearing black slacks and white shirts. No jacket or particular uniform had been issued, deliberately in an attempt to make them blend in. Most of the servers were from the security detail. He'd been looking to use the servers as an extension of his eyes and ears but hadn't expected a fake one to infiltrate from the outside.

And he should have. Matt frowned and shook his head. Celeste gasped when she saw the food laid out, drawing Matt out of his reverie.

Henry stood behind the massive table, a beaming smile on his face. When he saw the ladies, he gasped, and a torrent of Spirent, his native tongue, rolled out. But it was obvious that whatever he said was complimentary. In fact, he appeared to be completely bowled over by the women in their finery. He opened his arms and cried out, "Beautiful. The three most beautiful women in the world."

"Take a look around and see if you sense anything wrong," Matt murmured to Celeste and the others. "Based on that champagne, search for a similar energy, so we don't poison anyone here tonight."

Celeste quirked a smile and, in a low voice, said, "Henry's abilities wouldn't allow it. The food is safe."

Matt stared at her, then at Henry, who nodded as if he understood, then at the food. "In that case, I'm starved," Matt said.

CHAPTER 28

CELESTE ENJOYED THE next hour immensely. She ate, drank, and was surrounded by people she loved. Now that the confrontation with Grandfather and his family was over, everyone who came up to the sisters appeared to be friendly and happy to meet them. In fact, the heavy pall over the entire room had lifted. Lots of people asked her about Granny's life and abilities and how the triplets had lived, growing up. No one had heard about them being sold as children or all of Grandfather's attempts to steal their heritage, which he'd been doing for decades.

Several of the men openly commented to Matt about it.

"I presume this will be taken care of and what belongs to these young women is returned to them," said one blustery older gentleman, several of his cronies nodding in agreement.

Matt smiled. "We're working on it. Grandfather and his forebearers have been squatting on stargazer land for over a century now, and charging others for the privilege."

"Then it's time to be put right. That man is a menace, I tell you. He came to me, looking for investment money a dozen times over the last decade, always saying land was available for those who were part of his investment schemes." The gentleman snorted. "He never came out and said what land was available or who would get what. He's more than a little bit slimy, that one."

Celeste had to agree. "It's a good thing you never got involved," she said. "Many people bought land that wasn't theirs to buy. And I'll be reclaiming it all. Purchasing stolen goods does not give anyone compensation."

"Damn, I like her," the older man said, brushing his mustache with his fingertips. "You've got quite a big investigation ahead of you, Matt." He glanced around, as if asking his cronies for advice.

Celeste leaned closer with curiosity, as she saw the cronies nod.

"We might be able to help you out with a list of names of those who were involved in damn-near every one of Grandfather's deals."

The older gentleman nodded. "Interesting times ahead." He went to turn away, then leaned closer. "And watch out for that sister of Grandfather's. Selling these triplets was bad, but it wasn't the first time, and I suspect she's had enough nasty deals going on to match her brother. Best to be rid of the both of them."

"Now, if only they'd truly disappear," Celeste said in wry tones. "I suspect they'll be around to badger me for a long time to come."

With a pat on her shoulder, he walked away, leaving her with one parting shot. "You're up to the task, my dear. No worries there."

She watched in bemusement as the group slowly shuffled away.

"Seems that the weather in town has shifted for the better," Genesis said, from her side. "There is definitely a change in attitude."

"True. Some of it is envy though."

"From the men at our side, the dresses everyone is dying

to get their hands on, or the massive inheritance we now stand to gain?" Tori asked, with a laugh. "Speaking of dresses, anyone else been asked where we got them from?"

Celeste shook her head. "No, I haven't."

"Well, I have," Genesis said. "I told the truth. That they were gifts from our granny."

"I did too," Tori admitted. "Most of the women were shocked. And very jealous."

"Not my problem," Celeste said. "I'm just so grateful Granny knew to leave them to us."

"Hear, hear."

The lights dimmed just then, and music—a slow pulsating beat that lit Celeste's blood and made her skin shimmer with heat—thudded through the big hall.

Matt's voice rang over the sounds of the audience. "I thought a little dancing might be a great way to spend a couple hours. Or maybe I want an excuse to hold my beloved in my arms for a little while." And he hopped down, the crowd surging back, leaving him standing alone in the middle of the dance floor.

"Oh no he didn't," Celeste muttered. "As if I know how to dance."

Matt grinned, holding out his hand to her.

Shit.

"Go," Tori urged. "Remember. We have power shoes."

Celeste blinked in remembrance, then smiled a slow, sexy smile that stopped Matt in place. She handed over her glass to her nearest sister, then stepped onto the dance floor, swaying her hips to the heavy beat of the music, as she walked toward Matt. He loosened his tie, and she shook her head, her hand closing over his and wrapping his arm around her waist.

"You asked for this," she whispered, knowing the audience was watching them intently, "and now you'll pay for it."

He threw his head back and laughed in delight. "Bring it on, sweetheart. There is nothing you have that I can't handle."

And the music jolted into a hot and heavy beat, as he swung her around in a circle on the floor. She matched him step for step. On one turn she caught sight of her sisters and their men dancing alongside them.

This would be a night to remember.

By the time the evening wore down, Celeste was tucked up against Matt's side at the front door, saying goodbye to the first wave of guests. Before too long, most of the partiers had left, but still a dozen or so hung about.

"Did we learn anything?" Celeste asked Matt in a low voice, as they walked slowly back to the buffet table, where she picked up several canapés and put them on a small plate.

"Mopsy had no triggers. Neither did anyone else yet, including Scott."

"Damn."

"But I suspect we will have more trouble still to come tonight. The enemy may not have necessarily wanted to cause a widespread panic here, but now that the numbers have dwindled …"

"*Hmm.*" She wasn't so sure. If it had been her, she would have used the spirit animals to find out what she needed to know and then planned an attack for later.

Something tugged at the back of her brain, but she couldn't place it.

She pondered what was escaping her thoughts for a long moment, while she ate. Then slowly put down her plate and reached for Matt's hand. When he turned to face her, a questioning look in his eyes, she asked, "Did you consider that spirit animals might be left behind? Not ours, but someone else's, in an attempt to gain access later tonight?"

He frowned, his gaze searching. "I hadn't considered that. Can you tell if other spirit animals are here?"

She nodded. "There are, of course, as many people brought their pets tonight on the assumption that they wouldn't disturb anyone."

"And did they take away those same animals again?" he asked intently.

She frowned, sensing something, a strange energy here, but it was hard to tell, as the place was overrun with foreign energy. It was a perfect foil. "I'm not sure they did."

"And just how much damage could a spirit pet do?"

"Remember the gorilla that hurt Jessie?"

His frown deepened, and he spun around, as if looking for that monster. "Are you saying that some aggressive animals could be here now?"

"We were so busy that I never thought of it," she admitted. "And I've been trying to contact Silky and Minkel for the last few moments. and I'm not getting through."

In fact, … she felt a deep dark surge of power inside the hall. She spun around. It was coming from the downstairs. "Someone, something, is here. It's in the research labs. Where we found my sisters."

Matt grabbed her arm and jumped from his seat. "Stay here."

She shook her head and rose to meet him. "No, this is about spirit animals. This is too big for you alone. I have to be there."

Celeste could tell that indecision held him back. But he looked to be on the verge of bolting anyway. "Fine, but you have to stay safe," he said in frustration. "I can't do all this"— he waved his arms around—"and end up with you getting hurt anyway."

"No time," she snapped and raced toward the elevator. Behind her, she heard Genesis and Tori call out, but she knew they would follow regardless. They waited briefly at the elevator doors, but the transporter was taking too long, so they headed to the stairwell She raced down the stairs, wishing she had on her runners, then squeaked in surprise when her stilettos changed to sneakers before she'd jumped to the step below. With Matt right behind her, she raced to the research lab and wasn't surprised to find the security off and the door wide open.

Someone had gained access in such a way that had made it look like child's play. The energy locks had been blown apart by something powerful from within.

She heard Matt's angry spluttering behind her, but she skidded to a full-on stop, before she hit something way bigger than she could handle.

Holy shit.

The others poured in behind her. She held out her arms to stop their full onslaught.

"What the hell is that?" Matt said on her left.

"It's a snake," Connor said in shock, "but I have no idea what kind. Since when did they come this big?"

"It's been fed dark energy to make it grow," Celeste answered in a soft, pained voice. This was no normal snake, regardless of its size.

"Is that Twitch in front of it?" Devon cried out in anger, stepping forward.

Celeste held him back. "It is, and Darbo, Silky, Remi, and Jessie." She frowned at the almost nonexistent energy field over their beloved spirit pets. "In fact, he has almost every spirit pet who is here at the Center full-time."

"And what will he do with them?" Matt asked in a low voice, anger pulsing in his tone.

The massive snake opened its mouth and hissed at them. Then, unhinging its jaw, it lowered its head, as if to eat the long line of unconscious spirit pets.

"No," she shouted, stepping forward. "Stop."

The snake stared at her, its eyes glowing balefully at her. She stared at it, hoping to see the energy center whence this animal came. She determined it was a he, and he'd been good at one time.

"You cannot hurt those animals."

The snake wasn't speaking like a normal spirit pet, but, inside her mind, she heard his thoughts. His anger. The absolute hatred he held for anything and anyone.

"I don't know why you are so full of hate," she said in a calmer voice, sending out waves of healing, loving energy, "but you will not hurt those animals."

He rose up high, until he towered above her. She refused to be cowed.

"Ah, Celeste …" Matt said, his voice full of warning.

"No," she said. "He's been poisoned by the black rocks somehow. Whether accidentally or deliberately, he is now infected … by the same darkness."

"Can you help him?" Genesis asked.

"Help him?" Connor cried out. "I think you mean, can you kill him?"

"No," Tori said in a sad voice. "Killing him only perpetrates the same negative evil. It's what we've been fighting all this time." She reached out and grabbed Celeste's arm. "Easy, Celeste. The person who did this did so deliberately. The snake is angry. But more than that, he is—"

"Hurting." Celeste nodded. "And healing him will be a

much bigger issue."

"How about instead you find out who did this to him, and let us go pick them up," Matt growled. "They can stop this asshole."

"I'm not sure if that person can even control him now," Celeste said absentmindedly, her gaze on the huge snake that had the ability to wipe out all their spirit pets with one nasty swallow.

"What?"

She nodded. "It's already too big and too swollen with black energy to control. The owner would have to be deadly strong."

"Can you help?" Devon asked. "Storm is looking to take matters into his own hands. And I highly suspect that, although Storm might have the heart of a warrior, this snake is too much for even him."

"He can't do this alone," she said. "Call him back. I'll try first, and if that doesn't work ..."

"Yeah, then what?" Matt asked sharply. "What if he goes after you?"

"My sisters are here," she said. "They will help."

❧

"HELP? THERE IS no *helping* this." Matt growled—anger and, yes, fear, tinging his voice. Not for him but for Celeste, who appeared to be ready to walk where only angels would go. He shifted to his side, and, using much of his own energy, he tried to build a protective wall between Celeste and the monstrosity of a snake.

Until Celeste placed her hand on his. "We cannot fight this with fear or more negativity. We can only offer love and healing."

"Like hell," he muttered, determined to do whatever was required to keep her safe.

"You'll see," Celeste murmured. "The snake will only absorb the negative energy, and it will make him stronger. More powerful. That will take longer to heal then. Much longer to help him."

"Only you would talk about trying to help him."

"She's right," Tori added, "and I can help her. He is of the woods too. One of nature's creatures, and that is my domain."

"He's part of all our domains," said Genesis. "I'm a healer first and foremost, and this creature needs healing."

"Shit," Connor whispered. "And what are we supposed to do? Stand here and watch, while you knock yourselves out trying to do this?"

"You can help," Tori said, her answer surprising him. "In fact, we'll need your help."

"How?" Devon asked. "What can we do?"

"Let go of the anger. Realize this animal didn't ask to be like this. Send your energy to us, and we'll use it to help him." Genesis stepped up beside Celeste, Tori matching her on the other side.

Devon said, "*Um*, hang on here a moment ..."

But the women all raised their hands, shutting up the men.

Matt walked forward, until he stood beside the women. "I presume you know what to do, so let's get on it. Let's save our pets."

"Oh, it's well past the pets now," Celeste whispered. She closed her eyelids and did something that tugged at Matt.

He felt his energy being pulled into a torrent, created by Celeste. Like a small hurricane, she was creating a funnel of energy that he presumed would be blasted at the snake. Only, when she released it, the actions it took surprised him. The energy wafted toward the snake with a gentle, loving motion, before it settled atop him, like a blanket cuddling a child ready for a nap.

As if.

He wasn't a great believer in a light touch, but the snake appeared to be confused by it. Maybe that was good. Maybe. … Matt narrowed his gaze and wondered if he could do something more to help. He brought out his probe and sent it gently toward the mix-up happening in front of him. Maybe Matt could find out who had done this to the poor snake.

This poor snake? At his thought, he froze. Was he thinking that the animal had been treated harshly by someone else? As if that justified what the snake had become? No, but it did ease back his hatred—his fear—of the abomination in front of him. The snake was still huge and deadly, but Matt did understand it a little better.

He sensed a pat of approval from Celeste. Was the healing energy directed at the snake having an effect on him as well?

Damn.

Who would have thought?

CHAPTER 29

CELESTE CONTINUED TO swaddle the huge snake with warm cosseting energy, as she approached, her body movements calm and gentle. She needed to keep him distracted, while the other spirit animals collected their injured friends. Storm had already retrieved Twitch and moved him back to the far side of the room. Storm was back again, trying to save another one. Mopsy showed up behind him. Smurg the owl perched on the far side. He wasn't big enough to collect any others beside Darbo and Silky, but, if he could remove them from harm, that would help Storm.

Celeste couldn't let herself be distracted by the others.

The snake rose higher in a weird shaking movement to discard the healing energy off him faster than she could pour it over him. She frowned, unable to see that her efforts had any reasonable effect on the snake.

But, as he rose, she noted the glowing heart of him. Instantly she narrowed her stream of energy and focused on that spot, pouring as much of the energy that she could into that organ. Filling him with as much goodness in her world, that light of love and peace, as she could. She wasn't sure the snake had ever experienced such a thing. Not all spirit animals were blessed with great beginnings.

The glow widened, as she poured more energy into it.

"It's working," Tori whispered. "More, let's pour in

more."

In a concerted effort, the women shoved in more energy, as they tried to shift the snake's energy into a positive balance.

Slowly the energy of the snake approached the middle of the scales of balance. But the snake was fighting it. He had lived with so much negativity for so long that it was normal for him. Uncomfortable in these uncertain circumstances, he searched for a way back to what he knew. To the comfort and security he was used to.

They were approaching the most dangerous part. He could lash out now, in one last attempt to return to the status quo. As soon as the thought arrived, the snake coiled tighter and tighter.

"More," Genesis shouted. "We need more."

And the snake lunged.

Hitting a wall.

Celeste shook her head. "If you'd drop that wall, then we could pour in more energy faster."

"And you'd have been attacked right now," Matt snapped beside her.

"The animals are almost safe," Tori whispered.

Taking a quick glance, Celeste realized that all the spirit animals, with the exception of Darbo, had been collected. But he lay there still, unconscious. The pet she'd loved and lost and then found again. He was the closest to the danger and, therefore, the hardest to rescue.

"Damn it," Matt snapped. "Let me rescue him."

"Not necessary," Celeste said and upped the wattage of the power stream heading toward the snake.

"What happens if this doesn't work?" Matt muttered.

"The snake dies," she answered calmly, registering Matt's shock at her words. "It's energy. It can't be destroyed, but the fight is no good for it either. Only one side can dominate at a time. One must give way to the other."

"And if that doesn't happen easily?"

"That fight can consume the soul of the person or the animal involved. The result is madness, psychological breakdown, and eventually—sometimes immediately—death."

"Good. Can we get to that point now, please?"

"Only if we fail to turn him." Inside, she was tiring. The snake was damn strong. "It's so damn powerful."

"Or we're damn weak," Genesis said, with a tired groan.

"Or the opposite," Tori snapped. "Someone is helping the snake."

Celeste gasped. "Yes, that's it. Well, almost …"

She shifted slightly, so she could see what was going on behind the snake. She'd wondered why the snake had been capable of absorbing so much good energy. Someone else must be feeding it more negative energy and siphoning off the positive energy. It was the only way the snake could maintain this fight.

Therefore, Celeste had to plug that drain, in order to save the snake. And somehow she had to track that energy back to the source, if she could. And then there was the wall that Matt had built. She should be able to go into it and out the other side.

She took a step toward the energy storm in front of her. She heard the others protesting, but she needed to do this.

Needed them to let her do this.

Needed them to know she was okay.

And she stepped into the storm.

The energy buffeted all around her. Her hair flew out wildly behind her, as the energy wrapped her up into the vortex.

She tilted her head back and smiled up at the ceiling and the sky beyond, before taking another step into the eye of the storm. It was calmer here. Not peaceful though, as if a huge expectation of something to come existed. Taking a deep breath, she took another step, her soul resisting leaving the Center and moving deeper into the havoc. With her soul in a position of love, she took the step anyway.

And opened her eyes.

There. A tight powerful black hole was pulling loving energy out the back of the snake. The energy was represented as white and dark, as if it were a two-way highway. She marveled such a thing existed. Moving carefully, she stepped in front of the flow of the energy and blocked the hole.

Like a valve that had been shut off, the energy immediately stilled. Calm once again reigned. The snake lowered slightly, his body wavering, as confusion hit him. He would adapt. As the good energy continued to pour in, and, with her controlling the plug, she could release the black energy. She had to find a way to block it entirely, but she had no idea how.

Then Celeste laughed. She didn't have to plug it. Once the snake was filled with loving, positive energy and turned into the kind of spirit animal she knew well, that darkness could never reenter, as the snake's energetic balance would be all one way.

"Celeste?" Matt's worried voice called her.

"I'm fine," she said calmly. "Keep pouring in the energy. He's almost there."

At her words, there was a final shift, and the snake lay down to rest.

MATT LET HIS breath out slowly, as if afraid the snake would rise up into that damn monster again. But it lay on the ground, a fraction of its original size, and, from the shaking of its body, it appeared to be having difficulties. He stepped closer to Celeste. "Is it okay?"

She shook her head. "I cut him off from his owner." She held out her arms. "I didn't have a choice. The owner was feeding him dark energy, while siphoning off the loving energy we were pouring into it."

"Will the good energy have an effect on that owner?"

"No." She lowered her arms. "Not with the bond cut."

"Celeste is right. It won't." Tori walked around them and bent over for a closer look at the snake. "Chances are the person is very adept at shifting energy to do what they did here. That means they have a way to deal with the good energy so that it won't affect them. This person has spent a lot of time and effort learning to control dark energy. They want this. They don't want healing energy."

Celeste reached out a hand to touch the snake. He shivered at her touch but didn't react in any other way. Matt hadn't even tried to stop Celeste from touching it, as it looked so different—a weak, limp version of the monster he'd first seen.

"This shouldn't be allowed," Devon said. "If we don't look after our spirit pets, who will?"

Matt allowed himself a small grin. Devon only recently got a spirit pet of his own, and that lethal-looking cat seemed to have acquired a pet of *its* own, if Storm's instant attachment to Twitch was anything to go by.

"Matt?" Connor asked. "Maybe we need to look at some kind of regulation, or at least consequences, for hurting these spirit animals."

"We're certainly seeing more of it now than we ever used to," Genesis said. "Again though, all in the last year. And that could be from the imbalance triggered by Granny's death."

"Or rather was triggered by our inability to step into Granny's place," Tori said in dry tones.

"No one expected you to be able to do that. At least not without training," Devon protested. "There is only so much anyone can do."

"People always have expectations. Then they are upset when they can't have what they want," Matt said. "They just have this thought, and it sounds like what they want, so they go for it, expecting to get it."

"Selfish."

"No," Celeste said. "Just people."

Matt sighed. "The question of regulating spirit pet owner-ship is something we can discuss at a later date. What will we do with this snake now?" He crouched and scooped up Darbo and tucked him against his neck, where he was safe. "The snake likely shouldn't be alone, should he?"

"No." Celeste frowned. "I'm wondering if his owner will try to retrieve him. Try to reconnect."

"I hadn't considered that." Matt didn't like the concept. "If he abused the snake in the first place, wouldn't he just do so again?"

"Most likely. Besides, if the snake did have some weapon as well, then the owner might want it back."

"But we don't know that, do we?"

"What are the chances that the snake was out in the woods that day, and the gunmen saw him, and that's what scared them to death?"

"Maybe accidentally," Celeste said. "The snake didn't show us anything to indicate that's what happened."

"Unless the snake had never been used to kill anyone before, and that was the first time. Those gunmen acted as the snake's first targets. A trial, if you will."

"Why kill their own men?" Tori shook her head. "That seems counterproductive."

"Because the gunmen had screwed up. Because they couldn't do what was asked of them. Or because they'd become a liability in some other way?"

"Depending on the person we are dealing with, maybe because the owner was pitting one killer against another. Wondering who would be stronger, faster, better." Celeste turned to look at the others. "Think about it. What if the gunmen were sent to the woods to hunt me and so was the snake? If the gunmen found and killed me—great. But, if they didn't, it was a perfect opportunity to pit the snake against them."

"And that would explain the cloud of darkness we saw there at the same time." Matt frowned. He didn't like the concept of disposable employees. Good men were hard to find. Then again, useless idiots were everywhere.

"Exactly," Devon agreed.

"But we didn't see the snake turn any weapon on us," Genesis said slowly. "I'm not against your hypothesis, I just want to make sure that you keep your mind open to all possibilities."

"Understood."

Matt tried to cast his mind back to that day. He remembered the cloud and the look of horror on the men's faces. "I still feel like whatever they saw had them frozen in place." He motioned to the snake. "Was the snake capable of that?"

"Yes, perhaps just due to his size. But the gunmen had also lost a lot of energy. Drained perhaps. That is definitely something the snake could do. In fact, carrying that much negativity, he'd be compelled to gain more. The horror was likely that the gunmen realized the snake was stealing the very life force from them, and maybe the snake didn't know what was happening either—especially if he'd been given any of those black rocks. We already know the rocks can steal healing energy on their own. That they are compelled to in order to rebalance their own systems."

"I wonder if the owner could see through the spirit pet's eyes? Use the snake as a personal weapon at its own directions?"

Celeste shrugged. "This person is already very strong and has already utilized its spirit pet in ways I have never seen or understood before, so it is possible. Sure."

"Then why didn't the owner do it here?" Matt countered, pointing to the large group standing together.

"There were too many of us," she countered. "And we're all energy workers. Maybe it doesn't work on us."

"I think it also couldn't control the energy in here, with all the security locks in place," Tori suggested. "The snake's owner might have started this setup as a trap that backfired. It's one thing to practice this in the woods, but not behind this much steel and cement walls, not to mention all the security measures in place."

"And don't forget the immediate wall of healing energy directed at it," Genesis added.

Matt nodded. "I think that's the reason for siphoning off the healing energy, while still trying to pour black energy into the snake. It was trying to gear up for that moment where the snake would steal our life forces, but we stopped the snake's one trick, without realizing it."

"If that's true," Connor said in a hard voice, "what will the person behind this do now that he or she has been thwarted, yet again?"

CHAPTER 30

Back in the main hall Celeste found the place empty, except for the staff cleaning up. She'd forgotten to ask Matt for a follow-up on the server who'd tried to poison her. Right now, she didn't care. She was hungry. That last energy drain had wiped her out and had left her needing to refuel—like all energy work did. She walked over to the buffet table being cleared of food and quickly filled a plate for herself. She was exhausted, her energy stores dangerously low. She needed sustenance. She glanced up to see Matt and the others following her example. By the time they had all filled their plates, there was almost nothing left for the servers to put away.

She walked outside with her plate and sat down on the porch. It was a stunning night. She should feel exhilarated, but instead she was depressed. The things humanity did to each other sucked. On top of that, the things they did to their pets …

"Is the snake safe to leave alone?" Genesis asked, sitting in the chair beside her.

Her mouth full, Celeste nodded, chewed, and swallowed. "It will be okay, but it will never be the same, and neither will it live long. Unless we can get it to the healing pools."

"Is that something we should do?" Connor asked, leaning against one of the veranda's support beams.

"I think the other spirit pets could take it there. In Granny's cottage, the snake would live longer. Might even recuperate, but I doubt he'd ever really heal from that damaged bond. I broke it, but it was the only way." And, if she kept saying that, she might eventually believe it.

"It's not your fault," Matt said patiently. He'd said the same thing a half-dozen times before.

"I know, but I feel like I should do more." She took a bite of a small pastry. "Maybe the other animals will."

"It tried to annihilate all the spirit animals. Why would they help it now?"

"Because, more than any of us, the spirit pets are pure energy, and they know the snake was filled with darkness, but not of his own making. And now that he is no longer under his owner's influence, then they would understand. I wouldn't be at all surprised if some of them haven't already done something to hel—" She paused midthought, then chuckled. "Right. Minkel and Smurg have taken the snake to the cottage, where they have dumped it in the healing pool." She shrugged. "Mother Nature taking care of itself in the best way possible."

"Will it survive the pool?" Matt asked. "The snake had a lot of darkness in it, and the pools were quite agitated over just the black rocks being thrown in."

She studied his face. "True, but they are healing pools, and they healed themselves, as they also healed everything else. They would have eventually healed the rocks, if they'd had enough time, but we stepped in and removed them, making it easier on everyone. It might have taken the pools decades to reverse that much negativity, but they would have done it eventually."

"And, of course, they have no time constraints. Only people do that."

She nodded. "I'm wondering if we could entice the snake to help us trap its owner. The thing is, to do so"—she swallowed and took another bite, while trying to marshal her thoughts—"to do so, means trusting that the snake has fully healed and will no longer be susceptible to the owner's dominant energy again."

"That's asking a bit much," Connor said, seated across from her. "And so soon."

"Maybe, but the owner already knows where the cottage is and now knows that we have the snake," Celeste said. "If the owner puts those two bits of knowledge together in the same place, then it's quite possible that it will attack the cottage again, and this time plan to use the snake from the inside out." Then she froze, her voice rising in panic. "Oh, my God. If that's the case, we've played directly into this person's hands."

Genesis and Tori hopped to their feet, shock on their faces.

"Whoa, what?" Devon stood at the doorway, a larger heaped plate than any of them in his hands. "What was that last bit?"

"The snake was a trap. Not just downstairs but now inside the cottage." She turned to her sisters. "We have to go."

They took off running toward the hovercraft.

Celeste called out from behind them, "We don't have time for that."

She snagged Genesis's arm. "We have to go now." She turned to see Tori, still sprinting for the hovercraft. "Tori, come here!"

Out of the corner of her eye, she saw Matt almost reach out for her. She threw up an energy block. "No. You can't come this way."

Tori grabbed her hand. "What are we doing?"

"What we have to do," Celeste cried out. "There's no choice." And she raised her sisters' arms in the air, and let the ancient song run through her body. "Use the cloud dresses."

"What?"

She heard their shock but felt the dresses power up, energy racing through her feet and her legs, connecting one place on her body to another, flowing through with the same message of the ancients. It twisted and bent and rolled right through the three of them. Creating a pulsing vortex of power.

When she couldn't control the maelstrom inside anymore, Celeste cried out, "Now."

A weird popping sound came. Then silence reigned.

She opened her eyes.

To see Granny smiling at her.

"Granny?" She gasped in joy, glancing sideways at her sisters. They too stared at the mirage in front of them. "Why are you here?"

"You might need help, child. All of our help."

And behind Granny, faces peered out of the fog. The one behind her, standing out in particular.

"Mom?" Celeste cried out, tears in her eyes.

"Oh my!" Genesis burst out, crying.

Tori reached for her mother. But the energy was faint, distant. Behind their mother was a long line of women fading into the distance. Their ancestors. They had to be. Celeste stared in awe at the beautiful loving features of the beloved woman who had gone before them. Her granny, who'd died while raising them, and the long line of stargazers who'd done the same for their daughters.

"Oh my God," Celeste whispered. "We are all one."

"We are all one," Granny confirmed, with a stunning smile on her face, in her eyes, and, yes, in her voice. "We are all connected, and we always will be."

"Do we need you now?" Tori asked in a small voice. "What are we up against?"

"Evil, child. Negative energy. It's always there. Always around. But this time it thinks you are weak. Thinks you are young. And thinks to destroy that which cannot be destroyed." She smiled. "But, if you know that we are here and that we can help if you need us, … then you are stronger than even you know."

She hated to ask, but Celeste had to know. "If the cottage can't be destroyed," she whispered, "why are you all here?"

"Because you can be destroyed. And then there would no longer be a stargazer here to keep Glory safe."

The blood drained from her face, taking the warmth with it. Inside, she was so cold. She knew they could die in this fight, but it hadn't been brought home to her so starkly, not until she'd heard Granny say it out loud.

"We came to support you," Granny said, her voice a whisper. "To keep you safe and to help vanquish this evil once again in our midst. We have all faced it before, at least once in our lifetimes. We have all seen it, felt it, been damaged by it. And still it rises once again."

"Why can't we stop it forever?" Genesis cried out. "Then we can all live happily and safely in peace."

"Because Mother Nature is a balance of two sides. For all the positive energy in the world, there is negative energy as well, but, as soon as things go out of balance, then the negative is given an opening to rise again."

Celeste nodded and turned her attention just a little bit farther down the line. She couldn't tear her eyes away from the beautiful woman standing behind Granny. Standing *behind* because she had gone *before*. "Mom, if I don't get another chance …" She gulped back the tears clogging her throat. "I love you and missed you every day of my life. But Granny?" She shook her head. "She did a wonderful job and kept you alive in our hearts all the time."

"I missed you so much," Tori cried out.

Genesis could hardly speak for the quiet sobs in her voice.

Their mother smiled, warmth and caring and love radiating from her gaze. She moved her mouth, and the words, "I love you all," echoed around them. Celeste felt nearly full to bursting with joy.

What a moment.

Celeste also knew they were heading into danger. Knew that one of them could join their ancestors on the other side after today, but, Lord, she hoped not.

"It won't happen today, child." Granny beamed at her. "But you needed to know we are here for you." And she started to fade slightly, as if taking a step back.

"Wait," Tori cried out. "We need you."

"We're here and are not going anywhere, ever. But, until you need us to step in, we'll wait and see how you handle this. So far, you are doing very well."

"Thanks for the dresses, Granny," Celeste rushed to say. "They are the best."

"And you'll need them now too." And, with that, she took a step farther back.

Celeste choked back a sob, as her beloved mother's face disappeared into the clouds.

What a blessing, and one she realized was part of that heritage she'd hated growing up with. She couldn't see anything special about it—until now. Lord, she'd been away far too long. But she was home now, and their lives had been enriched in more ways than she could ever begin to count.

The sisters looked at each other, sniffling and wiping away the tears, but smiling.

"Did that just happen?" Tori asked softly.

"It did." Celeste shook her head. "I'm not sure how or why, but it did."

"Oh my God, that was too freaking touching," a snide voice broke in. "Now, if only I could restrain myself from breaking up this emotional scene."

The sarcastic voice was female.

And one they all recognized. After all, she'd been at the Center earlier that night.

Chelsea.

MATT SHOUTED, "NO, don't."

But it was too late. A thick, rich fog surrounded the triplets, even as he watched. The early morning light of a summer sunrise was breaking off to the side. Offering just enough to make out the fog so dense that he could barely see the women in front of them. He reached out a hand where they should have been, only his hand went right through the field to … nothing.

"How can they be gone?" Devon asked.

Connor looked at Matt, reminding him that Devon hadn't been in the hovercraft with them, when the triplets had pulled the last trick with the hovercraft.

"They transported in the same way the spirit pets travel from one place to another."

Devon shook his head. "I heard what you all said, but I didn't believe it, not really. I'll have to see this to really believe it."

Connor walked around the space where the women had been. The fog had dissipated, leaving a vibrant green circle behind. There weren't even footprints in the grass.

Matt turned and started to run. "We're late. Let's go."

They raced toward the hovercraft. "Can we land without the women?"

"We'll have to try." Matt opened the pilot's side door, calling over his shoulder, "We have no choice."

He had the hovercraft in the air in record time. The other two men were still trying to lock down their seat belts, when Matt was already flying over the Center. He hit the juice and sent the machine as fast as it could go in the direction of the cottage. He couldn't believe the women went without him. Surely they could see that they needed help. That they couldn't do this alone. It might be stargazer business, but that didn't mean that the triplets' partners weren't there for no reason. And that the men weren't useless.

He understood that the triplets were used to being alone. Used to handling difficulties on their own. Used to not thinking in terms of having men to help. Also not used to using the tools around them, but this was ridiculous.

He was here. So were Connor and Devon. And they were all pissed.

The GPS locator signaled that they'd reached the cottage location. And, of course, he couldn't see it. "Anyone see anything?" he asked, hopefully studying the green terrain below.

"No."

"I'm asking the animals," Connor said. "Surely they can unlock the stealth mode and let us in?"

"Is that safe though?" Devon asked. "We could be opening up something the women need to stay hidden. We don't even know where the sisters are."

"Neither can we help them, if we can't see them." Matt turned to look at the others. "We need to land." He'd asked this question before and had never got an answer. But he knew this was the place, and the answer was about to come. After a single deep breath, he slowly lowered the hovercraft. "Hope I don't hit the roof," he muttered.

"Actually …" Connor pointed to the woods around them. "It looks like we're in the wrong place."

"No, it's the right place, but the cottage is hidden from us still."

"Does that mean the sisters are here, but we can't see them?"

Matt turned off the engine and opened the door. He saw nothing but the woods. And not ones he recognized.

"Where the hell are we?"

CHAPTER 31

CELESTE TURNED VERY slowly to stare at Chelsea. The same girl they'd gone to school with. The same woman whose husband had been killed after he'd attacked them. And the same woman who'd been in the hall tonight, professing her and her family's innocence.

She wasn't protesting anything right now.

Instead she stood, casual and elegant as always in front of them, oozing self-confidence like she always had.

No weapons in her hand, nothing but a smug look on her face.

And, of course, that sneer that she'd worn all through high school was front and center.

"Hello, Chelsea." There. Celeste had spoken with a light, airy voice. "What are you doing here?"

Genesis stepped forward. "And why?"

"Why what?" Chelsea snarled. "Do you think I wouldn't want retribution for Mason?"

"You knew what the odds were," Tori snapped. "You were okay to kill me and my family. Why is it that you're surprised when life didn't turn out the way you planned it to?"

"I'm okay with the loss of Mason honestly." Chelsea shrugged. "He was my husband and a good man in his own way. At least he took orders well." She smiled. "But he was getting to be a bore."

Celeste gasped. "He was your husband. Your lover. How can you say that about him?"

"Of course he was those things," she snapped. "But he was simple. Didn't have vision. Was happy with a smaller payout."

"And you wanted more? Bigger? Better?" Celeste asked in a dry voice. Of course she did. Chelsea was nothing, if not greedy.

"Of course. I want it all."

"When your grandfather dies, you'll get whatever he has left."

"Oh, that's not a problem. I already got everything."

The sisters exchanged glances in silence.

What did that mean? Celeste had an inkling, but surely Chelsea wasn't that cold-blooded?

Genesis got it though. "You mean, Grandfather's already dead?"

Chelsea nodded. "Him and his sister. And her husband of course. Couldn't let any of them live. Certainly not any in that generation. They wouldn't understand."

Confused, Tori asked, "With Grandfather being in the state he is—was—now, what was the point of killing them? They are your family."

Apparently that word didn't mean the same thing to Chelsea as it did to Celeste and her sisters.

"They *were* family." Chelsea nodded her head. "But ones long past their due date." She snorted and flung her arm out wide, a strong wave of energy rippling past Celeste in a simple demonstration of her power. An unconscious power that she wielded with grace.

"I'd have had to wait forever to get my inheritance, and, by then, they'd have lost it to you. Fools," she snapped. "It should never have gone this far. But they didn't want to do what was necessary." She glared at Genesis. "Especially after Grandfather's swim in your healing pool."

"What was necessary?" Tori asked in a hard voice.

"Killing you all years ago." She snorted. "Before you polluted the high school with your taint."

Celeste took a small discreet step back. She didn't have a plan, but she had to assume that Chelsea had something up her sleeve, and they were too close for comfort. "Of course," Celeste said, with a smile. "You were always jealous of us."

"Jealous?" Chelsea gasped in fury. "Of what? You three? You have nothing. Are nothing. And always will be nothing. You are discarded property, bought and sold like the damaged products you are." A proud look settled on her face. "I come from leaders, not crones."

"You come from liars and cheats, thieves and murderers," Celeste said quietly. "Nothing to be proud of in that. Then you married a failure. So, not good at picking men either."

"We got that down pat," Genesis said smoothly. "And, of course, you're on the lookout for another one now."

Something about Genesis's statement sent Chelsea into a rage. "You might have them, but you will not keep them. At least not the one I picked out for myself." She swept her gaze over Celeste from head to toe and dismissed her. "I *will* have Matt. Anyone else is beneath me."

"I think Matt might have something to say about that," Celeste said quietly. "I guess his announcing our engagement tonight really burned your ass, *huh*?"

"Not at all. He can play for a little while." She smiled. "But he'll be mine, soon enough."

And that was enough of that. "What do you want from us?"

"Oh, nothing. Except for you to die ..." She pulled her

arm back and threw something.

Fireworks exploded beside Celeste. She never moved, having put the shield in place earlier, when she'd seen the casual wave of energy slide so easily off Chelsea's hand. That was the one thing she felt was lacking in her experience. She'd not been taught to fight. Or to partake in energy battles.

The next blast was a direct hit. And stronger by a large magnitude.

"Shit," Genesis whispered.

"Double shit," Tori snapped. "I got this." She closed her eyes, and the whispers rolled out across the ethers. *Walk away. Forget about the stargazer sisters. Walk away. Live a life of peace.*

Chelsea cackled with wild abandon. "Not happening, Tori." She swatted the energy back right at her. "I can see the energy coming from a mile away. You'll have to be much more subtle than that." She snorted. "You three think you're special, and you're not. A lot of us can work energy. And even more of us specialize in it. We're not just good—we're beyond good. I can see energy. Track it. Stop it. Steal it." And she laughed again. "Mason didn't even know what I could do. Or what I could get *him* to do."

"What good will attacking us do?" Celeste asked curiously. "You still can't own the land. It must stay in stargazer hands. Killing us won't change anything."

"Exactly," said Chelsea, with a big smile. "Nothing changes. As in, everything stays the way it is right now. And, with my being the next in line to Grandfather's estate, it will be all mine."

"So Matt was right—it was all about the inheritance," Celeste said, scorn in her voice. "Do you really think it is that easy? That we are so easy to kill?"

"You haven't shown any talent yet." Chelsea sneered. "I've

been developing mine for decades. You're naught but children in my world."

"All of which means what?" Genesis snapped. "I'm ready to go home, thank you very much. It's been a long day, and you're just pissing me off."

"Oh, don't worry, dear," Chelsea said in a low voice, dripping with acid. "It will be all over soon."

She stared behind the women. Then called out, "Sith, it's time."

<hr>

"THERE HAS TO be a way to find them," Matt said in frustration. He tilted his head back to the sky. "Granny, we need help."

"Or not. Storm is here," Devon said. "He says something ugly is going on."

"Can he undo the settings for the cottage? Ask the women to do so?"

"Hang on," Devon whispered. "I think I've got it. Jessie is busy at the door."

And suddenly the cottage appeared beside them. And so did the women, standing near the cottage.

"Whoa." Matt raced toward Celeste. "What's going on here?"

"Oh, nothing," Celeste said sarcastically. "Chelsea has just planned on killing all of us and hooking up with you. She's already killed off Grandfather and several other of her family members, clearing the way for her to inherit everything—particularly as she figures that, by killing off the three of us stargazers, she'll inherit it all."

Matt studied Chelsea. Gentling his voice, he said, "You know that won't ever happen, right?"

"It will, if I do everything right." She waved her hand. "I'm not alone, you know?"

"We know," Matt said. He smiled. "Only your partner is no longer capable of helping you."

"He's a killer." She shook her head. "I trained him. You have no defenses against him."

Matt wrapped his arm around Celeste. "You don't understand," he said, sending a beautiful smile toward his love. "See? Even when I wanted to kill your partner, Celeste here wouldn't let me. She wanted to believe in the beauty of love. Of healing and of peace."

Chelsea rolled her eyes. "Oh, brother. Sith, get your ass out here. It's time. I felt you at the Center, playing at being hurt, but I know you. That couldn't happen. You're too strong. I made sure of that. Enough games," she finished, with a snarl.

"And those plans need to be reworked," Matt said gently. "Sith is inside the cabin."

She frowned. Brushing past the women, she strode to the cottage door. "Let me in."

The door to the cottage opened up silently. She strode inside.

Matt whispered, "How did she get in?"

"I let her inside," Celeste said. She raced after Chelsea.

Matt crowded into the kitchen behind her. Like hell she would walk away from him again.

"Happy now, Chelsea?" Celeste wandered through the kitchen in a casual manner, leading her victim in one direction. "By the way, what are you looking for?"

"My spirit pet should be here, waiting. I know he's here. I can sense him." She opened doors and checked behind each inside, before circling the living room in frustration. "He has no choice but to be here. He is under orders to be here."

Celeste walked ahead of Chelsea and motioned to the last door. "I think you want this door."

"Why?" Chelsea snapped. "What's in there?"

"Sith, I believe."

Chelsea shot her a disbelieving look and pushed open the door. Instantly Celeste pushed her forward—right toward the healing pool.

Chelsea let out a strangled cry, and, even as she toppled over the edge of the pool, the healing waters reached up and wrapped tightly around her limbs and held her firm, dragging her down into their dark depths.

She screamed, the sound cut off as she disappeared below the surface. The waters were too strong. Too fast. Too determined.

Matt raced to the edge of the pool and cried out, "Where is she?"

"The healing pools have taken her," Celeste said calmly. "They will deal with her as they see fit."

Connor came up from behind the group. "And that means, ... what?"

She shrugged. "You have to understand how the pools are ancient. They deal with ancient. The evil that Chelsea operated from is their domain too. Once the spirit animals brought Sith here, it was part of Chelsea's plan for Sith to turn rogue and to destroy us from within. Only she didn't know that the pools are love. They are healing. And, in Sith's case, with all his black energy gone already, he was easy to heal."

"Chelsea, on the other hand ..." Tori said, quietly staring down at the bottomless depths of the pool, "is beyond saving."

"But I've been in that pool," Devon said in shock, moving closer to the edge. "It had a bottom. I could sit and stand. Yet, she went straight into the water and disappeared."

"What happens to negative energy when it's overwhelmed with positive?" Genesis asked gently. "It …?"

"Turns to positive energy," Connor said.

"And becomes absorbed by what's around it," Matt whispered. Holy shit. Finally Matt understood. Chelsea's penance for all her evildoings was to spend the rest of eternity healing others as part of the healing pool.

"Is she in here now?" he asked. "Dispersed into such small particles that she is no longer herself?"

"Yes. And already sent to the healing pools below," Celeste said, with a smile. "As the water circulates, her energy is now one with all of Mother Nature and will circulate as well."

"And Sith?" Devon asked. "Did anyone remember him in all this?"

The sisters grinned and pointed. There, lying on the windowsill, soaking up the late-afternoon sun, was the fattest, happiest snake they'd ever seen, his body a gleaming rosy-pink color.

Lying on top of him, his belly to the sky, was Twitch. And, beside him, as if happy to stand guard over his new friend, was Storm.

"This is Sith's home now," Celeste said, with a laugh. "He was treated terribly and won't ever be quite as strong as he could have been if he'd had a loving environment all this time, but he's fine and will always be welcome here. He has friends now. And he won't ever be alone again."

Celeste was so damn special, as were her sisters. Matt knew they had a mess to clean up, and it wouldn't be easy. But now they could do it—together. All of them.

Matt reached out a hand to clasp Celeste's. "And neither will you ever be alone again."

He opened his arms, loving how easily she stepped into them. Where she belonged.

With him.

Forever.

This concludes Book 3 of Glory: *Celeste.*

Read the first chapter of Tuesday's Child: Psychic Visions Series, Book 1

Tuesday's Child: Psychic Visions (Book #1)
Chapter 1

March 18 at 2:35 a.m.

SAMANTHA BLAIR STRUGGLED against phantom restraints. *No, not again.*

This wasn't her room or her bed, and it sure as hell wasn't her body. Tears welled and trickled slowly from eyes not her own. Then the pain started. Still she couldn't move. She could only endure. Terror clawed at her soul, while dying nerves screamed.

The attack became a frenzy of stabs and slices, snatching away all thought. Her body jerked and arched in a macabre dance. Black spots blurred her vision, and still the slaughter continued.

Sam screamed. The terror was hers, but the cracked, broken voice was not.

Confusion reigned, as her mind grappled with reality. What was going on?

Understanding crashed in on her. With it came despair and horror.

She'd become a visitor in someone else's nightmare. Locked inside a horrifying energy warp, she'd linked to this poor woman, whose life dripped away from multiple gashes.

Another psychic vision.

The knife slashed down, impaling the woman's abdomen, splitting her wide from rib cage to pelvis. Her agonized scream echoed on forever in Sam's mind. She cringed.

The other woman slipped into unconsciousness. Sam wasn't offered the same gift. Now the pain was Sam's alone. The stab wounds and broken bones became Sam's to experience, even though they weren't hers.

The woman's head cocked to one side, her cheek resting on the blood-soaked bedding. From the new vantage point, Sam's horrified gaze locked on a bloody knife, held high by a man dressed in black from the top of his head down. Only his eyes showed, glowing with feverish delight. She shuddered. Please, dear God, let it end soon.

The attacker's fury died suddenly. A fine tremor shook his arm, as fatigue set in. "Shit." He removed his glove and scratched the exposed skin.

In the waning moonlight, from the corner of her eye, Sam caught the metallic glint of a ring on his finger. It mattered. She knew it did. She struggled to imprint the image before the opportunity was lost. Her eyes drifted closed. In the darkness of her mind, the wait for Death was endless.

Sam's soul wept. Oh, God, she hated this. Why? Why was she here? She couldn't help the woman. She couldn't even help herself.

Sam welcomed the next blow—so light, only a minor flinch undulated through the dreadfully damaged body of this woman. Maybe the poor woman had passed on. Sam's tortured spirit stirred deep within the rolling waves of blackness, struggling for freedom from this nightmare.

With one last surge of energy, the woman opened her eyes and locked on to the killer's gaze staring back from within the mask. In ever-slowing heartbeats, her—and Sam's—circle of vision narrowed, until the two soulless orbs blended into one small band, before it blinked out altogether. The silence, when it came, was absolute.

Gratefully Sam relaxed into the woman's death.

Twenty minutes later, Sam bolted upright in her own bed. Survival instincts screamed at her to run. White agony dropped her in place.

"*Ooooh*," she cried out. Fearing more pain, she slid her hands over her belly. Her fingers slipped along the raw edges of a deep slash. Searing pain made her gasp and twist away. Hot tears poured. Warm sticky fluid coated her fingers. "Oh, God. Oh, God. Oh, God," she chanted.

Staring in confusion around her, fear, panic, and finally recognition seeped into her dazed mind. Early morning rays highlighted the water stains on the ceiling, shining through the slapdash coat of whitewash on there, and Sam's banged-up suitcases, open on the floor. An empty room—an empty life. A remnant of a foster-care childhood.

She was home.

Memories swamped her, flooding her senses with yet more hurt. Sam broke down. Like an animal, she tried to curl into a tiny ball, only to scream again as pain jackknifed through her. Torn edges of muscle tissue and flesh rubbed against each other, and broken ribs creaked with her slightest movement. Blood slipped over her torn breasts to soak the sheets below.

The smell. Wet wool fought with the unique and unforgettable smell of fresh blood.

Sam caught her breath and froze, her face hot, tight with agony. "Shit, shit, and shit!" She swore under her breath, like a mantra.

Tremors wracked her tiny frame, keeping the pain alive, as she morphed through realities. *Transition time.* What a joke. That always brought images of New Age mumbo jumbo to mind. Nothing light and airy could describe this. Each blow leveled at the victim had manifested in Sam's own body. This was hard-core healing time for Sam—time when bones knitted, sliced ligaments and muscle tissue grew back together, and skin stitched itself closed.

Sam understood her injuries had something to do with her imperfect control, paired with her inability to accept her gifts. Apparently, if she could surmount the latter, the first would diminish. She didn't quite understand how or why. Or what to do about it. Her body somehow always healed; the physical and mental scars always remained. She was a mess.

The physical process usually took anywhere from ten to twenty minutes—depending on the injuries. The mental confusion, disconnectedness, sense of isolation took longer to disappear. She paid a high price for moving too soon. Shuddering, Sam reached for the frayed edges of her control. It wouldn't be much longer. She hoped.

Nothing could stop the hot tears, leaking from her closed eyelids.

This session had been bad. Apart from the broken ribs, there were so many stab wounds. She'd never experienced one death so physically damaging. Nervously she wondered at the extent of her blood loss. If she didn't learn how to disconnect, these visions could be the end of her—literally.

Just like that poor woman.

Sam hated that these episodes were changing, growing, developing. So powerful and so ugly, they made her sick to her soul.

Several minutes later, Sam raised her head to survey the

bed. The pain was manageable, although she wouldn't move her limbs yet. Blood had soaked the top of the many Thrift Store blankets piled high on the bed. Her hollowed belly had become a vessel for the cooling puddle of blood. Shit. The stuff was everywhere.

The metallic taste clung to her lips and teeth. She rolled the disgusting spit around the inside of her mouth, waiting. She wanted to run away—from the memories, the visions, her life. But knowing that pain simmered beneath the surface, waiting to rip her apart, stopped her. Weary, ageless patience added to the bleakness in her heart.

Ten more minutes passed. Now she should be good to go. Lifting her head, she spat the bloody gob onto the waiting wad of tissue and noted the time.

Transition had taken fifteen minutes this morning.

She was improving.

Oh, God. Sam broke into sobs again. When would this end? Other psychics found things or heard things. Many of them saw events before they happened. She saw violence—not only saw it but experienced it too.

Occasional shudders racked her frame from the coldness that seemed destined to live in her veins. The odd straggling sniffle escaped. She couldn't remember when she'd last been warm. Dropping the top blood-soaked blanket to the floor, Sam tugged the motley collection of covers tighter around her skinny frame. Warmth was a comfort that belonged to others.

She wasn't so lucky.

She walked with one foot on the dark side—whether she liked it or not. And that was the problem. She'd been running for a long time. Then she'd landed at this cabin and had been hiding ever since. That was no answer either.

Her resolve firmed. Enough was enough. It was time to

gain control of her *gift*. Time to do something, even if just reading more books on psychics, maybe finding one she could talk to. This monster had to be stopped.

Plus, Christ, she was tired of waking up dead.

Book 1 is available now!

To find out more visit Dale Mayer's website.

https://geni.us/Dmtuesdayuniversal

Author's Note

Thank you for reading Celeste! If you enjoyed my book, I'd appreciate it if you'd leave a review.

Dear reader,

I love to hear from readers, and you can contact me at my website: www.dalemayer.com or at my Facebook author page. To be informed of new releases and special offers, sign up for my newsletter or follow me on BookBub. And if you are interested in joining Dale Mayer's Reader Group, here is the Facebook sign up page.
http://geni.us/DaleMayerFBGroup

Cheers,
Dale Mayer

About the Author

Dale Mayer is a *USA Today* best-selling author, best known for her SEALs military romances, her Psychic Visions series, and her Lovely Lethal Garden cozy series. Her contemporary romances are raw and full of passion and emotion (Broken But ... Mending, Hathaway House series). Her thrillers will keep you guessing (Kate Morgan, By Death series), and her romantic comedies will keep you giggling (*It's a Dog's Life*, a stand-alone novella; and the Broken Protocols series, starring Charming Marvin, the cat).

Dale honors the stories that come to her—and some of them are crazy, break all the rules and cross multiple genres!

To go with her fiction, she also writes nonfiction in many different fields, with books available on résumé writing, companion gardening, and the US mortgage system. All her books are available in print and ebook format.

Connect with Dale Mayer Online

Dale's Website – www.dalemayer.com
Twitter – @DaleMayer
Facebook Page – geni.us/DaleMayerFBFanPage
Facebook Group – geni.us/DaleMayerFBGroup
BookBub – geni.us/DaleMayerBookbub
Instagram – geni.us/DaleMayerInstagram
Goodreads – geni.us/DaleMayerGoodreads
Newsletter – geni.us/DaleNews

Also by Dale Mayer

Published Adult Books:

Shadow Recon

Magnus, Book 1

Bullard's Battle

Ryland's Reach, Book 1

Cain's Cross, Book 2

Eton's Escape, Book 3

Garret's Gambit, Book 4

Kano's Keep, Book 5

Fallon's Flaw, Book 6

Quinn's Quest, Book 7

Bullard's Beauty, Book 8

Bullard's Best, Book 9

Bullard's Battle, Books 1–2

Bullard's Battle, Books 3–4

Bullard's Battle, Books 5–6

Bullard's Battle, Books 7–8

Terkel's Team

Damon's Deal, Book 1

Wade's War, Book 2

Gage's Goal, Book 3

Calum's Contact, Book 4

Rick's Road, Book 5

Scott's Summit, Book 6

Brody's Beast, Book 7

Terkel's Twist, Book 8

Terkel's Triumph, Book 9

Terkel's Guardian

Radar, Book 1

Kate Morgan

Simon Says… Hide, Book 1

Simon Says… Jump, Book 2

Simon Says… Ride, Book 3

Simon Says… Scream, Book 4

Simon Says… Run, Book 5

Simon Says… Walk, Book 6

Hathaway House

Aaron, Book 1

Brock, Book 2

Cole, Book 3

Denton, Book 4

Elliot, Book 5

Finn, Book 6

Gregory, Book 7

Heath, Book 8

Iain, Book 9

Jaden, Book 10

The K9 Files

Jenner, Book 16

Rhys, Book 17

Landon, Book 18

Harper, Book 19

Kascius, Book 20

The K9 Files, Books 1–2

The K9 Files, Books 3–4

The K9 Files, Books 5–6

The K9 Files, Books 7–8

The K9 Files, Books 9–10

The K9 Files, Books 11–12

Lovely Lethal Gardens

Arsenic in the Azaleas, Book 1

Bones in the Begonias, Book 2

Corpse in the Carnations, Book 3

Daggers in the Dahlias, Book 4

Evidence in the Echinacea, Book 5

Footprints in the Ferns, Book 6

Gun in the Gardenias, Book 7

Handcuffs in the Heather, Book 8

Ice Pick in the Ivy, Book 9

Jewels in the Juniper, Book 10

Killer in the Kiwis, Book 11

Lifeless in the Lilies, Book 12

Murder in the Marigolds, Book 13

Nabbed in the Nasturtiums, Book 14

Offed in the Orchids, Book 15

Poison in the Pansies, Book 16

Quarry in the Quince, Book 17

Revenge in the Roses, Book 18

Silenced in the Sunflowers, Book 19

Toes up in the Tulips, Book 20

Uzi in the Urn, Book 21

Lovely Lethal Gardens, Books 1–2

Lovely Lethal Gardens, Books 3–4

Lovely Lethal Gardens, Books 5–6

Lovely Lethal Gardens, Books 7–8

Lovely Lethal Gardens, Books 9–10

Psychic Visions Series

Tuesday's Child

Hide 'n Go Seek

Maddy's Floor

Garden of Sorrow

Knock Knock…

Rare Find

Eyes to the Soul

Now You See Her

Shattered

Into the Abyss

Seeds of Malice

Eye of the Falcon

Itsy-Bitsy Spider

Unmasked

Deep Beneath

From the Ashes

Stroke of Death

Ice Maiden

Snap, Crackle…

What If…

Talking Bones

String of Tears

Inked Forever

Psychic Visions Books 1–3

Psychic Visions Books 4–6

Psychic Visions Books 7–9

By Death Series

Touched by Death

Haunted by Death

Chilled by Death

By Death Books 1–3

Broken Protocols – Romantic Comedy Series

Cat's Meow

Cat's Pajamas

Cat's Cradle

Cat's Claus

Broken Protocols 1-4

Broken and… Mending

Skin

Scars

Scales (of Justice)

Broken but… Mending 1-3

Glory

Genesis

Tori

Celeste

Glory Trilogy

Biker Blues

Morgan: Biker Blues, Volume 1

Cash: Biker Blues, Volume 2

SEALs of Honor

Mason: SEALs of Honor, Book 1

Hawk: SEALs of Honor, Book 2

Dane: SEALs of Honor, Book 3

Swede: SEALs of Honor, Book 4

Shadow: SEALs of Honor, Book 5

Cooper: SEALs of Honor, Book 6

Markus: SEALs of Honor, Book 7

Evan: SEALs of Honor, Book 8

Mason's Wish: SEALs of Honor, Book 9

Chase: SEALs of Honor, Book 10

Brett: SEALs of Honor, Book 11

Devlin: SEALs of Honor, Book 12

Easton: SEALs of Honor, Book 13

Ryder: SEALs of Honor, Book 14

Macklin: SEALs of Honor, Book 15

Corey: SEALs of Honor, Book 16

Warrick: SEALs of Honor, Book 17

Tanner: SEALs of Honor, Book 18

Jackson: SEALs of Honor, Book 19

Kanen: SEALs of Honor, Book 20

Nelson: SEALs of Honor, Book 21

Taylor: SEALs of Honor, Book 22

Colton: SEALs of Honor, Book 23

Troy: SEALs of Honor, Book 24

Axel: SEALs of Honor, Book 25

Baylor: SEALs of Honor, Book 26

Hudson: SEALs of Honor, Book 27

Lachlan: SEALs of Honor, Book 28

Paxton: SEALs of Honor, Book 29

Bronson: SEALs of Honor, Book 30

Hale: SEALs of Honor, Book 31

SEALs of Honor, Books 1–3

SEALs of Honor, Books 4–6

SEALs of Honor, Books 7–10

SEALs of Honor, Books 11–13

SEALs of Honor, Books 14–16

SEALs of Honor, Books 17–19

SEALs of Honor, Books 20–22

SEALs of Honor, Books 23–25

Heroes for Hire

Levi's Legend: Heroes for Hire, Book 1

Stone's Surrender: Heroes for Hire, Book 2

Merk's Mistake: Heroes for Hire, Book 3

Rhodes's Reward: Heroes for Hire, Book 4

Flynn's Firecracker: Heroes for Hire, Book 5

Logan's Light: Heroes for Hire, Book 6

Heroes for Hire, Books 19–21

Heroes for Hire, Books 22–24

SEALs of Steel

Badger: SEALs of Steel, Book 1

Erick: SEALs of Steel, Book 2

Cade: SEALs of Steel, Book 3

Talon: SEALs of Steel, Book 4

Laszlo: SEALs of Steel, Book 5

Geir: SEALs of Steel, Book 6

Jager: SEALs of Steel, Book 7

The Final Reveal: SEALs of Steel, Book 8

SEALs of Steel, Books 1–4

SEALs of Steel, Books 5–8

SEALs of Steel, Books 1–8

The Mavericks

Kerrick, Book 1

Griffin, Book 2

Jax, Book 3

Beau, Book 4

Asher, Book 5

Ryker, Book 6

Miles, Book 7

Nico, Book 8

Keane, Book 9

Lennox, Book 10

Gavin, Book 11

Shane, Book 12

Diesel, Book 13

Jerricho, Book 14

Killian, Book 15

Hatch, Book 16

Corbin, Book 17

Aiden, Book 18

The Mavericks, Books 1–2

The Mavericks, Books 3–4

The Mavericks, Books 5–6

The Mavericks, Books 7–8

The Mavericks, Books 9–10

The Mavericks, Books 11–12

Standalone Novellas

It's a Dog's Life

Riana's Revenge

Second Chances

Published Young Adult Books:

Family Blood Ties Series

Vampire in Denial

Vampire in Distress

Vampire in Design

Vampire in Deceit

Vampire in Defiance

Vampire in Conflict

Vampire in Chaos

Vampire in Crisis

Vampire in Control

Vampire in Charge

Family Blood Ties Set 1–3

Family Blood Ties Set 1–5

Family Blood Ties Set 4–6

Family Blood Ties Set 7–9

Sian's Solution, A Family Blood Ties Series Prequel Novelette

Design series

Dangerous Designs

Deadly Designs

Darkest Designs

Design Series Trilogy

Standalone

In Cassie's Corner

Gem Stone (a Gemma Stone Mystery)

Time Thieves

Published Non-Fiction Books:

Career Essentials

Career Essentials: The Résumé

Career Essentials: The Cover Letter

Career Essentials: The Interview

Career Essentials: 3 in 1